SILVER MOON

SHADOW CITY: SILVER WOLF

JEN L. GREY

CHAPTER ONE

The man—who could pass as my brother—stood over Griffin and me as my mate held me in my wolf form. The joy of having Griffin beside me eased some of the aches that racked my body, despite his concern wafting through our bond.

I loved him so damn much.

The full moon was high in the sky, shining as if informing me we'd been in battle longer than I realized. It had to be just after midnight, and there was still a chill in the late spring air that felt good on my hot skin.

Because of the full moon, my wolf body was twice the size of a normal wolf, which made me a larger target; that was partially why I'd almost been shot in the first place. Julius had just pushed me out of the path of a bullet fired by one of my enemies, but the reason why was worse than death.

In fact, he was the worst enemy here. A man from my own race, working to hand me over to someone who wanted to use me as his personal breeder.

Someone who wanted to take me from my fated mate and hold me hostage for personal gain.

Who wanted to rule over my race—the rare silver wolf—because we had ties to the moon and were stronger than other wolf shifters.

Who wanted to breed his own personal army.

It was a future that I refused to accept. I'd rather die than submit to someone like that.

The only person whose children I'd ever bear was my mate, Griffin's.

You're hurting. Griffin's deep, sexy voice rang in my head. *We have to get Rosemary to heal you.*

I'm okay. The words were bitter despite them not being spoken aloud. *Julius...knocked me out of the way.* I'd almost said *saved me*, but that wasn't what he'd done at all. He wasn't saving me from evil—he was just making sure that I survived long enough to fulfill the evil plan that would benefit him.

I bared my teeth at Julius, allowing my wolf to surge even more. We were in some sort of stare-down, and this asshole wouldn't win. Whether he realized it or not, I was more dominant—my brighter silver hair told us everything.

He'd also mind-linked with me, which shouldn't have been possible.

I lay in the grass only a few yards away from three fighters dressed in all black. Two of them were still shooting at Killian and Sierra, while the third held a phone to his ear. I couldn't hear what he was saying, though, because I was in some sort of stunned state when I *should* have been ripping out Julius's throat. It would be so easy while he was in human form and I was still a wolf. It would eliminate yet another threat—but I couldn't get myself to do it. The bond that had formed between us was causing both of us issues.

His silver eyes had darkened to a gunmetal gray, and his smoke-colored hair was disheveled from all the fighting. Only alphas and their bloodlines had silver hair, with the true alphas having the lightest shade, like mine.

"I'd heard you caused problems, but I didn't believe it until now." Disgust wafted off him and into me through whatever demented bond we shared as he clenched his hands at his sides. His scent—a mix of Mom's and Dad's—made my eyes burn. "But the world revolves around you, so I shouldn't be surprised." *She must have done something to me.*

Griffin growled, "If you say one more word about her, I'll kill you even slower than I'd already planned."

Wait...

Julius thought *I'd* done something to *him*. The idea was laughable. I'd been minding my own business—trying to live my life and move on from the slaughter of my pack—and he'd kidnapped me. Now he blamed *me* for something happening to *him*? Annoyance flared through me, calming some of the inner turmoil. *I haven't done a damn thing to you.*

Eyes widening, Julius stepped back like I'd slapped him. "Stop doing that."

"Like hell I will." Griffin's hazel eyes glowed with his own alpha wolf.

My mate thought Julius was talking to him, but it was me.

Before I could intervene, black wings whooshed past me, and someone slammed into Julius, forcing him past me. Rosemary screamed with unbridled rage as she punched him in the jaw and kept swinging. "There's more where these came from if you don't get in line." Her long mahogany hair fell over her shoulders, and her large angel wings stretched behind her. She turned her head, and her purplish twilight eyes scanned me for signs of injury.

Watching her punch Julius bothered me way more than it should have. After all, she'd refused to kill him earlier because she'd been raised to protect silver wolves. However, she wasn't using fatal blows, so he wasn't at any risk of dying.

The ski-masked gunman dressed in all black, who had just fired at me, must have been in shock because he suddenly yelled, "What the hell, Julius? We were told to kill her if things got out of hand."

Of course they'd be more upset over Julius knocking me out of the way of the bullet than care that he was getting the shit beat out of him by the angel. And the idiot just stood there like he expected an answer.

Gunfire hadn't ceased, even if it felt like time had stopped for those few moments. Bass Guitar and the other gunmen continued to fire at Killian and Sierra, ensuring they couldn't advance here to help us, while the gunman Julius had thwarted continued to gape at him.

"Get her off me," Julius grunted at me as he grabbed Rosemary's wrists, restraining her for the moment. *She's going to stand there and do nothing.*

The angel used her wings as weapons, curling them around her body and stabbing him with the tips of her feathers. For feathers that looked so silky, they sure turned into armor or a weapon when she needed them to.

His pain radiated through me, and I hated that the silver moon had connected the two of us tonight. Our mind-link was going to cause problems.

But once again, how were we able to link? We weren't mates or pack. This shouldn't have been possible. *Maybe you shouldn't have tried to capture your own kind,* I retorted back to him.

He gasped and released his hold on Rosemary, his eyes searching for me. One eye was already swollen from her attack, and blood dripped down his arms. *This is so strange. Why do you keep talking to me like this?*

My heart broke with the realization that he must have been raised as a lone wolf for him not to understand how mind-linking worked—but at least that meant he couldn't link with anyone else to alert them to what was going on. Or he was playing some sort of demented game? I couldn't rule out the latter.

The guard who had just shot at me raised his gun, pointing it at Rosemary. *No!* I screamed in terror.

"Move, Fallen," Julius growled. "He's aiming at you."

Rosemary paused and snarled, "Don't call me that." She jerked her head toward the guard and wrapped her wings around herself as he fired at us once more. The bullet bounced off her, leaving her unharmed.

"What the hell?" The guard's eyes widened, and he glanced at the gun barrel.

How I wished the damn man would shoot himself in the eye. What an idiot. You never pointed a gun at your face —even if it was empty.

I got back to my feet and forced myself to step away from Griffin's warm embrace.

"Hey, easy," Griffin said softly.

Yeah, I was about to piss him off, but the battle wasn't over. Pushing away the pain, I raced toward the gunman who'd attempted to shoot me and then Rosemary. The other two guards were still focused on keeping our allies at bay, so this guy didn't have help.

He pointed the gun back at me, but it was too late. I lunged at him, and he fell back and shot skyward, completely missing his mark. I landed on top of him and ripped out his throat, and even more blood coated my silver fur, mixing with that of the bear shifter I'd killed just minutes ago.

For whatever reason, these men were trained to fight with guns and knives and not their animal sides. Using my wolf was always my first instinct, with my knife being second. I'd been trained with weapons because we couldn't ignore them...but these people used their animals only as a last resort. It was a weakness that we'd been able to exploit in our defense.

"If you want my help, you better stop beating the shit out of me," Julius rasped to Rosemary. "Their numbers may be dwindling, but they should've already called for backup. We've got to get out of here."

My stomach sank. Just when we had only two opponents left...the threat of more coming meant we'd be back to being outnumbered. He was right, we needed to leave. I wasn't sure we could last another round.

But did that mean he planned on coming with us? Surely not.

"And we should trust you *why*?" Rosemary asked. "You could be trying to trick us so you can attack when we're fighting."

We didn't have time for a strategy discussion. I turned my focus to Bass Guitar, who had just smelled his friend's blood. He jerked his head in my direction, then stiffened and winced a little, probably due to the pain of his shoulder injury from where he'd been shot. That little bit of a reaction was all the extra time I needed to get to him.

"Ernie, we're the last two left right now." Bass Guitar's voice didn't sound quite as deep with panic setting in.

Great, he was going to get his buddy to help take me down. Maybe I wouldn't make it out alive after all, but that would be a better alternative than some mystery asshole thinking he could use me to make a silver wolf army.

"They're going to kill her if we don't help." Concern laced Julius's words, and it must have been enough for Rosemary to somewhat trust him.

She stood and hissed, "One wrong move, and I'll punch *you* without a moment's hesitation."

The two guards stopped firing as they turned their focus on the most immediate threat. Bass Guitar's dark eyes flicked toward Julius. "Get her. Don't just stand there." He turned his focus back on me and put his finger on the trigger, but Griffin lunged straight toward him.

His sculpted face was tense with anxiety, and his normally perfectly styled honey-brown hair flopped with each step. His light, hazel eyes with flecks of green locked on Bass Guitar. My mate was twice as large as my attacker— his six-and-a-half-foot frame towered over the guy, despite him being about twenty feet away.

Griffin aimed his gun, ready to take on the enemy. Seeing him like this, with so much raw power, filled me with adoration. Despite us not having the same sort of training growing up, Griffin was formidable with a gun.

A millisecond before Bass Guitar pulled the trigger, Griffin shot the guy through the head. He crumpled dead on impact.

Another gunshot fired, and I turned to find Rosemary's wings wrapped around her once again. I was jealous of her ability—getting shot hurt like hell.

Griffin turned toward the man focused on the angel and shot him between the eyes. The last guard in black dropped.

Do you know how damn anxious I've been? Griffin ran

back to me and pulled me into his arms. *That blood. Are you injured?*

His unique scent of leather and myrrh filled my nose, easing a part of me now that I was back in my mate's arms. Just minutes ago, I hadn't known if I'd see him again or feel his skin on mine once more. I rubbed my head against his chest, needing him close. The fight wasn't over—not yet— but I needed to take a moment for my own sanity. Being in human form would have been ideal right about now, but if I shifted back, I'd be completely naked, and I wasn't comfortable with that.

"We've gotta get out of here in case what he said is true," Rosemary said as she marched toward Julius again.

I begrudgingly pulled away from my mate, but I needed to shift back to human form. *I need my extra set of clothes.*

Griffin nodded. "I'll be right back." He jogged off in the direction of the car as Killian came into view.

Killian's warm, dark-chocolate eyes lasered in on me, and his jaw relaxed. He rushed over, his cappuccino hair flapping in the wind. He stopped when he reached me and looked me over. "Next time, I'm with Griffin. This was way too stressful. I can't do that again."

My head nearly came to his shoulder tonight as I nuzzled against him, letting him know that I was fine. Nothing bad had happened—well, except for everyone we'd had to kill.

Before Griffin reached the tree line, Sierra stepped from between the cedars and redwoods and passed him with a black duffel bag hanging from her shoulder. Her gray eyes sparkled as if all the stress had left her body. Her sandy-blonde ponytail bounced with each step she took as she raced toward me, with Griffin following close behind.

He reached for the bag, and she turned, leaving him to

grab air. She winked at me and threw the bag in front of me. "He's pouting," she said. "He wanted to bring you your clothes, but I was coming back with the bag already. I saw you shift and figured you might need this."

I nodded and took the bag in my mouth, then ran into the trees. I quickly shifted back to human form and dressed, listening to Griffin get louder while talking about Julius. "You expect me to just let this asshole walk away after he planned to kidnap my mate? She almost died—yet again—because of him!"

"We can't kill him," Rosemary said, upset. "I'm supposed to protect them."

"You just punched the shit out of him, girl." Sierra chuckled. "I'm thinking that doesn't count as protecting him."

"Well...I didn't kill him," Rosemary retorted. "I mean, I wanted to do much worse, and if he doesn't tell us all he knows, then I might make an exception."

"I can't stay here." Julius tensed. "I have to go with you."

"Nope," Killian growled, sounding almost as upset as Griffin. "He can't be trusted. We leave his ass here for someone to find him."

"No!" The word was out before I could take it back. But I couldn't let anything happen to Julius. The two of us were connected, and I wanted to understand why. What if he really was my brother and had been kidnapped at birth? It wouldn't be his fault that he'd wound up like this, if that was the case. I locked gazes with Griffin. *He saved me.*

So he could give you to the asshole who wants to control you, Griffin growled, and his jaw twitched with rage.

Maybe, but he and I can mind-link. He had to understand that this was important to me. That if Julius was hurt, I'd feel his pain, too. *My hands are tied.*

Griffin closed his eyes and rubbed a hand down his face. *This keeps getting better and better.*

"Look, if I don't go with you, I'm dead," Julius slurred from behind a fat lip. "One of them called their alpha and ratted my ass out while I was preoccupied with Sterlyn. Besides, I know how these guys work, so I can be an advantage to you." One of his eyes had swollen shut. "Backup will be here within thirty minutes. The farther away we get, the safer we all will be."

"We?" Killian laughed maniacally. "You think you're actually going with us?" He walked over to Julius and clenched his fist.

It was time for me to do something before things got out of hand.

CHAPTER TWO

I stepped in to stop Killian before he punched Julius and made things worse. Since my friends and I weren't all one pack with mind-links, no one but Griffin realized that Julius was the only reason I wasn't dead. "Stop, please." I winced, preparing for his inevitable reaction. "He saved me from being hit by a bullet."

"So he could hand you off to God knows who!" Killian didn't budge. "This asshole better be glad that you and Rosemary want him alive, or I'd rip out his throat right now." He turned to Julius. "Who is after Sterlyn?"

I understood why he was reacting this way. He was the first person I'd met in this group. He'd found me floating on a log in the flood-swollen Tennessee River, asleep after nearly drowning while running from the men who had decimated my pack. He'd pulled me out and taken me in. We'd become close in that short amount of time while we were pretending to be a couple; he felt like a missing part of my family I'd never known about until that fateful day. Because of him, I'd met Griffin, my fated mate and the love of my life. "Look, he's a silver wolf, which means I'm not alone." I didn't want to spill my guts in front of Julius, so I was choosing my words carefully. "But I agree." I spun around to Julius. "Who are you working for?"

Julius glanced at me, and something unreadable crossed his face. He knew we had a connection, but I didn't want him to know how much that affected me. He said, "If you take me with you, I'll consider telling you."

"Not good enough," Griffin rasped as he punched Julius in the eye and dropped him back to the ground. "We want to know everything you know. Now!"

"Girl, this asshole doesn't care that he's silver." Sierra shook her head, looking disappointed. "They're still coming after you, and he's helping them. Don't go making me think you're not as smart as I thought. I'm not sure my heart can take it."

"He's coming with us." Rosemary nodded, backing me up. "And I'll keep watch on him the entire time—but one way or another, this asshole will tell us everything."

Killian growled, low and threatening. "He's coming over my dead body."

"Well, that can be arranged," she retorted. "I agree with Sterlyn. We can't kill him, and he admitted to knowing he'll be dead if we leave him behind. So, if he comes with us, he'll have to answer our questions, or I'll kill him myself once we get settled."

"Dude, why am I the only one getting all up in arms?" Killian asked as he turned to face Griffin, looking for an ally. "She's your mate. Don't let me be the bad guy."

"I'm not thrilled about any of this." Griffin rubbed his temples and closed his eyes. "But Sterlyn wants him to come with us, and if that's what she wants, then so be it. The closer we keep him, the more easily we can keep an eye on him."

"Are you fucking serious?" Killian's mouth almost hit the ground. "What, is she your alpha now?"

I'd never seen Killian act this way, and his words cut deep. I tried to hold in my hurt, but it flowed into my bonds with Griffin and Julius, which pissed me off even more. I marched over to Killian and slapped him, stealing some power from the moon to make a point.

His head snapped back, while Sierra gasped.

Emotions were becoming charged, and horrible things were going to be said if I didn't keep a level head. "You're being an asshole. How dare you speak like that to your best friend, who would do anything for you *and* me?" I glanced at my mate, who gave me a tiny nod. "But it doesn't matter. You're outvoted. And even if you don't like that answer, I don't care. He's coming with us. We'll keep him under watch the entire time if that's what it takes." I stared Killian straight in the eye, ready to make him submit if that was what it came down to. I never liked playing the alpha card, but I'd do whatever was necessary to do what was right. And everything inside me told me Julius coming with us was just that.

Killian rubbed his cheek and grimaced.

"Sterlyn's right," Griffin said as he took my hand, scowling at his friend. "If she hadn't slapped you, you'd be dealing with me right now. You don't get to disrespect her that way, even if it's because you're afraid of losing her." *I'm actually kind of disappointed that you beat me to it. I've been wanting an excuse to punch him ever since I learned you two weren't romantically involved, but I've been trying to be the bigger person.*

My heart warmed, and some of my anger disappeared, nearly making me chuckle. I was afraid that we'd fight over

Julius, but once again, Griffin proved that what I needed was the most important thing to him. *I love you.*

And I love you. He squeezed my hand affectionately. *If I hadn't proven it before, this should damn well show you how much.*

The man had taken a bullet for me. *You have nothing to prove.* I kissed his lips, pouring my love into him.

"Really?" Rosemary wrinkled her nose. "They're doing that even at a time like this?"

"Have you ever been in love?" Sierra countered. "You know what? Never mind. It's obvious you haven't. There's always time for kissing."

Rosemary was right, though. We needed to get a move on. Despite me wanting Julius to come with us, I didn't trust him, so we needed to spend a few minutes making sure bringing him wasn't putting us even more at risk. "Are you part of anyone's pack?" He'd seemed surprised earlier that I could hear his thoughts, but I couldn't assume that meant he wasn't linked to anyone else.

"No, I'm not." Julius met my gaze as if he didn't have anything to hide. I watched for any signs of abnormalities beyond the horrible sulfuric smell of a lie, but nothing seemed out of sync with his natural inclinations.

Dad had taught me that over ninety-nine percent of society couldn't hide the obvious stench of a lie, but there was less than point one percent that somehow could manage to mask that standard tell. However, no lie was completely perfect, and the slightest change in heartbeat or breathing for a split second—or even an abnormal swallow—could give it away.

"Then how are you mentally stable?" Even during the short time I'd been rogue, I'd shown signs of going insane.

"Why wouldn't I be mentally stable?" He shrugged, his brows furrowing. "Is that some kind of wise crack?"

Sierra gestured at Julius. "He obviously isn't mentally stable since he's working with sick assholes."

His eyes darkened. "And you guys are so outstanding. I mean, you just killed a ton of men yourselves."

"To protect ourselves," I countered. This was once again turning into a highly volatile situation. "What I meant is, since you aren't part of a pack, how are you able to keep a sane mind?" I had to give Sierra some credit. He had obviously been manipulated, given how much hatred he held, but I didn't think it was his fault.

He chuckled darkly. "I've always been alone. I grew up that way. I haven't known any different."

Appeased, I turned my attention to my next task. This one would get the reaction from Griffin that Killian had given me. "Carter's brother is downstairs in the prison. We have to free him, too." The teen, Randall, had been taken hostage for leverage to force Carter to set me up to be kidnapped.

"Let's go." Griffin tugged me toward the car. "It's bad enough that we're taking dipshit over there, but now we're going to stay here even longer to rescue Randall and risk backup finding us?"

"That person is your responsibility because he's part of Killian's pack." Granted, Killian was Carter's direct alpha, but their pack protected one side of Shadow City. The very city that Griffin was supposed to be leading. "Killian's pack is our responsibility, and it's time we start acting like one pack and not two separate ones. Would you leave Killian behind?" A lot of the Shadow Ridge wolves felt slighted by the Shadow City packs...or that was the rumor I'd heard at the coffee shop. They were good enough to live outside the city and protect Shadow City supernaturals, but in return, the Shadow City wolves acted like they were above the Shadow Ridge pack. Now that Killian was taking over Shadow Ridge and Griffin was leading Shadow City, it was time to act like one pack again.

"You know I wouldn't," Griffin huffed, realizing that I'd already proven my point. "Fine, but dickhead here is going to go with Killian to get Randall instead of Killian having to stumble around, looking for the keys or a way to get him out."

"No, it's too risky." The best thing was to keep Julius right in front of us where he couldn't pull some sort of trick. "The keys to the jail cell are on the table. It shouldn't be hard to figure out."

"All right, I'll go. I'm linking with Randall so he doesn't get scared," Killian said as he ran off to the house.

I turned to Sierra and Griffin and said, "You two head back to the car."

"I'll keep an eye out for incoming vehicles. I'll be two miles southbound, so you shouldn't have any issues with hearing me if I see something." Rosemary took off into the sky, heading toward the road.

"They'll be here shortly," Julius growled, clearly annoyed. "We need to go or we're going to get caught. I offered to come with you all because I thought I'd get away from here faster, not be stuck waiting for my imminent death."

"With Rosemary gone, I'm staying here with you." Griffin crossed his arms, refusing to leave. "Sierra, hurry and go get the car." *After almost losing you, I can't leave you right now. And that way, two of us are watching Julius.*

His words softened me. He'd already agreed to so much, despite not being thrilled about it. *Okay.*

"Uh, why me?" Sierra asked and pointed at him. "You have two legs."

"You know Griffin would never leave here without me," I said. Sierra also wasn't the best fighter, so for her to not be in front of the house if their backup rolled up would be ideal, but I also didn't want to offend her. She'd been loyal and jumped into danger to help and be part of the team. Disregarding her would be a mistake. "We need you to get the car ready so we can get the hell out of here if things go south. Or worst case, you'll still be free and can get help if the rest of us are caught."

"Oh, okay." Sierra nodded, and her back straightened. A glint of determination darkened her irises to charcoal. "I can do that." She pulled the keys from her pocket and headed toward the car

I kept my gaze on Julius to avoid looking at the bodies that littered the ground. If I paid attention to them, I'd have flashbacks of my own slaughtered pack, and unlike these people, we hadn't done anything to warrant an attack.

When Sierra disappeared back into the tree line, I stepped toward him. "Now tell me who's after me. Who are you working for?"

"Why would I tell you now?" Julius sneered. "You could just leave my ass behind. I need to make sure you're invested in keeping me around."

Griffin clenched his fist. *That jackass.*

Yeah, I couldn't disagree with that sentiment. "We could still leave you here. Maybe you should give us something so we know your knowledge is worthwhile."

He smirked arrogantly. "Yeah, I'm not falling for that." There was so much animosity wafting off him, it was almost suffocating. I had no clue what I could've done to make him hate me so much.

The problem was that Julius knew he had us. We couldn't risk leaving him behind in case he actually did know something. And even if he didn't, I couldn't turn my back on one of my own. It would've been so much easier if I'd never found out he existed.

The front door swung open, and Randall and Killian ran outside.

Randall's shaggy brown hair clung to his face, sticky with greasy sweat, and when he saw us, his moss-colored eyes widened in horror, emphasizing the light purple bruise around his eye. "He's still here." The spicy smell of fear emanated from him.

Then Rosemary's scream filled the air. "Incoming!"

CHAPTER THREE

Her words rattled me as we sprang into action.

We crossed the gravel driveway, and Randall was able to keep up, despite the younger wolf's injuries. If his face was bruised like that, I could only imagine what the rest of his body looked like. They hadn't given us any food or water since I'd been there, so there was no telling the last time he'd eaten, which would slow his healing. A weaker shifter might not have been able to push through.

More confident in Randall's stamina, I kept my eyes forward, trying to ignore the corpses lying all over the ground. Even though we'd killed in self-defense, death still haunted me; there had been too much of it, and I was raised to always mourn the dead, regardless of the situation. In our attackers' minds, they weren't the bad guys, and in fairness, we could be viewed as the bad guys through another lens. It was all about perception.

By the time we reached the tree line, the rumble of an engine was purring faintly in my ears. Shit, they were getting here faster than I'd anticipated. They couldn't be more than a couple of miles away now.

Wings flapped overhead, and I glanced up. Rosemary's dark feathers almost blended into the night sky, which was saying something, given my better-than-normal vision. She grunted, "Hurry up. They'll be here in minutes if not sooner."

Even if the trees hid us, they'd pick up our scent easily. It was fresh and strong, and though Julius and I could easily outrun them on a night like this, we would be held back with Randall's injuries. He might be a trooper, but they would catch up to us, even with our head start.

Griffin ran faster as the crunching of gravel grew closer. The other two kept a steady pace behind us.

The only reason I wasn't panicking was because since I could hear the engine of the car Griffin had rented to trail my kidnappers' car from the coffee shop where they'd grabbed me, which meant we were getting closer to Sierra. We'd known the kidnapping was going to happen because Carter—the shop's manager, and my boss—had informed us this time around. We couldn't risk our enemies identifying Griffin's or Killian's vehicles, so we'd rented one and left it in the school parking lot overnight. Griffin had driven me to work at the shop like usual in his car so that nothing would seem suspicious, and then he, Killian, and Sierra had been able to stay under the radar in the rented car. Rosemary had followed in the sky.

Fortunately, the plan had worked. They'd remained undetected until we had to act when four additional men came here a day earlier than expected to retrieve me from Julius.

The trees grew thicker, helping to cover us from the silver moon's bright light. That would buy us a few minutes before the new arrivals realized what had happened. Well, maybe not that long—the bodies were easy to see.

A small break in the trees came into view. That had to be where they'd hidden the vehicle. *How close to the road is it?* Maybe we'd have a chance to get out of here after all.

It's a cutout, so not even a quarter-mile, Griffin answered, not missing a beat. *I want you in the front seat with me, okay?*

Julius needed to be in the far back seat so he wouldn't be close to a door. *I wouldn't have it any other way.*

The enemy vehicle had arrived at the house, and the sound of doors opening and closing made my skin crawl.

"What the hell happened here?" one guy asked, clearly at a loss for words. His baritone voice sounded worried. "How the hell did this happen with Julius being a fucking silver wolf?"

"I don't know," another guy spoke as he sniffed. "But they aren't far away. He must be chasing them because his scent blends with theirs. Do you smell how fresh it is?"

They would be on us soon if we didn't move our asses. They wouldn't be able to catch us, but if they were anything like the others, they had guns and could blow out the car tires.

Black peeked through the thinning trees, revealing the rental car about fifty yards ahead. They'd rented a Chevrolet Traverse to go unnoticed. The car didn't stand out, and no one would expect these young alphas to drive something so standard; everyone was used to Killian's fancy truck and Griffin's Navigator.

Our group increased the pace, but one guy's raspy voice yelled, "She came this way."

"What do we do then?" the baritone asked.

"We were instructed to kill the Shadow City alpha, too, if he interferes," the raspy guy answered. "Don't chicken out now. We're in too deep."

Don't chicken out? And now Griffin was a target. My being his mate had put a target on his back. The realization sank in before I could do anything about it.

"I'll distract them," Rosemary huffed, and flew toward them, trying to buy us time.

I hated that she kept putting herself in danger for me, but I'd gladly take her help. I normally wouldn't be as accepting, but her wings protected her in ways that none of us could equal.

Our breathing grew ragged as we rushed ahead. I could now see Sierra jump out of the driver's seat and dive into the back. She was as ready to get the hell out of here as the rest of us.

"Angel!" the baritone screamed. Rosemary must have begun her attack. "I'll take her, the rest of you go after them!"

At least that would keep one of the guards busy. Gunfire started once again, which wasn't surprising. These guys had the one consistent way of fighting, which still seemed so strange to me: they fought like humans instead of animals. Yes, guns were deadly, but our animals empowered our magic and made shifters the most formidable enemy. I used my wolf as much as possible, which I believed was one reason we kept winning, despite being outnumbered.

We reached the car, and Griffin pointed at the front seat. "Sterlyn goes there. The rest of you get in the back." He ran straight to the driver's seat and got in. "Sierra, move so that Killian can sit in the far back with Julius."

Sierra nodded and climbed into the middle bench seat as I opened the back door, hoping to help speed up the process. Julius frowned, pausing.

Get your ass in there. He obviously didn't want to sit in the very back, but he was going to have to learn his place in our circle...sooner rather than later. *I might have pushed for you to come, but if you put my family at risk, I'll leave you here without a second thought.* I shoved forward those feelings, wanting him to know that I meant them. *If you don't believe me, then test it.*

He huffed and climbed over the middle seat into the back while his conflicted feelings of both respect and hatred hit me. I wasn't sure why he felt either, but I could analyze all that later.

Killian and Randall reached the car door, and the poor kid jumped in headfirst, no doubt desperate to get out of here. I couldn't blame him. My skin crawled after being in that basement half a day, and he'd been there for a week, if not longer.

Grunting, Killian climbed over Sierra and into the back with Julius. He growled, "No funny business, jackass. One strange look, and I'll kick your ass."

The three guards darted toward us and broke through the thinning trees. They raised their guns and fired at us as Sierra reached for the door.

Griffin gunned the engine, causing the SUV's wheels to spin and fling dirt before we lurched forward.

"Close the door," Julius yelled, as Sierra bent and grabbed the door handle.

"I'm doing it, dumbass," Sierra growled back as another shot fired and Killian yelped in pain. The door slammed shut, but the metallic scent of blood filled the SUV.

Our attackers continued to shoot as Griffin spun onto the road, taking off toward Shadow Ridge. The bullets hit the plastic of the SUV, but luckily didn't hit the tires or any spots that would make the vehicle stop. Though their shots continued, we were out of harm's way as Griffin pushed the car, making the engine redline.

Since we were out of immediate danger, I turned around and scanned Killian, looking for the injury, as Randall leaned over the back of the seat to help his alpha. Killian bent forward, helping Randall survey the injury.

Blood soaked Killian's shirt at the shoulder. "Did the bullet exit?" I asked. The memory of when I'd been shot flashed through my head, the sensation of the phantom bullet turning my stomach. Griffin had gotten it out, but the extraction had hurt like a bitch, worse than when I'd been shot in the first place. But it was better to get the bullet out before your shifter healing set in, instead of having to reopen the wound later.

"I have no clue," he whispered, in pain.

"Aw." Sierra glanced over her shoulder, her face slightly pale. However, she felt good enough to make a jab. "Do you need some tissue?"

Ignoring her, Julius rolled his eyes. "Of course he doesn't. Lucky for you, I had to learn how to tend to injuries," he grumbled as he leaned over and lifted the sleeve of Killian's shirt. The material was soaked and sticking to his skin, and I was surprised when Julius gently moved the fabric away, taking care not to hurt him even worse.

Killian hissed and grimaced.

"What are you doing?" Randall asked, and shoved Julius away.

The silver wolf's hand dropped, yanking the shirt with it.

"Damn it," Killian huffed as his face tensed. "That hurt."

"You asshole," Randall yelled as he punched Julius in the face. "I'm going to kill you." There was so much hatred in his voice, it unnerved me.

Get him off me, or I'll hurt him, Julius linked. *I swear to God, I'm about to lose it.*

"Randall!" I shouted, leaning over the center console and catching his arm. "Stop. He wasn't hurting Killian. He was checking out the bullet wound and needed to move his shirt. Of *course* it's not going to feel good." I barely knew Randall, and I hated talking to anyone like that, but he needed to get his shit together. There was no telling what he'd endured in that house—and Julius probably deserved his anger—but there was too much going on to be acting this way.

"She's right." Killian backed me up. "He wasn't doing anything on purpose to hurt me. At least, not this second." Mistrust dripped from each word.

"Can I proceed, or are you going to start hitting me again?" Julius's jaw twitched, and he sneered at the young man.

"Fine," Randall snapped as he jabbed his finger in Julius's face. "But one wrong move, and I'll punch you again."

"Do you think you could actually beat my ass? Don't you remember what happened back in that house?" Julius's expression filled with disgust. "I'm holding back because you all let me come with you, but that's it. Do one more thing out of line, and I'll hit back. And you know my punch is going to hurt you worse than yours did me."

"Boys!" Sierra snapped her fingers and gave each one a level look. "Behave, and concentrate on the man who's injured and not the pissing match you two have going on. There are more important things than revenge and personal agendas."

At that moment, I could tell that Sierra was an oldest

child. She'd obviously helped look after her siblings, and thus, she knew how to put misbehaving idiots in their place.

Griffin glanced in the rearview mirror at Randall and said, "Julius is going to check Killian because he's the one with experience. If he pulls any funny shit, I'll handle it. Got it?"

"Yeah." Randall nodded and sat back in his seat, crossing his arms. His lips mashed together as he glanced out his window, staring into the darkness.

"Okay, let's try this again." Julius rolled his neck from side to side and reached across Killian's body. This time, he was able to move the shirt completely out of the way while Killian gritted his teeth.

"He'll be fine." Julius put his shirt back in place and sat back in his seat. "There's an exit hole, which you can see at the back of his shoulder. I wanted to make sure it was there. The wound is far enough from any main arteries, so it may hurt like a bitch for a while, but he'll be fine."

His heartbeat remained steady, nothing indicating a lie. "Thank God." I blew out a breath as I looked at the man who was my brother in every sense except biologically. "You scared the shit out of me."

"Welcome to our world," Killian said through clenched teeth. "Now you know how you make Griffin and me feel at all times."

I didn't want to keep the focus on his discomfort, so I smiled and turned back around in my seat.

"Dude, don't even try to compare yourself to me," Griffin teased, trying to ease the tension. "She's my fated mate; there's no competition. Think about how I've been suffering."

"Yeah, okay." Killian snorted. "She's my sister, so it's pretty much the same thing."

Julius huffed loudly in the back. *He's your brother?* He laughed bitterly in my head.

Not by blood. For him to act this way pretty much confirmed my suspicions. He didn't like Killian calling me sister, but there was no reason he should care...unless *he* was my brother. But how could he know about me and not try to find us? The questions were on the tip of my tongue, and my mind reeled. There were so many damn unknowns.

"No, it's not." Griffin wrinkled his nose. "When you meet your fated mate, you'll understand."

"Okay, boys." Sierra chuckled. "We got it. You both care about her. Can we just be quiet, for the love of God? After all that commotion, a little silence would be nice."

"I agree." I leaned my head back on my headrest and closed my eyes.

"Uh...what's going on?" Griffin's words startled me from my doze. "Killian, those are some of Shadow Ridge's police cars."

I blinked a few times before reality came crashing back in. We were passing by Shadow Ridge University, and there were indeed a few police cars parked in front of the school with flashing lights. My chest tightened.

What the hell had gone wrong while we were away?

CHAPTER FOUR

The flashing blue and red lights reminded me of a scene from a movie or some horrible news clip on television. We were still far away, but the lights were almost blinding in the darkness.

Killian groaned, still in pain. "This night keeps getting better. I'm covered in blood and injured. Isn't that bad enough?"

"It's nice to see my alpha being so strong and brave." Sierra snorted.

"Well, we can't leave the Navigator there. It's already been over twelve hours at this point." Griffin's knuckles turned white as he clutched the steering wheel.

Ugh. Once again, it felt like we were in an impossible situation. My mind began to race, causing my sanity to crack. I was so damn tired of us being put in difficult positions.

No. I couldn't break down. Not now.

"Let's park somewhere downtown and take the woods into the school," I suggested. "We can climb over the fence relatively easily." The huge gate and fence were only for the front part of the campus, in order to appear secure for the humans coming to visit, despite them never being admitted. This was a supernaturals-only college, but I knew they had to keep up the charade that everyone had a chance of attending. In truth, because of Griffin's father leading the charge, supernaturals from all over the world could attend. The admissions staff just weeded out the human applicants. Living this close to a powerful, hidden supernatural city would raise human suspicions and threaten to expose our races' presence to the human world.

Though we were much stronger than humans, they outnumbered us by leaps and bounds. And the few humans who had learned about us had developed weapons that could take us out. We didn't remain hidden for noble reasons—it was a means of survival.

"I can't go in there," Julius insisted. "We need to go somewhere else and forget about your damn cars."

"Except that Killian and Griffin disappeared, leaving their cars behind. This could be all about finding them." I had been so arrogant. I'd suggested they get a rental car so they could follow me without easily showing up on the enemy's radar. I'd thought that we'd return before nightfall, but I'd underestimated my enemy and might have caused this new situation. "If that's the case and we don't get their cars now, it could escalate things. You two should check in with your packs."

"Then how are you going to explain me?" Julius's voice took on a wild edge. "The people who are hunting you— well, now us—have spies everywhere. I can't be spotted."

"Killian introduced me at the university, and it wasn't a huge deal." He was freaking out over being seen, which made me wonder who was involved. Maybe this was a bigger group than we realized...or there were more people we trusted who could be wrapped up in this. What had those people done to Julius? "It's not like they're going to be able to tell you're a silver wolf on sight. If that were the case, they would've known about me."

Julius snapped, "We need to keep a low profile, which is the opposite of strolling up to police officers with a new person in tow, another who's been missing for weeks, and a Shadow Ridge alpha who's been shot up."

My stomach dropped, and bile rose in the back of my throat.

"What are you trying to say?" Griffin stopped the car in the middle of the road and turned toward the back. "That we run and hide? You obviously don't know Carter well. If none of us show up with his brother, he'll start running his mouth to anyone who'll listen."

"Regardless, if they're looking for Killian and Griffin, the longer we wait to show up, the more cops they'll have searching everywhere, which means you could be discovered, anyway," I said.

"It's not like I can hide in the trunk. They'll smell my scent. I guess I need to make it on my own." Julius's nostrils flared.

"Not happening," Griffin growled, and his eyes darkened. "Do you think that after you tried kidnapping Sterlyn multiple times to hand her over to some self-absorbed prick, we're going to trust you and let you go? There's no way in hell. In fact, you're going to tell us who the prick is, or we'll beat it out of you when we finally get back to the house."

"He must think we're idiots." Killian's face tightened, and he glanced at Julius, giving a small flinch as the only sign that his shoulder pained him. "Maybe we should just kill him and lose the threat."

"That wouldn't be smart." My chest squeezed at the

thought of something happening to Julius, but I couldn't let my emotions factor into this any longer. I needed to keep my head on straight but make sure I didn't lose my heart.

Dear God, if Dad knew how many times I'd repeated his little teaching moments that I used to roll my eyes at, he'd tease me and tell me he was smarter than I ever gave him credit for. But that was the problem with pure warriors who pushed their hearts aside. For whatever reason, they left their hearts outside the equation and made decisions based on logic, and that was when what was right became blurred concerning what they wanted done. Both parts were equally important—one shouldn't outweigh the other. "Right now, let's figure out our first problem, because he's afraid."

Julius's gaze met mine, and his pointer finger tapped on his leg.

He was uncomfortable that I'd called him out. Being afraid was hard for silver wolves to admit. Being confident and steadfast was ingrained in us.

"Okay, she has good points," Sierra jumped in, surprising me. She normally stayed out of strategy conversations. "So what do we do?"

"I still say kill the asshole," Killian grumbled and scowled. He looked a little green and sweaty, and I wondered if his wound was feeling worse.

Randall lifted a hand. "Hey, if that's what my alpha wants, who am I to disagree?"

Despite the horrible situation, his response made me smile. There was a little bit of Carter's smart mouth in him after all.

The sound of fluttering wings notified me that Rosemary was near. She tapped on my window, and I rolled it down.

She crossed her arms as she glared at me. "What the hell is going on? You're sitting in the middle of the road, stopped after midnight, not far away from a school crawling with Shadow City and Shadow Ridge guards."

"Shadow City?" Griffin leaned back against the headrest. "I figured it was only Shadow Ridge."

That could mean they were looking for Griffin. "What do we do? We can't show up with Julius as our prisoner and Killian injured."

"I'll take Julius with me to Griffin's." Rosemary rolled her shoulders as she prepared for his extra weight. "And I'll heal Killian. As long as you have an extra shirt, we should be good."

I kept forgetting she could heal. "Are you sure? You've been sticking your neck out for us a whole lot more than I could ever ask of you."

"That's one reason I don't mind doing it." Her gaze softened, and her beauty became even more breathtaking. She was so gorgeous that someone should have erected a statue of her. "You embody everything Mom told me about silver wolves, and thus, it's an honor to help you." She cleared her throat, seeming uncomfortable with her moment of vulnerability, and yanked open the back door on the passenger side. "Pull your shirt off," she ordered, and leaned over Randall toward Killian.

"Uh..." Killian seemed baffled for a second, and he swallowed nervously, still looking a bit green. He moved toward her, lowering his voice as if that would make any difference with all our supernatural ears. "I mean...I'm not saying no, but is now the time? Maybe a date first—"

Uh...does he have a thing for Rosemary? I snorted, somehow keeping the noise solely inside mine and Griffin's heads.

Griffin's shoulders shook, and his amusement flowed into me. *Not that I'm aware of, but who knows? I've never heard him say something with so much sincerity.*

I knew they'd gotten closer, but I hadn't realized it had come to this. Normally, races stuck to their own kind, but the thought of those two being together didn't bother me. They'd make a great team.

"Oh, dear God." Rosemary's eyes sparkled with humor before her perfectly veiled expression snapped back into place. "Didn't you just hear that I'm going to heal you? Your shirt is drenched with blood, and it works faster if I touch the actual wound."

Killian laughed loudly and winked, but I suspected he might be trying too hard to convince us. "Of course. I totally knew that."

He slowly removed his shirt, and Rosemary made a point of locking eyes with me as if she were making sure we knew that she wasn't watching him, which seemed odd. *Something has to be going on between those two.*

"Damn it." Killian groaned as he pulled the shirt over his head. "That still hurts a lot. Shouldn't I be healed more by now?"

"They laced their bullets with wolfsbane," Julius muttered. "To make you die more painfully."

Great, we had sick, *sadistic* assholes hunting us. No wonder Killian still looked shaky. I shouldn't have been surprised—they *did* want to capture me to either force me into birthing babies or kill me. Little did the general wolf population know that silver wolves reproduced at a slower rate. That was one reason why Dad and Mom had only me...and, well, Cyrus. Even the males were affected by a low reproductive rate. A regular wolf could birth a baby a year, but it took a silver wolf ten years, if not longer, to conceive once we began to try, and our window of fertility was drastically reduced, as well. Realistically, Griffin and I would most likely have only one child, two max. My pack had been the only one in existence, and we'd kept how little we could reproduce a secret. We were already living in hiding since we'd always feared people would hunt us for this exact reason—to manipulate us and use our strength and magic against everyone else to control all the races.

Dad had told me that we were gifted by the moon to not only be stronger but to also make us pure in intent. Great power comes with responsibility, and magic had a way of balancing itself. Silver wolves would never want to rule over the supernatural world because we wanted the best for everyone, not just ourselves or our race.

"Lovely," Rosemary retorted as she placed her hands on Killian's wound. Her hands glowed an iridescent white as she pushed her magic into his injury. "Thankfully, that won't impact my magic."

"Oh, thank God." Killian sighed as his body began to heal in earnest. "That was almost unbearable."

She kept her hands on him for a few more seconds, then dropped them and stared at Julius. She commanded, "Get out. You're coming with me." Glancing at Griffin, she added, "And get the hell out of the middle of the road. You're lucky no one else has come through here yet."

"It's the middle of the night." Griffin lifted both hands. "We should be good."

Julius blew out a breath and squeezed past Randall out of the car.

Rosemary still blocked most of the doorway, proving I was right to trust her to take the silver wolf. She knew that if she moved even a foot too far away, Julius could take off. Yes, she was fast, but on a full moon, he could outrun her.

Thankfully, she could outfly him, but she needed to stay close and always on alert.

When he climbed from the SUV, she grabbed his arms and took off toward the sky. "I'll meet you at Griffin's!" she called, but they were out of sight before I could respond.

I watched as Sierra climbed into the far back seat by Killian then started digging through the trunk as Griffin followed Rosemary's instructions, pulling to the side of the road.

"Here. Please." Sierra tossed Killian a shirt and covered her eyes with her hands. "You're like a brother to me, and I prefer you clothed."

I cringed, trying to keep my eyes adverted. Killian was an attractive man, but I viewed him as family now. And no one wanted to see their brother naked.

"Me too," Griffin deadpanned and winked at me, trying to help with the emotions he could feel brimming inside me.

I loved him so much for it, but I wouldn't feel at ease until we were back home safe in our bed. "It might be best if Sierra and Randall don't come to the university with us. Maybe they can hang out in the woods until we come back and pick them up. It would be safe for them here, especially in wolf form."

"We can shift and run back to the pack neighborhood. It's only about a twenty-minute run from here," Sierra said as she stretched and patted Randall's arm. "I can drop Randall at his house. And I bet I'll still beat you back to your place."

"Yeah, I linked to Carter now that we're close enough." Randall rolled his eyes. "He's a hot mess and needs to see me. I love him, but damn, he can be high maintenance."

"Thanks for that." Killian groaned. "He's been nagging nonstop."

"Wait...isn't it supposed to be the younger brother bugging the older one?" Sierra climbed back to the middle row and gestured for Randall to get out.

Randall laughed, but it held an edge. "Yeah, that's what I always thought, but that hasn't been the case."

"I hate to ask, but before you go..." I turned my body, wanting Randall to feel my sincerity. "Do you know or remember anything that could help us?"

"I don't think so." Randall exhaled and grimaced. "I mean...it was those five guards most of the time. Julius only dropped by every now and then. They talked about some guy in charge that only showed his face to Julius, but they were all promised large sums of money and a nice place to live. Other than talking shit about each other, they were kind of tight-lipped."

That didn't surprise me. They wouldn't want to divulge too much in case Randall did get free. But I'd had to at least try. "Well, if you think of anything later, let us know."

He opened the door and got out, then paused. "Thank you all for saving me." His attention locked on me. "And I know it's because of you that I got out. If you hadn't seen me..." He trailed off, and his face filled with horror. "I...I don't know what would have happened." He moved out of the way, heading to the tree line.

"I'll see you at Griffin's." Sierra climbed out of the car, but before shutting the door, she stuck her head back in. "And be careful. The three of you attract crazy like I've never seen before." She slammed the door and hurried after Randall.

"You know, you could go with them." Griffin put the car in drive but didn't press the gas. "And keep an eye on them."

In other words, he wanted me to stay protected. But they were safe in the woods, and we both knew it. The enemy wouldn't have regrouped yet. They would attack again—and soon—but not tonight. "Did you mean it when you said you want us to lead your people together?"

His shoulders tensed, knowing his answer would only reinforce that I should go with him. Instead of answering, he blew out a breath and turned back toward the university.

"If you're going to be mad at anyone, it should be fate." Killian chuckled behind me, but it was devoid of humor. "She's the one who put you together with a headstrong, independent fighting machine." I heard shuffling as he moved from the far back onto the middle seat.

"Yeah, but I wouldn't have it any other way." Griffin rubbed his eyes and sighed. "The truth is, we protect each other. Not just her and me, but you, too. We're stronger together."

The truth of his words hung in the car the entire way to the university. We *were* stronger together. The three of us were not just friends, but family...a pack. It was about damn time we started seeing each other that way. The divide among shifters, particularly our kind, only weakened us. It was a self-inflicted injury.

The university came into view as we followed the black wrought-iron fence to the empty guard station. Griffin pulled the entry card from the rental's glove box and scanned it, opening the gates.

He slowly pulled to the front of the main office building. Guards shouted at our approach, not familiar with the SUV, and Dick Harding marched out in his black suit with a guard right behind him.

I sucked in a breath. Of course Dick would be here. He was a council member and vying for Griffin's top spot, even though my mate hadn't quite figured that out yet. But he was beginning to.

If that asshole was on campus, that meant he was using whatever situation we'd just driven into to gain more control. But I wouldn't let Griffin fall victim to some narcissistic, power-hungry douchebag. It was time to take a stand together in front of everyone. The moment to show that Griffin and I would lead together without outside influence was now.

In other words, it was time to take back what was rightfully Griffin's.

CHAPTER FIVE

Dick tugged at the lapels of his black suit as he marched toward the rental car. The windows were dark, so he couldn't see in. His salt and pepper hair was over-gelled to the point of looking greasy, and he ran his fingers through his dark scruff as his ebony eyes squinted, like that would help him see inside.

Dumbass. He didn't have X-ray vision, just wolf vision.

"Whoever the hell it is, get out of the car," Dick growled, his face squinched. "Now."

You better roll the window down before this gets out of hand. This entire situation was odd. Why were there so many cars out there? And the fact that Dick was here in the middle of the night didn't add up.

Griffin rolled the window down, and when his face came into view, Dick's eyes slightly widened as his musky sandalwood scent floated into the SUV.

"Griffin?" Dick asked, sounding truly shocked. "What are you doing here?"

"Uh...I go to school here and needed to get my car. I left it here today." He arched an eyebrow at his fatherlike figure, then looked at a guard who'd joined Dick. "Is there a problem?"

"Of course not, sir." The face of the guard stretched into a smile. He extended his hand to my mate. His black clothes were crisp with no signs of wrinkles, and his matching black hat sat on dark chestnut hair that spilled from the edges. The hat was marked with a crescent of two buildings and an upside-down paw print above it, the logo for Shadow City. "My name is Lars. We've been searching for you."

"For me?" Griffin tapped his chest. "Why?"

"Because Carter called, informing us that Dove disappeared," Dick said, as he gestured to me. "And then you couldn't be found."

"Did you expect him to just sit back and twiddle his thumbs when his fated mate had gone missing?" I asked. I bet he hadn't. In fact, I'd have wagered that he'd hoped that Griffin got hurt along with me. I mean, here he was, in the middle of the night, dressed to the nines. He'd put time and thought into what he wore on campus, which signaled some kind of power play. "Would you wait around if your mate went missing?"

"Probably," Killian chuckled, causing Dick to flick his gaze to the back seat. However, Killian didn't miss a beat as he continued, "They're chosen, anyway, so they don't have as strong of a connection."

I bit my cheek, desperate to find a way to keep my smirk from spreading. Killian had pretended to justify why Dick wouldn't feel as passionate about his wife by effectively reminding everyone that he had a chosen mate rather than a fated one. Every shifter knew that a fated mate made a person stronger in a way that a chosen mate never could. He'd weakened Dick's status compared to Griffin's with me by his side.

"That doesn't make a difference." Dick's nostrils flared as he glowered. "I'd..." He trailed off.

He and his mate barely get along. Griffin linked. *They're good at pretending, but behind closed doors, they're awful. They live next door to my family in Shadow City, and we can hear them yelling through the walls. But Dad and I never confronted Dick about it.*

That was information that I could hold close to use when it might be advantageous. Sometimes, keeping the tidbits quiet helped make a bigger impact later when you needed it. For now, Killian had sufficiently called Dick out, and I didn't want to anger the beast more than he already was. He might explode...

Hmm...that made it so much more tempting.

"Well, he's here," I said. If we kept pushing Dick, he could play the victim, claiming that he'd stormed the halls, looking for their alpha, and all we'd done was show up and insult him. He'd use whatever he could to cast Griffin in a bad light to prove that he wasn't fit to actually lead. "And thank you for your concern. It's nice to know that Griffin has people who have his back." I smiled sweetly because I knew Dick understood that I hadn't been referring to him, but rather to myself and Killian. He'd soon learn he wasn't the only one able to play the nice guy.

"Of course." He forced a smile, but all it accomplished was making him look constipated.

"So, what happened, sir?" Lars took a few steps closer.

If we wanted to sniff out who was behind all of this, we'd have to be vague and keep our ears alert. That way, if anyone knew more specific details, we could identify them. I needed to be careful and make sure I didn't say anything that could be a lie. "We're not sure, exactly," I said before Griffin could answer Lars. "Someone put a bag over my head, so I couldn't see much, but I know my kidnappers drove me about an hour east from here. Luckily, these two guys"—I beamed at Griffin and then Killian—"found me before anything truly horrible happened."

"Oh, man." Lars's sea-green eyes sparkled with admiration. "You're lucky that they found you in time. Do we need to go check out the area? And what's with the rental car?"

"We don't have jurisdiction over that area," Dick growled. "So unfortunately, we can't check it out. The last thing we need to do is get more involved and make our city a target."

Of course Dick didn't want us to check it out. Every meeting with him made him more suspicious than the last.

"Are you sure the city is a target? Or is it just my mate?" Griffin asked, his brows furrowed.

Don't push too hard. We didn't want to alert Dick that we were suspicious of him. *He needs to hang himself naturally.*

Dick laughed loudly.

Fine, I'll let him off the hook, Griffin replied. "As for the rental, we thought it'd be nice to have something different so people couldn't easily identify us." He shrugged and reached over the center console, taking my hand as he stared lovingly at me. "Good thing we had the crazy idea, or we might not have been able to track her, since they'd probably have recognized my car."

"You're going to have a hard time returning it." Lars gestured to the back of the SUV. "You have at least three bullet holes on this side."

An older man ran out the front door of the school, heading straight to the car, his bald head glistening in the moonlight. A brown shirt with the Shadow Ridge crest of a paw print on the front covered his large, muscular chest. He was only slightly smaller than Griffin, which meant he was huge by wolf standards. His face was lined with concern as he beelined to us. "Are they okay?"

"Yeah, Billy." Killian's voice softened to the tone he only used for me. "Sorry if we caused a problem."

"As long as you three are safe, that's all that matters," he replied. Goodness radiated off him, especially standing next to Dick. This must be the man who'd been holding things down on the Shadow Ridge side since Killian's parents passed.

"Well, as you can see, they are." Dick nodded curtly at us. "So you and the other guards are dismissed." He wrinkled his nose as if speaking to Billy was beneath him.

Billy lifted his chin, and his acorn eyes narrowed. "Shadow Ridge guards were here before Shadow City's personnel. If—"

"Now listen here." Dick pivoted toward the beta, looking ready to unleash the rage he was barely containing.

Do something, I encouraged Griffin. It was important for him to be the one to put Dick in his place, not me. The Shadow City guards needed to see their true leader take control. *We should be one pack, not divided.* I must have sounded like a broken record, but going against the established norm was hard. I finally understood how Dad felt all those times our pack rolled their eyes at him being insistent the day would come when we'd need to fight and protect not only our own kind, but the entire supernatural world. None of us had believed it because nothing had happened for centuries. Now here I was, harping at the guys, trying to encourage them to embrace change.

Maybe nagging them was more accurate, but...harping sounded a *little* better.

"No, he's right," Griffin said. "If Shadow Ridge arrived

here first, they deserve to be part of this conversation. After all, not only were Dove and I at risk, but their alpha, too." Griffin straightened his back, his trepidation wafting into me. *You're right, but damn, why is this so hard?*

Because it's easier not to upset anyone. And I had a feeling the more we rattled Dick, the quicker he'd show his true colors. But a confrontation had always been inevitable. That man was determined to take control. He'd been going slower and easier only while Griffin had been compliant. *Especially someone you grew up believing had your best interests at heart.*

Dick huffed, and his jaw twitched as his composure slipped. "Now, Griffin, you asked me to handle things while you finished school and goofed off. Why don't you stay out of this and let me take care of it like usual?"

God. He was such a prick. He'd purposely used that term to undermine Griffin in front of everyone. I opened my mouth to defend my mate, but he surprised me.

"You're right. I did." Griffin's face was smooth as if he didn't have a single worry, but the vein in his neck bulged. "And effective as of this moment, Dove and I plan to become more involved."

You handled that perfectly. If he had told Dick we were ready to take back control, it would have pushed him over the edge, and we weren't ready for that. Not yet. We needed to move the needle slowly and gauge the fallout. Someone as vile as Dick could cause even more chaos for us, and the others needed to see Griffin begin to take the reins so they'd feel comfortable backing him when the time came.

Dick's mouth dropped before he closed it, and his beady eyes landed on me—Griffin had taken him by surprise. He swallowed hard and rolled his shoulders as if the suit was suddenly too much. "I think you have something to do with that decision."

I'd never had someone look at me with such disgust. It both unsettled and thrilled me. Dad always said that whenever someone met you, if they didn't either love or hate you, you'd done something wrong because you'd blended into the background—been unmemorable. Silver wolves were about taking a stance and doing the right thing, so we should never go under the radar unless we did so purposely. Between Dick and his daughter, Luna, I'd definitely followed Dad's advice. "Nope, this was all Griffin." And that was the truth. I'd only grounded him, which enabled him to see what the future should be.

"Whether she did or didn't is irrelevant," Griffin said with annoyance. "The fact remains that it's solely my decision to make. On that note, my mate has been rescued, and we almost didn't make it through, so I think it's best if we get our cars and head home. We'll take care of the rental tomorrow."

Dick's jaw twitched, but he nodded, unable to do much else.

"Billy..." Killian leaned forward and placed a hand on my shoulder, effectively showing I was under his protection too. "We need a handful of guards available at Griffin's in case something goes awry."

Unlike Dick, Billy flashed a proud smile. "I can send them there now."

My body tensed. Julius was there. If the guards saw him, there was no telling what kind of problems that could cause. I understood we needed protection, but if the enemy found out where Julius was staying, they could try to kill him. We had no clue yet who was working against us—we needed those answers from Julius. And the fact that there were at least two people who'd killed themselves rather than be caught spoke volumes about what his controllers would do if they got ahold of him.

The thought of Julius being injured upset me way more than it should.

It'll be fine. Griffin obviously understood what was roiling inside me. *Rosemary should already be there with Julius. I gave her a key this morning in case we had to split up, so no one will see him come in.*

I hadn't considered that. The enemy wouldn't expect an angel to be flying Julius around. Having the guards could work in our favor. I heaved a sigh. We should be okay.

"If you're okay with that plan, I'll link them myself." Killian rubbed my shoulder for a second before removing his hand.

"Kill, they're your pack." Billy patted the hood of the SUV. "You don't need my permission to act as the alpha."

And that was the largest difference between Dick and Billy. I already liked Billy and could easily view him as a friend or even a family member in the future.

"Lars, do you mind coordinating a few Shadow City guards, too?" Griffin didn't even bother looking at Dick and spoke directly to the guard. "It would be good for the two forces to work together."

"Of course, sir." Lars's face reminded me of a kid's on Christmas morning.

"Wait." Dick shook his head as his hands clenched. "Why do we need to involve our guards when Shadow Ridge's can do the job just fine?"

"Because pooling resources is always smart, and Shadow Ridge has already given lives to the cause," I said. I hated the man. "Why should Shadow Ridge always risk themselves and their pack for both cities? Don't you think there should be more of a partnership?"

"This is how things work," Dick spoke through gritted teeth. "I don't expect you to understand."

"Excuse me." Griffin's voice laced with alpha will as he stared the prick down. "You will not speak to her like that again. Do I make myself clear?"

Dick grimaced and growled. "Perfectly."

"As I was saying, please send at least two guards to help out the Shadow Ridge guards," Griffin said stiffly to Lars. "If you have any questions or problems, link me directly."

Lars's head bobbed like a doll's, and Griffin pulled forward, heading straight to the vehicles.

This whole day had been a shit show, and it still wasn't over.

GRIFFIN PULLED his vehicle into his garage, passing three pack members standing guard out front.

The guards had officially circled the house, which both stressed and comforted me. As long as Julius didn't do anything stupid, we should be safe. But he seemed to be a hothead, and the moon was still full, despite it descending in the night sky.

The two of us climbed out of our vehicle just as Killian entered the garage. As the door lowered, I exhaled and relaxed, feeling so damn glad Rosemary was near. We might not have made it out of that place if not for her. She was a powerful ally, and I wanted to know why she was helping us. Why would her mom be so insistent that they should help protect the silver wolves? We were missing a chunk of the story.

"I said get out of their room now!" Rosemary commanded so loudly we could hear her in the garage. "You might be a silver wolf, but I *will* kick your ass."

Just when I thought I might be able to crawl into bed, there was already another fight brewing. I ran toward the interior door, needing to know exactly what Julius was snooping for. Maybe he was one of the less than point one percent of our population that could lie, but I couldn't fathom it. My gut said differently.

There was only one way to find out, so I marched into the house.

CHAPTER SIX

The commotion was coming from mine and Griffin's bedroom, so I stalked through the kitchen, down the hallway past Sierra, who was flipping the station on the TV, and into the room. Griffin and Killian were only a few steps behind me, ready to fight.

Usually, this room, with its warm blue walls that reminded me of the ocean and the dark walnut furniture that reminded me of the forest, was my sanctuary.

But not today.

Julius had dug through Griffin's room and found the family album, journal, and notes that I'd hidden under the bed. Angst, confusion, and hurt swirled inside him, spilling into me.

The album lay on the floor, open to the picture of Mom holding my brother and me on a bed. Blood spotted our bodies, proving that we'd just been born. Dad had his arms wrapped around Mom's shoulders, and they both looked so damn happy.

Each time I looked at this photo, it stole my breath.

My brother having been stripped from us was horrible,

whether it was due to death or kidnapping. The man who sat on the floor was rocking himself as he read Dad's journal, his face crumpled in agony.

For him to be looking so desperately for answers, he had to be Cyrus.

Rosemary stood over him, her body coursing with anger. The angel wasn't the most empathetic person, and being ignored didn't sit well with her.

"You heard her," Griffin growled as he appeared to the right of me, with Killian flanking me on the left. "Get the hell out of here. What do you think you're doing?"

All they could see was a threat inside our house, but I saw a lost, broken man. "He's looking for answers." It was that simple.

He wanted to find himself.

"Well, this is the wrong fucking way to do it." Griffin waved his hands around the room. "He's in our bedroom and digging through my drawers."

Sierra entered the room with a smile—or grimace—I wasn't sure. She arched an eyebrow at me as she inhaled sharply.

"I'm so sorry," she said in her usual talking-shit voice. "But when you say drawers, do you mean the shelf or your actual underwear?" She waved a hand to the still-open drawer with his boxers shoved to the side and spilling out. "You can see where I'd be confused."

Killian closed his eyes and shook his head. "Now isn't the time."

"Get out," Griffin rasped with rage, directing it toward her and away from Julius. "Now."

I couldn't help but grin, appreciating Sierra diverting some of his anger toward her. But Griffin would have to come to grips with Julius. He wouldn't be leaving anytime soon, and there was too much other shit to focus on for us to waste energy on something that wouldn't change. *Hey, give me a moment alone with Julius.* I already knew how he'd react to that comment, but I needed a chance to talk to Julius alone.

Hell, no. Griffin turned his icy glare on me. *Not happening.*

His outright refusal pissed me off. *That wasn't a request,* I snapped. *But if you'd rather I leave with him, that can be arranged.* I wasn't some meek mate who would bend to his will—I was my own person. Whether he liked it or not, I made my own decisions.

He organized a kidnapping to hand you off to some limp-dick prick who hoped he could get a hard-on long enough to impregnate you. Griffin's body was so tense, he could pass as a statue. *So excuse me if I'm not thrilled to leave you alone with him.*

Forcing myself to take a deep breath, I thought through my next words. He was my mate and deserved some sort of consideration for how he was feeling. I had forced him to watch me walk into a dangerous situation earlier today, and he saw Julius as a continuation of that threat. *I understand, but I can feel him spiraling out of control. Stay right next to the door, and if anything feels wrong, you can barge right in. Just give us the illusion of privacy.* I knew in my heart that he loved me and that he was reacting from fear.

"Why aren't you listening to me? I told you to get the hell out of here." Rosemary faced us with her brows furrowed. She pursed her lips as she tilted her head. "Do you think he's deaf? Can wolves suddenly go deaf?"

"It's called selective hearing," Sierra hollered from down the hall. "All men suffer from it. I'm surprised it took you so long to learn this."

"She can't keep her mouth shut," Killian grumbled, and ran a hand down his face. "It's like she gets worse instead of better. She used to only be this bad with Olive."

Olive—his late sister. She'd died a couple of years ago, along with the rest of Killian's family. He rarely spoke of them, so for him to say her name startled me.

Griffin sighed, making it clear that he wasn't happy. "Let's give Sterlyn a few minutes alone with *him*."

"You wolves have such a weird sense of humor," Rosemary said as she crossed her arms and stared at Griffin. His somber expression didn't change. "Wait...you aren't joking?"

"No, unfortunately, I'm not." Griffin's voice was strained, and he stomped over to Julius, sneering, "But one wrong move, and we'll be back in here in a flash. Don't get any stupid ideas."

Julius's irises darkened to gunmetal as a stormy expression crossed his face. "I'm here with a stronger silver wolf and an angel. That alone would give anyone pause." He made it clear that he wasn't scared of Griffin and Killian.

Great, these guys were going to have a power struggle, which wouldn't result in anything good. Just more anger and tension. "Okay, we got it. You're both strong alphas. Noted," I said. "Now I'd like to have a few minutes with him."

Rosemary strolled over to me and spoke into my ear. "Do you think that's wise?"

"Yes, I think it might help," I replied, and placed a hand on her shoulder. "But thank you for your concern."

Her face tightened, and she picked at her nails like she was suddenly uncomfortable. "I just...like you better than most. Even those of my own race."

My heart seemed to keep growing, making room for

more people. Whether the angel admitted it, she cared for me and probably every other person in this group. She and Killian didn't argue nearly as much as they had when I'd first met her, and she'd even smiled at some of Sierra's absurd comments. This was one reason the great divide among the races had to come down. Inherently, we'd always remain more separate, but we didn't have to work against each other. "I feel the same way about you, but I need you to trust me."

"Fine. Shout if you need me." She nodded and marched out the door, not even giving a backward glance.

Why couldn't Killian and Griffin be that conciliatory?

"If you so much as fart weird, Griffin and I are in here," Killian warned Julius as he pulled me into a huge hug, wrapping his arms securely around me. "And I swear, you're trying to see how far you can push us."

I returned the embrace, knowing that this whole situation had been hard on him, too. "Not on purpose. I promise."

"All right, let my mate go," Griffin grumbled, and he kissed my cheek. "You don't have long. That's even pushing it, considering the way I'm feeling."

That was something to start with. Julius and I wouldn't be able to discuss everything in one conversation, anyway, and I was exhausted. Now that the bed was only a few feet away, all I wanted to do was climb into it with Griffin. "Okay."

One thing out of line, if he's even breathing funny, you let me know. Griffin linked, staring deep into my eyes, looking like he could see into my soul. *I can't chance losing you again.*

I'm not going anywhere. I kissed him gently. *He has to be my brother. I need to talk to him and connect with him.*

Otherwise, he's not going to help us. He's vulnerable right now, and he needs me.

Griffin nibbled on his bottom lip and looked away. "Come on, man," he said to Killian.

The two of them exited, and Griffin glanced at me one last time before shutting the door.

The room somehow seemed overwhelming with just Julius and me inside, despite there being fewer people.

He didn't acknowledge me, but instead kept flipping the pages of the photo album. I casually walked over to him, trying not to seem threatening. This was something I couldn't alpha out of him. He needed to come to grips with it on his own terms, but that didn't mean that nudging him in the right direction was out of the question.

Pictures of me at my first birthday party was where he'd gotten to in the book. A birthday he should've been a part of.

"I didn't know you existed until I found the album and journal barely a week ago." I sat next to him and pointed at a picture of me with pink icing and chocolate cake all over my face. Mom and Dad stood on either side of me. My eyes had been more purple then, before the silver set in, and my silver hair was pulled into short pigtails. I had a large smile on my face, proving that I was happy and loved. However, now that I knew about my brother, I noted a sadness in my parents' eyes. That must have been both a horrible and joyful day for them, remembering the death of one child while celebrating the life of another.

His jaw flexed, and he flipped the page to the next set of pictures. "Do you think that makes me feel better? It makes it worse."

"Did you know that you're my brother?" And yet, he'd still tried to hand me over to God knew who.

"My parents gave me up because they only wanted you. The girl alpha." Disgust and hatred rang clear in his words. "I was reminded daily by the person who took care of me that I should be grateful that I had them, since my parents didn't want me. That despite my uselessness, they still took me in."

My heart hurt for him, but he couldn't be angry with me over that. "Did you not hear the part about me not knowing you existed until a few days ago?" Maybe Rosemary was right. Could he be hard of hearing?

"And what's *their* excuse?" He pushed the picture album away. "They didn't even tell you about me."

"They thought you were *dead*." His accusation stunned me. "The witch assigned to heal Mom told them that you died while she was cleaning us up. The witch *had* to be in on it. She brought you back out with me, and you didn't have a heartbeat. She must have spelled you or something."

"I want to hear this from them." He climbed to his feet and waved his arms around. "I'm assuming they'll be here at some point. They wouldn't want to leave their precious *daughter* unattended for long."

Wait. He thought our parents were still alive? He had no clue that they were dead. But then who else was in play? I wanted to break the news to him gently, but I wasn't sure how that was even possible. In some ways, their death would be worse for him because he'd never have the opportunity to know them. At least I'd had that, and selfishly, I wouldn't change it for the world. "They're no longer living."

"What?" He sagged against the wall. "They're *dead*?"

"Yeah." I couldn't hide the pain in my voice. I missed them so damn much.

"But...when?" The strong young man I'd met today now

looked broken. Like every bit of hope he'd clutched had been destroyed.

"A few weeks ago." I should tell him more, but I wasn't emotionally ready for it. If I tried, I'd fall apart. And that was something I couldn't do. Not in front of him. Not yet. I didn't trust him, and the only people you should ever show weakness to were the ones who had your back even in the worst of times. Killian, Griffin, Rosemary, and Sierra had proven that. I deflected the situation. "I'm curious about who raised you in their absence, though."

"Just some person who was paid and forced to do it. Don't worry, she wasn't the one who wanted you. When I got old enough to take care of myself, she disappeared just like everyone does with me." He frowned and glanced around the room like the answer would magically appear. "How did you find out about me?"

I wanted to push the conversation more, but there was so much pain in his words. Besides, this was where I'd hoped we'd land from the very beginning. He could read the stories in Dad's own words. That would mean so much more than coming from me. He'd be able to read the heart-break in them and maybe find a sense of peace over time.

I gestured to the journal that lay closed on the shaggy carpet. "In there. I found the journal and album back at my pack house." I grabbed it and opened it to February fourth of the year we were born, then handed it to him. "Here, read it."

Julius took the worn leather book in his hands and turned it around. As his eyes scanned the pages, my heart broke in two, watching and feeling his pain.

His hands tightened on the book, and I forced myself to remain quiet. I didn't want him to hurt the pages, but he had to go through his process, and I didn't want to interfere.

His jaw clenched, and he began to swallow like his throat was dry. When his eyes watered, I wasn't surprised; everything he'd ever wanted to know was right in his grasp. But sometimes, no matter how badly we wanted the truth, we weren't nearly as prepared for it as we thought.

"This has to be some sick joke." Julius slammed the book closed but didn't put it down. "There's no way that happened. You're manipulating me, trying to turn me into one of your brainless followers like those idiots out there. I won't fall for this act."

I could only imagine what he was going through. I took a deep breath and sighed. "Cyrus—" I hated calling him by his fake name.

"No!" he yelled, and his face turned red. "Do *not* call me that! That's not my name. And even if it was, your lying ass better not call me that. All those years, my caregiver told me the truth about you. You're just a piece of shit who'll do everything possible to be on top. You're only good for breeding an army." He shook his head and marched to the door. "I can't do this."

He yanked open the door, revealing Griffin. My mate snarled, "What the fuck is your problem? You can't yell at her like that."

And he was right—Cyrus couldn't, but only I would be able to demand his respect. Griffin couldn't command it for me, so I knew exactly what I had to do.

CHAPTER SEVEN

I grabbed Julius's shoulders and slammed him into the wall, causing the door to rattle. I allowed my wolf to surge and felt alpha will begin to bubble within me, but I pushed the urge down, needing to make him respect me without that influence.

Alpha will should be used only as a last resort, when nothing else would work, or if there was a deadly risk if someone did not obey. Respect should be earned, not forced, whenever possible.

"I get that you're upset." I did. Hell, I was upset, too. My life hadn't been bad, and though he'd had it a lot worse than I had, my past hadn't been a walk in the park, either. "But you can't act out like that. I didn't cause this. Why would you think I was involved? I would've loved having a sibling growing up."

He held his chin high in defiance as his lips flattened. Despite the rage pouring from him into me, he held the picture album and journal tight against his chest and snapped, "Are you going to let me go now?"

Keeping my gaze locked on his, I shook my head. "Not until you tell me that you understand."

Griffin stepped beside me and cracked his neck from side to side. "And apologize before I have to make you."

Oh, dear God. *Please stop. You're going to make this worse.* I loved that Griffin wanted to have my back and support me, but all he was doing was antagonizing Julius—and all I wanted *him* to do was calm down. He needed time to process his emotions, but not in an explosive, disrespectful way. All we'd done was help him.

"You and what army?" Julius sneered at Griffin, while a faint glow lightened his silver irises.

They were having yet another pissing match. "Yeah, we get it. You're a big, mean, silver wolf." I let the sarcasm drip from each word. "But I'm one, too, and stronger than both of you." I glared at Griffin as well. There, I'd insulted both of their manhoods. Maybe that would wrap things up more quickly.

If I didn't love you, that would infuriate me, Griffin linked.

All strong wolves desired to be the strongest alpha. That was how most supernaturals were wired and one reason why there was so much corruption in our world. In wolves, alphas not only wanted to be the strongest, but also to protect their pack. It was an internal struggle that was always at the core of our wolf.

Dad had taught me that each supernatural race had some sort of inherent conflict it struggled with. Angels had their lack of emotional range—they were built to be warriors and tended to be colder and more closed off, making them seem heartless at times. Vampires were born or turned with humanity, but they had a thirst for blood and power that was always at war with their empathetic side. The list went on and on.

For silver wolves, strength and weakness were tied to the same thing: the moon.

The larger the moon, the more powerful we were, but the less the moon glowed until it waned to a new moon, the weaker we were. Our power grew and lessened. Naturally, our kind had dubbed the full moon "the silver moon."

"You don't think I know that?" Julius growled as his nose wrinkled in disgust. "Your power is the only reason you kept escaping."

"That's not true." Strength was great, but that wasn't how I'd survived. Maybe it had been at first, but not now. "I have a mate and friends who love me and would sacrifice anything to keep me safe. Because of that, we brought you with us. You should remember that, since you were afraid of being killed." He needed to come to grips with the fact that we'd saved him.

He thrust out his chest and remained silent.

Yeah, this was pointless. Me holding him here would only make things worse with us relationship-wise. "I'm going to let you go, but if you treat anyone in this house, including me, horribly again, then I'll kick your ass. You can be angry, stomp, cry, or scream at the moon, but not at any of us. Got it?"

Just when I thought he wasn't going to acknowledge me, he negligibly nodded his head. *Got it*, he linked with me, probably not wanting Griffin to hear.

I wanted to roll my eyes at his childish antics, but I'd scolded him enough for one night. I wasn't his parent, after all, and he was an adult. I couldn't help but wonder who'd raised him. Someone had put a roof over his head, but he was packless and had abandonment issues, so they'd messed with him. That was the one thing I knew for sure.

Not wanting Griffin to chime in, I linked with my mate as I released my hold on Julius. *He said he got it, using our strange bond.*

Of course he did. Griffin wasn't pleased.

None of us were happy at the moment. Too much shit was going on, and even though we'd gotten closer to the bad guy, we still had no clue who we were up against. Time to try to gain some knowledge. "So...we're here, and you're safe," I said to Julius. "Who's trying to kidnap me?"

"That information is the only reason for all of you to keep me around." Julius sneered. "I'm not telling you a damn thing until I learn more about who created me. If you want information, then I need mine first."

Dear God, this was going to be never-ending. But I wanted to try to cooperate with him—after all, he was my brother.

Rosemary stepped into the room. Her face was set into her customary mask of indifference.

"Is everything okay?" Griffin asked as his shoulders sagged. Lately, it seemed like we couldn't catch a break.

"Yeah." Rosemary arched an eyebrow. "I wouldn't walk in like this if there was something we had to address."

And there was my blunt angel friend. She could come off as aggressive, but I found her refreshing. She didn't shy away from the truth or confrontation. "I think what he meant to ask was is there something you need?"

"No." She pointed at Julius. "I figured I could take him to sleep in my room. I can keep an eye on him."

That, actually, was the best plan. We couldn't trust Julius, so we needed someone to watch him. Since she was the strongest of us, it made sense. I was just glad she'd offered instead of one of us having to make the request. "Okay, you know where the extra covers and pillows are if you need them." Under normal circumstances, I'd have offered to get the blankets and help out, but I was exhausted; I wasn't sure how I was still standing. Before I could crawl into bed, though, I needed a shower. Being locked in that cell for half a day hadn't been pleasant—the entire basement had smelled like piss and body odor.

"Or he could just sleep on the floor without any luxuries." Rosemary shifted her weight to one leg as she looked at Julius with cold disregard. "I mean, after all he's done, that's better than he deserves."

I didn't have the energy to argue with her, nor was she wrong. I turned and headed toward the bathroom and waved a hand. "Do what you have to do." At the end of the day, as long as he was safe, that was all that mattered. Maybe being a little harder on him would make things more bearable for him. He seemed to struggle with us being nice, like he was afraid that we'd take it back.

"Come on, Beta," she teased. "Let's get you settled."

Julius *harrumphed* but followed the angel out of the room.

I'm going to make sure he doesn't cause any problems. I'll be back in a minute, Griffin linked as I made my way into the bathroom.

Don't be long. I needed him after the day we'd had. For a second, I'd thought that I wouldn't be able to make my way back to him.

I removed my pale pink tennis shoes and socks and relished the cool gray tile that my feet now touched. Walking past the dark granite bathroom sink, I turned on the shower and pulled off my clothing.

Steam billowed from the top of the glass door of the

shower, and I climbed into it and let the warm water hit my tight, sore muscles for a moment before quickly washing myself. Even though I wanted to stand in there forever, my body required sleep.

After getting clean, I wrapped a fluffy white towel around myself and strolled back into the bedroom. Clean clothes in hand, I dropped the towel right as Griffin came into the room.

He shut the door quickly and took a rapid intake of breath before the spicy scent of arousal hit my nose. *I'm so damn lucky*, he rasped.

My body responded to his smell and sexy voice, and I turned to face him.

His lips parted as he erased the distance between us. He kissed me with so much passion, my mind grew hazy.

I can't risk losing you again. His arms wrapped around my body, and his fingers dug into my ass. *I almost went insane. It gets worse each time.*

Our bond strengthened every time we had sex or spent time together. I'd heard that mates fell in love more each day, and now I knew it to be true. At first, it was lust, with love taking root within our hearts, but the lust never went away. Fated mate bonds ever deepened within each other.

You know I wish things weren't like this. In a perfect world, we'd have only regular pack issues to take care of, not someone breathing down our necks, wishing captivity or death on me. *Maybe fate messed up, putting the two of us together.* Griffin deserved to not live under constant threat. He should've been given a mate who could not only make him happy but didn't put him at constant risk.

He growled and lifted me, his body pressing my back against the wall. One hand snagged my wrists and held them over my head. *Don't ever talk like that again.* He pulled his mouth away from mine and kissed down my neck, all the way to my breasts.

Last time we'd almost lost each other, he'd demanded slow and tender lovemaking, so when he bit my nipple, I gasped in both surprise and delight. His tongue flicked out, giving me the sensation of both pleasure and pain, and my fatigue left me.

All I wanted and needed was him.

My wet hair clung to my shoulders as I leaned my head against the wall. He nipped and teased me as one of his hands slipped between my legs.

Now that one hand was free, I took a fistful of his hair, pulling his head toward me. I wanted to taste him.

No, he chastised me as his fingers increased both the pressure and pace, rubbing the place that built the friction inside me faster.

My breathing grew ragged as his mouth devoured me and his hands pushed me toward the peak. Every time I tried getting closer to him, he pulled away and bit and touched harder. My body was teetering so damn close to the edge. *Fuck me now.* I growled.

I was done playing nice. There was only one way that I'd get fully sated.

Take it back, then. His teeth grazed against my skin, making my body somehow warmer. *Tell me you're glad that you're mine.*

Of course I am. I had trouble even forming the words in my mind—my body had never been through so much torture and excruciating pleasure before.

Say fate had it right, he linked as he slipped a finger inside.

Right as my body almost contracted, he removed his hand, causing the building sensation to stall.

I bucked under his hand, wanting that release so damn badly.

Say it, he growled, commanding me.

I'd never been so turned on in my life. As an alpha, I thought I wouldn't like being dominated, but Griffin was the exception to the rule. *Fate had it right, okay?*

Good. He stumbled back and yanked off his clothing. His scent of arousal was as strong as mine, though I hadn't even touched him. He grasped my waist and tried to turn me around so I wasn't facing him, but it was my turn to dominate him.

My wolf surged, and I pivoted so that we switched sides with him against the wall. His eyes widened, which meant my plan had worked. He thought he'd be in control the entire time.

I climbed him, and he bent his knees enough that my legs could touch the floor on either side of him. When he slipped inside of me, I rode him fast and hard. After the torture he'd just put me through, I wouldn't take it easy on him.

He thrust into me, slamming deeper, and soon, I was close to falling over the edge again. My fingers fisted his hair, and I pulled, wanting to give him a taste of the pain he'd given me as I sucked on his neck. He shuddered against me, making me feel even more powerful and sexy.

One of his hands slipped between us, pinching my nipples as I pierced his skin with my teeth. Our bond filled with raw attraction and need, and I could feel him as he orgasmed with me. Our bodies rocked in sync as he filled me, and we stilled as we floated back to reality.

Damn, that was amazing, he said huskily, as he started to pull back. He scanned my breasts. *I didn't hurt you, did I?*

Just the perfect amount. We'd done "fast and hard" before, but *that* was something a little different, raw and carnal. *And that was amazing.*

He chuckled and kissed my lips sweetly. *Yeah, you can say that again.* He scooped me up in his arms and carried me to the bed. He laid me down and pulled the covers over me. *Get some rest. I'm going to jump in the shower and then join you.*

My eyes grew heavy, and before he even made it into the bathroom, I'd fallen asleep.

I woke cuddled in Griffin's arms. On mornings like these, life felt normal. The exact way things should be.

His chest rose and lowered steadily, indicating he was still asleep, but he pulled me closer in his arms. I took a moment to breathe in myrrh and leather, his unique scent, which had quickly become my favorite smell in the world.

The essence of home.

But footsteps stomped down the hallway, and soon, we heard a loud knock at the door. Julius's urgent voice called out, "Sterlyn, we need to talk. *Now.*"

CHAPTER EIGHT

Griffin grumbled, and his arms didn't slacken. *Couldn't he wait a little longer before waking you up? You went through hell yesterday and need your rest.*

I glanced at the clock and saw that it was after ten in the morning. *In fairness, he kind of did, too. Besides, we need to get moving and get Julius to talk before something else happens.* One thing was certain: whoever it was who'd come after me would attack again. I couldn't help but suspect Dick, but I couldn't prove it yet, so I'd keep those thoughts close until there was more to go on. Griffin was already struggling with coming to grips that Dick wasn't as helpful to him as the man pretended to be.

"Sure, give me a minute," I called to Julius, and kissed Griffin. However, when I tried to pull away, he tightened his arms around me even more.

Just a few more minutes, he whined and buried his face in my hair. *I don't think we've ever been able to lay leisurely in bed together in the morning.*

We hadn't. With work, his class schedule, and everything in between, we were constantly on the go. *I know, but the sooner we can take down whoever keeps hunting us, the quicker we can live out that fantasy.*

Using logic on me shouldn't be allowed before noon. He groaned and released his hold on my waist. *I hate it. But the only reason I'm appeasing you is that I want to figure out who it is before they strike again. Allowing you to put yourself at risk is not an option.*

Annoyance surged through me, but I squashed the sensation down. He wasn't trying to be bossy but rather hated thinking we'd all have to go through this mess once more. However, I couldn't let the comment go by completely without addressing it. I didn't want him to think my silence was agreement. *I get it, but we all have to do whatever is necessary for the greater good of the people.*

His jaw twitched. Clearly, he wasn't thrilled with my response, either.

This was one of those situations where the two of us were going to have to agree to disagree and hope the situation didn't present itself. "I love you." I kissed his cheek, hating that he was already tensing up and we hadn't gotten out of bed. Hopefully, that wasn't a sign for how the rest of the day would go.

I love you, too. His face softened as his fingers ran through my hair.

My body protested as I pushed back the covers, but I persevered and quickly grabbed the pajamas that I never got to put on the night before. After Julius said whatever was on his mind, I'd get dressed for the day. I didn't want to chance taking too long and Julius doing something stupid.

I shut the door behind me and found the rest of the crew in the living room. The television wasn't on, and Killian stood in the corner of the room, leaning against one of the blue-gray walls. His white shirt and blue jeans contrasted starkly, making him appear even more on edge. He didn't even acknowledge me when I entered, as his gaze was focused on Julius.

The blinds were drawn against the wall of windows so no one could see in, but the tension in the room was nearly suffocating. If I didn't know any better, I'd think we had an enemy lurking in our midst.

In fairness, we could, but I meant a much bigger threat than just my brother.

Wow. That was still strange to say.

Rosemary perched on the large pearl-gray couch that sat across from the flat-screen television mounted on the wall. Her long hair was pulled into a braid, and her face was set in a scowl that she directed at Julius.

The only person who seemed like her normal self was Sierra. She sat on the matching loveseat perpendicular to the couch, dressed in her purple Dick's Bar shirt and jeans. She'd be leaving for work soon, and in a way, I was kind of jealous. Despite her getting involved in the craziness with us, she still had a somewhat normal life. The only thing that made me uncomfortable was that if Dick was, in fact, the person behind everything, he'd have a better opportunity to harass her.

"What's going on?" Maybe Griffin and I should've gotten up earlier.

"Well, Julius here is determined to go to your pack neighborhood." Killian frowned and cut his gaze to me. "And I told him there's no way in hell. That the last time we went, we almost didn't make it out alive."

My stomach filled with dread. I hadn't told them yet that Julius was my brother. After last night, he'd confirmed it, so there was no reason to withhold the information.

"Well, he was taken as a newborn, and he wants to see our family house."

"Family house?" Sierra parroted. "Are you saying you're *related* to him?"

"Yeah...he's my twin brother." The words felt weird passing my lips for the first time out loud.

A strange combination of hope and warmth exploded in my chest through the connection I shared with Julius. But after just a second, the sensations were replaced with skepticism, as if he were afraid to hope.

He cleared his throat. "I didn't realize we were going to let everyone in on that little fact." Discomfort wafted through him as if he didn't like them knowing. "But, yeah. Exactly, and I want to see the house I would've grown up in." Julius tensed next to the back door. "I at least deserve that."

"You don't deserve shit." Rosemary leaned over and gestured at him. "All that went out the window when you hurt your own kind."

"I never hurt her." He waved a hand toward me. "In fact, I tried to protect her as much as I could, despite knowing better. I don't know why, but it was like something inside me couldn't bear the thought of something bad happening to her. Hell, I saved her from being shot."

"True, but you were going to hand me over to some sort of sick, demented asshole." No matter how he tried to make it sound, he still wasn't truly protecting me. He just didn't want me to die, and honestly, that could've been because he didn't want the wrath of the big boss. There was a truthfulness to his words, but I had to be careful. I was desperate to connect with him—after all, he was the only blood family I had left. But I was still wary. I would keep that in mind moving forward.

"Wow. Now that you mention it, you two look similar, but, damn, your personalities are completely opposite. Ugh. I want to ask so many more questions, but I have to get to work," Sierra said as she leaned over, tying her tennis shoes. "This conversation is not over."

"Be careful." I was pretty sure she hadn't officially been lumped in with us by my enemy, but there had been times when we'd been watched and hadn't been aware. If she didn't show up to work, that would raise questions, so we were in one of those impossible situations where there wasn't necessarily a good choice. "If anything seems suspect, link with Killian and let him know." The fact that we all weren't linked was getting very inconvenient. There had to be a way to at least have our group interconnected.

Luckily, we didn't have to keep Sierra and Rosemary hidden like Julius. The guards wouldn't find it strange to see them coming in and out, as they'd been staying with us for a while.

"Of course." Sierra stood and hugged me, then went to the front door. "I'm heading over to my house to grab my car, and if you guys need me, don't hesitate to contact me."

The four of us watched her walk out. I welcomed the silence, trying to gauge how I felt. I understood both sides of this argument.

Our bedroom door shut, and Griffin strolled into the living room a few seconds later. He scanned the room, taking in the varying stances and body language. "What's he done now?" Griffin sighed as he turned toward Julius.

To prevent either side from starting, I jumped in. "Julius wants to go back to my pack neighborhood and get a feel for what the place was like before everyone died."

"What?" Julius gasped as his face went pale. "The entire *pack* is dead?"

"Like you didn't know." Rosemary snapped. "Don't even try to come off innocent."

Being a silver wolf was his only saving grace with Rosemary. She clearly didn't like him, never mind her mother's strong words about protecting our kind.

"But you said it was only our parents!" He blinked and swallowed, and I saw a suspicious glimmer in his eyes. "I had no idea that the pack was annihilated. They promised —" He cut himself off, as if realizing he'd already said too much.

"*Who* promised?" Griffin pushed up the sleeves of his mustard-colored shirt like he was preparing to fight.

"No, you have to be lying." Julius raised both a palm and his voice. "This has to be a sick game you're playing."

Each side accusing the other was unproductive; we could go back and forth like this all day. "No one is lying," I said. "We'd all know if we were. We're supernaturals, for God's sake." And if we wanted him to trust us, we had to give him a reason. One that wasn't convenient for us. Besides, I felt a tug to go home, too, now that the topic had been brought up. "I think we should take Julius back to the neighborhood. Besides, I'd like to find where they buried the dead." I glared at Julius. "But you have to give us something after this. Do you understand?"

My words hung in the air.

"If what you say is true, then I might be more inclined." Julius nodded, though he still wasn't committing.

Killian's shoulders slumped, and Rosemary placed a hand over her stomach as she sat upright.

God, I'm such an asshole. Griffin wrapped an arm around my waist, and regret wafted from him. *I hadn't even thought about that. You haven't gotten any closure or a chance to say goodbye.*

His simple statement was obvious, but I hadn't been able to nail down the negative emotions coursing through me.

Until him.

"Well, I guess that means we're heading to your pack house." Killian pinched the bridge of his nose. "But we need to be careful this time."

"I'll fly ahead." Rosemary stood and headed toward the back door. "Wait to hear from me before you drive into the neighborhood. I'll meet you at the entrance."

"Thank you." I hoped she could feel my sincerity. One day, I'd have to do something to pay her back for all she'd risked and done for us. "We'll be there shortly."

"See you soon." Rosemary exited the house.

"Okay, if we're going to do this, we have to be smart." We needed to get out of here with Julius staying hidden. "Griffin's Navigator is our safest bet. Julius can lie down in the back so none of the guards see him."

"You do realize some of the guards are going to want to come with us." Griffin pushed his shoulders back as he rubbed his fingers together. "What do we tell them?"

"That we have something that we need to do alone." Killian and Griffin were their alphas. It was as simple as that. "As long as you don't come off unsure, they won't challenge you."

"And we can reassure them that we'll link them if anything goes wrong." Killian shrugged.

"Fine. Let's just get this over with." Griffin bared his teeth at Julius. "One wrong move, and I'm bringing our asses back here."

"I figured that was coming." Julius rolled his eyes. "But I want to go too badly to argue with you."

They'd go back and forth all day if I let them. "Let's get

going. We'll be safer in the daylight, and we all know Rosemary isn't famous for her patience."

"You got that right." Killian clasped his hands together. "We'll never hear the end of it if she has to wait long."

I quickly dressed, and then the four of us made it to the car. Julius followed my directions without any prompting, lying down in the back with a blanket over his body so that he'd barely be seen if Griffin had to roll down his window. Killian took his normal spot in the middle row behind me as Griffin got into the driver's seat.

Once we were all settled, he opened the garage and backed out. Griffin rested his hand on the gear shift when he paused. After a second, he linked with me. *They're asking questions. Are we sure that it's smart to go there? The last time, we were attacked.*

I can't promise it will all be okay. For some reason, I wasn't too concerned about what we might face. *And this time, we have Rosemary standing guard. Killian wasn't able to alert us until it was too late. With Rosemary, we should be able to get in the car and out of the subdivision before they get close.*

"My pack wants to know where we're going, like we expected they would." Killian sighed. "At least they're asking through the pack bond and not in person."

Even though Julius should be out of sight, stopping would be risky. "Well, we'll get there and back quickly. We don't need to spend all day there." The longer we stayed, the greater our chances of someone ambushing us, but this was something Julius needed. Between the way he reacted to the entire pack being killed and learning that he'd been stolen, maybe this would be the final turn to get him to warm up to us.

Can I get up yet? Julius linked as discomfort slammed into me.

He always got more edgy when he connected with me telepathically. I guessed if I'd been a rogue my entire life, I wouldn't be enthused with someone having a link inside my head, either. Back in the day, I'd hated that the pack could have access if I wasn't careful when I got upset, and this had to feel completely foreign to him. *Give us another few minutes to get out of our neighborhood.*

As Griffin put the car in drive, six guards stood in his front yard with huge frowns on their faces, watching us pull away. I didn't need a pack link with them to know they weren't thrilled.

When we pulled onto the main road that would take us to my former neighborhood, I turned toward the back. "You can get up now. We're clear."

Julius's head popped up, reminding me of the whack-a-mole game Mom and I played together when I was little and she'd take me to the arcades. I turned forward before the smile broke across my face. Maybe things would be all right after all.

THE RIDE to my pack neighborhood took less than twenty minutes. As soon as Griffin neared the entrance, he stopped and waited for Rosemary to give us some sort of sign.

"Where is she?" Julius complained.

And here I'd thought Rosemary was the most impatient person I'd ever met. I'd been proven wrong. "We just got here. Give her a few minutes."

He groaned as he sat back in the seat.

"And I thought women were dramatic," Killian deadpanned, and leaned between the seats and over the center console with his fist pointed toward Griffin like he expected a bump.

I arched an eyebrow and glared at my mate as he raised his hand. I warned, "You touch his hand, and you'll see something dramatic." I was teasing, but at the same time, I was tired of the sexist comments that somehow got thrown my way.

Rosemary landed by my car door and scanned the area like she was expecting some sort of threat to jump out at her. When she chewed on her fingernail, it put me on edge. She was uncertain and nervous about something.

I rolled down the window and asked urgently, "What's wrong?"

The area around her eyes tightened as she looked at me straight on. "We have a problem."

CHAPTER NINE

If I never heard those four words again, it would still be too soon. There were so many damn problems—we didn't need to add more to the mix. "Are there enemy shifters here?" If there were, I was surprised that Rosemary hadn't started kicking their asses. Maybe she wanted backup; that would make sense.

"I'm not sure if *enemy* is the right word." She gritted her teeth, which wasn't like her. She normally ran her mouth without regard for what came out.

This change made my skin crawl. Something was horribly wrong. "Just tell us," I commanded.

She squinted at me, clearly not appreciating how I'd spoken to her, but she pushed it aside. "There are about fifteen shifters walking around your neighborhood."

"Of course there are," Griffin groaned. "And let me guess, they have guns."

"No, they don't." She pursed her lips. "One of them has darker silver hair, like Julius back there."

"Wait..." My mind raced to catch up. "Are you saying

one might be a *silver wolf*? But how? All the links are cold."
Unless...could it be my uncle?

"Based on finding both you and Julius, finding more
wouldn't be that farfetched at this point." Rosemary
shrugged. "If it was one of Julius's buddies, they'd be
loaded up."

"Maybe we should turn around," Killian said uneasily.
"Maybe having them pop up is fate's way of telling us to
stay away. We could stand to catch a break."

"No. I need to see them." Julius climbed into the center
aisle and out the driver's-side back door. "There might not
be another chance."

Everyone grew uneasy, which was affecting our logic.
We couldn't let emotions rule our decisions. That was how
mistakes were made. "If there are more silver wolves, they
could be allies," I said.

"But they might not be," Griffin countered, and pointed
at Julius, who surprisingly hadn't marched toward the
neighborhood.

A little bit of self-preservation was bleeding through his
eagerness. Good, I didn't need him running headfirst into a
bad situation.

"He has a point." Killian fidgeted in the back seat.
"Julius is a silver wolf, and he was definitely working against
us."

"I get your concern," I told him. Everything we'd experienced had taught us to be cautious, especially around new
people. Every time we turned around, somebody else was
trying to kill us. "But I think we have to check it out. If
there are more of us, we could have a hell of a lot better
chance of surviving and overcoming my would-be
kidnapper."

"You can't guarantee they'll work with you," Rosemary

said, and nibbled her bottom lip. "I didn't take you as over-confident."

Her words stung. Dick and Luna were overconfident; I'd never want to be lumped in with them. "I'm now the silver wolf alpha. My dad was the ultimate alpha, and his abilities transferred to me. My light silver hair signifies that. Worst case, I make them submit to me."

"And if they attack all at once?" Rosemary's forehead lined with worry. "I don't think we can hold off fifteen of them."

"If I challenge their alpha directly, it's against wolf nature to organize an attack." Only a coward would refuse or organize a group attack when faced with the alpha challenge.

Griffin swallowed and scowled. "If they're silver wolves, that doesn't mean they'll be ethical."

But it kind of did. I could feel the turmoil in Julius when he was solidly working with the other side. He was in constant conflict, and our bond only added to the chaos. It didn't create it. Like Dad had explained, our race was inherently good. I had to believe that. And if that was my uncle, maybe he'd have some answers. "Let's drive through the neighborhood. If we spot them, I can roll down the window and feel them out. If they charge or act shady, I'll tell you, 'Let's roll.' They might be fast, but they can't outrun a vehicle, especially for a long amount of time."

"Don't even bother trying to argue." Killian sighed and leaned between the center console yet again. "You know you're going to cave, and she does have a point. If there's a slight chance they're good—that they're on Sterlyn's side—we'd be stupid not to try."

"I know that." Griffin tapped his finger on the steering wheel. "But that doesn't mean I'm happy about the situation." He jabbed the button that rolled the window down and barked, "Are you getting back in the car or not?"

"Are you going down there?" Julius asked warily, but he opened the car door as he waited for a response.

Griffin groaned. "Yeah, she'd kick my ass if I didn't."

"I'll take to the sky and make sure nothing strange happens." Rosemary stepped back as her wings spread behind her. "If I see anything, I'll holler and let you know."

"Thanks." Every conversation I had with her always seemed to end the same way.

She took flight as Julius got back into the car. As soon as the door shut, Griffin rolled into the neighborhood.

He gripped the steering wheel so hard his knuckles turned white. "The first sign they might attack, I'm getting our asses out of here."

"Okay." If I fought him, he'd be even more hesitant to go. And honestly, he had a right to be wary. "But let's at least give them a chance."

"All you have to do is tell me," Killian grunted. "I'll roll the damn window up for her."

Those two were insanely protective of me. If I didn't love them as much as I did, I wouldn't be able to tolerate being around them.

"You do realize she can take care of herself, right?" Julius didn't sound amused. "If it weren't for her and the angel, you two would've been killed by now."

Not helping matters, I linked to Julius. *Let's not threaten their manhood when they're already going into a situation they aren't thrilled about.*

Agitation rolled off Julius. *If they can't handle the truth, they need to learn how to. Sometimes, the truth hurts.*

Says the guy who exploded on everyone last night when you learned about your past. You didn't know how to handle it. He had no right to get all high and mighty. Every single one of us had flaws, and in this instance, Griffin's and Killian's was that they cared so much about me. *Maybe some self-reflection would go a long way.*

He remained silent. In fairness, he couldn't have a good retort.

The modest brick houses came into view, and my heart twinged. With each house I looked at, the image of the family who had lived there popped into my mind. Every person meant so much to me. We'd been one large family, the way every smaller pack should be.

These houses were all one-story structures, similar to those in Killian pack neighborhood, but missing the Craftsman feel. These were simple and built to be low maintenance. The only sign that the town had been abandoned was the tall grass and weeds in everyone's yards, now that the weather was warming with spring.

Griffin drove slowly, but soon, we took the curve leading to the back of the neighborhood and my family home.

In front of my parents' house stood fifteen wolves. They didn't hide but rather stood side by side, staring us down.

The tallest man stood in the center of the group with seven flanking each side. His hair was a shade darker than Julius's but silver nonetheless. He appeared to be a few years younger than Dad and held himself in a similar way. And his golden flecked silver eyes zeroed in on me.

Could he be my uncle?

Griffin huffed as he turned the Navigator so that I faced the group head-on only a few feet away. When I rolled down my window, the faint floral, musky scent of the silver wolf filled the car.

I lifted my head high, making sure my posture exuded confidence. "Who are you, and what are you doing here?"

"Maybe we should ask you the same questions," the man who obviously was the pack alpha retorted. He lifted his head high, mimicking me. "You don't look as if you belong here."

A loud laugh escaped me. This had to be some sort of joke. "I grew up here."

"Really?" The alpha placed his hands inside his jean pockets and tilted his head. "You've let the place go to shit, then."

The insult burned. He was right. I should've done more. I shouldn't allow my childhood neighborhood to deteriorate like this. "I've been kind of preoccupied. Once again, who are you, and why are you here?"

"We thought we should check out the area." The alpha shrugged, but there was something strange wafting off him. His intent was good, but he was trying to hide some sort of pain. "See if we could find a place to land."

I wasn't in the mood to play games. Dad had told me that political maneuvers were an important piece of leading, but all they did was convolute things. I hated it. I got that there was a time and place, but now didn't feel like the time. "I'm Sterlyn Knight. Are you my uncle?"

Babe, I know you want him to be part of your family, but maybe you were a little too forthcoming. Worry pulsed from Griffin. *Now he could pretend to be your family.*

If he lies, we'll know. There were some things you couldn't hide. *He looks like my dad, and he's the right age.*

And he left for a reason. Griffin placed his hand on the gear shift, ready to pull away. *We don't know what it was.*

The alpha's mouth dropped open, and he quickly scratched his nose as if trying to cover up his reaction. "You cut straight to the point, huh?"

"I figure there's no reason to beat around the bush." I

scanned the entire group. The other men were around the same age as the alpha, so they weren't his children. There was no way a silver wolf could reproduce like that, and their mates couldn't be silver. "So my question is, what was my father's favorite dessert?" Dad's favorite was odd. Mom and I gave him hell, but he said his grandmother introduced him to it at a young age.

The alpha remained quiet for a moment, as if he were considering my words. "Jalapeno orange marmalade cupcakes. Grandma's specialty."

Even though I'd suspected this was my uncle, having him confirm it was surreal. "You're really him."

"And you're really her. I thought you died..." The emotion grew thick in his voice, and he trailed off, unable to finish the sentence.

"I escaped." I sounded like such a coward. "I was out in the woods when the attack happened. When I finally reached home to help, the slaughter was over. Dad was mortally wounded when he found me, and he told me to run. He had a huge gash—" I choked off.

"Look, I'm not trying to be an asshole," Griffin said, and glared at my uncle. "But why the hell are you here now?"

"That's a long story." He ran a hand through his hair, making it stand on end. His focus landed on Griffin and the other two men in the back seat. "And one that Sterlyn deserves an answer to. I was hoping to check out the house. Would that be all right?"

"How do we know we can trust you?" Killian asked. "If we walk in there, we could be walking to our deaths."

My uncle nodded his head in approval and looked at me. "Who are these two?" He gestured from Killian to Griffin. "They aren't silver wolves."

"No. I met them after I escaped." Even though we

might be family, I wasn't going to tell him my entire story. At least, not yet. Complete trust had to be earned, and I had learned that being family didn't always mean someone had your best interests at heart.

"And who's the other guy in the back?" my uncle asked.

"My brother." If he knew my name, then his reaction to this little tidbit would tell everything.

"Impossible." My uncle marched over to the car and scowled. "That's not funny."

His disbelief settled me. "Apparently, the witch who attended our birth spelled him to appear dead." I could throw Julius under the bus and tell our uncle that he'd been trying to kidnap me for the bad guys, but I wouldn't...for now. "We just found each other, but that's a long story. I'm more interested in why you're here now."

"Decades ago, murmurings arose about reopening Shadow City to the world, and the city's alpha began writing letters to your dad to see if he was interested in returning. We knew there was a chance that someone would try to control us, so since I was the pack beta, we decided that it would be best if I split off with a small number of wolves to form my own pack. This was a few years before you were born." He motioned to the fourteen men behind him. "About two years ago, your dad contacted me to tell me that he was heading to the city to meet with the alpha. We've checked in once a month since then as the murmurs got louder."

"That's why you're here." It'd been almost a month since I ran that day. "You reached out, and he didn't respond."

"Yeah." He clasped his hands loosely behind his back and stared at the ground. "When we got here, we searched the area and found several men dead in the woods. I'm assuming they were part of those who attacked the pack since they appeared to be military and had weapons on them, and they weren't silver wolves. And then we found—"

My breathing quickened. For him to not finish the sentence told me everything. "Did you find the bodies of my pack?" Last time I'd been here, with Griffin, Killian, and Sierra, I hadn't had a chance to find my dead because we'd been attacked again.

"We did." He closed his eyes and rubbed his forehead. "And it was awful. The way those assholes tossed them..." He blew out a breath and looked back at me. "Let's just say they're buried now in the cemetery."

"Are there markers so I can find them?" I opened the car door, wanting to see where they'd been laid to rest.

The shortest man behind my uncle took a step forward. His midnight-brown hair fell to the side like long bangs, and his blood-orange eyes glazed over with sadness. Dirt coated his arms and smudged one cheek. He was close to my height but thicker. "We put a cross in front of each and did our best to bury family members together."

"We were wondering where your body was." My uncle touched my arm. "I didn't let myself hope that you were still alive. I'm just so damn glad that you're here."

"Me, too." Having more silver wolves and finding my uncle was a very good thing, especially since my attackers shouldn't know about them. Not only that, but maybe he could help me get through to Julius so we could get some answers. We'd finally have something up our own sleeves. "But the question is, do you plan on staying?"

"We don't have a choice." My uncle lifted his arms and gestured around the town. "They tried to exterminate us. We won't take it lying down."

Good. I'd been worried they wouldn't feel that way, but they were here for a reason.

"Do you mind going inside the house with me?" My uncle glanced at the front door and then back at me. "There's something I need to show you."

Whatever he wanted to show me must be important, which made me wonder what we'd missed the other day when we'd had to rush away so quickly. Were there more secrets hidden inside?

CHAPTER TEN

Do *you think it's wise?* Griffin asked, feeling my determination through our bond.

I was glad he was challenging me. Sometimes, people needed to be questioned to ensure they were thinking things through. *I think if we don't go, and there's something in there that's valuable, we'll risk more by not finding out. Besides, I don't feel anything menacing coming off him like I do Luna, Dick, and even Julius.* I hated that my brother had such a darkness shrouding him, but it had to be a product of the environment he was raised in.

I met my uncle's gaze. "Are you sure no one's watching us?" I didn't want to get into the same situation as last time when we'd stayed in the house and couldn't get to the cars before we were attacked. "Our enemies have bird shifters on their team, and I overlooked them before."

"We checked for everything once we found all the bodies." My uncle shivered. "We're safe, and there are no recent scents."

"No odd noises that can't be explained?" Killian asked.

The last time, we hadn't smelled the bird because it had

stayed high in the trees, but it had knocked a branch onto the ground. I'd overlooked the odd noise then, and I wouldn't make the same mistake twice.

The man who'd spoken earlier raised his head. "We're good."

This time, we have Rosemary, I linked to Griffin.

"All right, let me park." Griffin put the car in reverse and backed up.

We pulled into the driveway, and the four of us were out of the car within seconds.

After shutting the door, I turned to find my uncle staring at Julius and me like he'd seen a ghost.

He shook his head as the corners of his mouth tipped downward. "You two look like the spitting images of your mom and dad. It's uncanny."

I'd been told that a lot. My pack always teased my parents, saying there was no mistaking that I was their child. Those comments used to irritate me, but not anymore. I cherished them. "Thank you."

A few of the silver wolves looked at me a little longer than felt appropriate, and Griffin placed an arm around my waist. "I'm Griffin Bodle, Sterlyn's fated mate."

My uncle's eyes twinkled. "A good mate always stakes his claim when it comes to other men." He laughed good-naturedly and took Griffin's hand. "My name is Bart Knight. It's nice to meet you."

That was when it hit me. I'd had no clue what my uncle's name was. At least Griffin got it out of him before I had to ask.

"And I'm Killian Green." Killian didn't budge, just stared each of the wolves down like he expected them to attack at any minute. "The alpha of Shadow Ridge, so if anything strange goes down, my pack will be here in minutes."

"Noted," Bart replied as he shook Killian's hand. "Which means you are Cyrus." Bart turned his attention to my brother, using his birth name. "I don't know how you two found each other, but thank God you made it out alive."

I cringed, waiting for the explosion, but nothing happened other than Julius stiffening before nodding his head.

"Yeah, that's me." Julius tilted his head and sighed. His demeanor reminded me of Dad so much that it hurt.

"Well, these are my men." Bart waved his hand at the fourteen people standing behind him. They were all over six feet tall and about as burly as Griffin and Killian, except for the one other guy who'd spoken earlier. My uncle gestured to him. "This is my beta, Darrell Hart." He did seem to have more confidence than the other thirteen.

"It's nice to meet you all, and I'm sorry to say that we don't have a ton of time to stay here," I replied. "We have to get back to Shadow Ridge before people get worried."

Even though we weren't trying to hide that Griffin was the Shadow City alpha, I wasn't going to offer that piece of information unless we had to. If Bart had split from our pack because of rumblings of Shadow City opening its doors, that could mean that he wouldn't be as forthcoming with Griffin in our presence—or potentially, even me—since we were mates. I wanted to see what information they had before risking them not sharing it with me.

Surprisingly, Julius hadn't ratted us out. My guess was that he was afraid we'd force him to leave before he got to see everything and that I would inform Bart and the others of exactly what his dear, sweet nephew had done. We both had leverage over each other, which worked for the time being. I hoped that one day, we could move past all that.

"All right, let's get moving." Griffin took my hand and led me to the door. "We do need to hurry." His expression remained indifferent, keeping his unease hidden from everyone but me, but it flowed through our bond.

I swung the sturdy red chestnut door open, trying to push away the suffocating sense of nostalgia.

The living room remained untouched from the last time we were here. The beige cloth couch still sat centered against the tan wall, with Dad's brown leather recliner in the corner. Mom's favorite orange-red throw was folded on the couch from when Sierra had slept there.

Sadness tried pushing through once again, but I couldn't appear weak, especially in front of these other silver wolfmen. I needed to be a confident alpha so they wouldn't second-guess my abilities more than they already did because I was female.

Dread filled me as I stepped on the dark walnut floor, and Mom's lavender scent caused my eyes to burn. God, how I missed her.

When I reached the center of the room, I blinked a few times to hold back tears before spinning toward the men marching in behind me. "So, here we are." Luckily, my voice sounded strong and didn't break.

Griffin winced as he sensed all the emotions raging inside me. He moved to stand next to me and reached for my hand, but I stepped back, which made him miss. Hurt etched on his face at my rejection.

I'm sorry. I hated that I'd made him feel that way and embarrassed him in front of the others, but I didn't have a choice. *If you comfort me, I won't be able to hold back my sadness. I feel safe with you, but I can't let my guard down in front of these strangers. Silver wolves or not.*

As long as that's the reason. He rubbed his hand on his pants leg.

As arrogant and vulgar as he'd acted the first day I'd met him in the coffee shop, I'd never have expected him to be insecure, ever. But there were hints like these that proved he still needed to realize the strength he had inside him. I was determined to get him to see the man he was. *I promise. Don't make me punish you for doubting me,* I teased, trying to make him smile.

As Bart's fourteen men began to enter the house, Bart commanded, "Stop. Spread out around the house and keep watch. Alert us of anything out of the ordinary."

Darrell's forehead pinched, showing he clearly didn't like being sent outside. Those two must have shared almost everything together, so not being privy to whatever Bart wanted to show me must not have sat well with him.

"Now." Bart's voice was laced with alpha will.

"Yes, Alpha." Darrell grimaced and turned, the last one to leave.

The door shut loudly behind them, and Bart nodded toward it. "Why don't you three go out there and help keep watch while Sterlyn and I have a few minutes to talk."

"Not happening," Griffin growled, shaking his head. "I'm her mate. I'm not leaving her side."

"And same." Killian marched over, flanking my other side. "Where they go, I go."

"Interesting." Bart tapped a finger against his lip as he faced Julius. "Why is Killian protecting her and not you?"

Silver wolves were intuitive, so the fact that Bart already caught on to my strained relationship with my brother didn't surprise me. I'd have been more worried if he hadn't.

"*He's* her brother," Julius spat and scowled. "Not me."

Great. We were going to let our family drama hang out with a man we hadn't even known for ten minutes. Things were already going so smoothly. "They can stay." I wanted to add *but not him* about Julius, but that would only make him feel more alienated. Whatever there was to find, Julius should theoretically have the same right to know as Bart and I.

"Okay, then." Bart shrugged. "You're the top alpha," he said without bitterness, catching me off guard.

I'd almost been afraid that he might challenge me for that title, but maybe there wouldn't be a problem after all.

Bart gestured to the hallway. "Let's visit the basement room."

"The basement room?" I had no clue what he was talking about. Maybe he wasn't who I thought he was.

He stepped back, looking startled. "Your father never showed you?"

I took a deep breath. I didn't like being left in the dark, especially since it sounded like I should know about it. "There's no basement room. This is a one-story house with a crawlspace." Either I was stupid, or he was. I had a feeling it was me, and that didn't sit well.

He lifted a hand for a moment and tilted it side to side as if he was trying to figure out what to say. "There's a secret room where our ancestry is hidden. Only the alpha heirs know about it. No one beyond them."

"If that's the case, then how do you know about it?" Maybe he would challenge me after all.

"Until you were born, I was the second in line to lead." He licked his lips and gazed at the wall above my head as if he was lost in memories. "I needed to learn everything about being alpha in case your father died. When you were born, you took my place. Now you're the true alpha with Cyrus as the spare. You two need to learn about our history. It's how things have always been done so no one is left without the knowledge."

Whether I liked the situation or not, Bart knowing about the secret room was a very good thing. That information could've been lost forever if both he and Dad hadn't been told. "Then why didn't he tell me?" Hurt laced my words. Dad had left me without all the facts.

"The transition should've happened by now, but knowing my brother, he wanted to protect you as long as possible." Bart rolled his shoulders, displaying his discomfort. "The more someone knows, the more at risk they are from people who are desperate to know all about us."

I laughed humorlessly. "At one point, I might have agreed with you, but not now. I was spared only because someone wants to use me as a breeder, so my limited knowledge hasn't saved me."

Bart's jaw twitched. "Some things never change. There's always someone out there trying to corrupt the world. It makes me sick."

"Maybe the silver wolves going into hiding wasn't the right call." I'd been thinking that for a while. We were meant to be just and fair. By running off to hide, had we allowed the supernatural world to become more corrupt? "We should've stayed and helped to fix the problems."

"You say that now, but you don't understand the whole story." Bart rubbed his hands together. "You're about to learn everything."

That was something I could get behind. "So where is this hidden room?" I'd grown up in this house and knew every nook and cranny. There was no way I'd missed it.

"Let me show you." Bart gestured to the hallway. "Do you mind if I lead?"

I waved him forward. "Go for it."

"But no funny business." Griffin straightened his shoulders. "There are four of us against you."

"Math is one of my strong suits." Bart chuckled and stalked down the hallway. "But thanks for clarifying."

"You stay here with us." Killian sneered at Julius.

Between Griffin and Killian, my brother sure couldn't feel the love. However, my uncle calling him by his birth name didn't seem to bother him. He was dying to fit in but wasn't sure how to go about it. Maybe if we let him come along, he wouldn't feel so alone. I couldn't fathom growing up without a pack; he'd had a rougher childhood than any of us could relate to. "No, let him come," I said.

"What?" Julius's lips parted as his breath hitched. "Is this some kind of cruel joke to get back at me?"

"You can't be serious." Killian ran his fingers through his hair. "He hasn't done anything to prove himself."

"Because we haven't given him the chance to. And Bart's right–he should know this, too." In order to prevent Julius from feeling any more uncomfortable than he already was, I took off after Bart.

There's no way in hell I'm letting you go down those stairs with your resurrected brother who's tried to kidnap you multiple times and an uncle who just recently appeared. Griffin sounded broken as he ran after me and took my hand. *Please don't ask that of me.*

Even though I hated considering breaking tradition, how could I tell my mate no after that? If anything, he and I were stronger together. *Fine, but just you.*

And Killian. Regret wafted from my mate toward me. *Because you can't take on two silver wolves on your own, and let's be real, I'm not even a match for just one. It'll be best if we don't split up.*

He was right. I had to think with logic, and beyond that, I trusted Killian and Griffin more than the two men in front of me. They'd proven they had my best interests at heart, and after all that we'd gone through, that had to mean something. I paused and waited for Bart to look back at me. "I respect that under normal circumstances, only Cyrus and I would go with you. But not many silver wolves are left, and Killian and Griffin are my family, too. I want them to be part of this as well."

Bart frowned but nodded his head before he took off again.

Griffin and Killian followed me, with Julius's hesitant footsteps several feet behind.

I glanced over my shoulder and watched my brother pause and look at every picture that he passed. Most of them were photos of me through varying stages of childhood, but then he spotted two family pictures of Mom, Dad, and me. I sensed his pain through our bond as he saw everything that he'd missed out on. And for some reason, that was what it took for me to understand even a fragment of his pain. How would it feel to look at pictures you should've been a part of but weren't? To see the life you could've had but that someone had stolen from you? If this didn't get him on our side, I wasn't sure what would.

I didn't want Bart to be alone for too long, so I quickened my pace and entered the very last doorway in the hall.

Bart had left the door open, and my parents' made bed immediately came into view. The navy-blue comforter was wrinkle-free, contrasting with the white bed frame and the sky-blue walls.

Bart stood in front of the white chest of drawers where

I'd found the hidden false bottom in dad's underwear drawer, which had contained the picture album, journal, and letters from Griffin's dad to mine.

The other three men entered behind me as Bart smiled and said, "This is when your entire life changes." He reached down to where the drawer had been and slipped his hand inside at the top. A loud *click* sounded, and the chest of drawers jerked.

Bart grabbed the right side of the heavy furniture piece and pulled it toward us. A large, gaping hole appeared with steps leading down to what must be the hidden room.

What was it with Dad and his fucking underwear?

CHAPTER ELEVEN

"Your dad's underwear has its own story." Griffin shook his head. "At least his hint was a good one."

Dad's words about a person's underwear speaking volumes about them made sense, especially now. Between the false bottom of the drawer and the button that unlocked the hidden door, his saying was obviously meant to stick with me to help me find everything. The only flaw in his plan was that I was pretty sure I wouldn't have found the hidden door if not for Bart. "You're telling me."

"Um..." Bart's brows furrowed. "I have a feeling that I don't want to know."

"Are we sure it's safe down there?" Killian walked to the door frame. He peeked his head through the hole, looking down the stairs.

Bart took the first step and looked over his shoulder. "Yes, the room is safe. Most likely a little dusty and small, but safe nonetheless. There's even a light switch, so we won't be in the dark."

I paused, taking a moment to collect myself. I had a feeling that whatever we'd find would alter my reality.

We don't have to go down there. Griffin comforted me. *We can head back home and come back later, or not at all.*

The idea was appealing, but leaving would be the coward's way. Whatever was down there was important, and it might answer some questions that had taken root in my mind. *That's not an option.* Even if I wanted it to be.

I'll be right here beside you, he linked as he placed a hand on the small of my back. *If it gets to be too much, we can head back up.*

Even if it became difficult, I'd push through. Not knowing things had been a problem this entire time. Everyone else was several steps ahead of us, and even though we were slowly leveling the playing field, time was running out. We needed something to use to our advantage instead of playing defense all the time. *And I love you for being right here with me.*

Bart continued the trek down the stairs with Killian right behind.

I rushed forward, following Killian before I lost my nerve. Griffin stayed close behind me with Julius taking up the rear.

The stairwell was small, even for me, and I was the smallest of the five of us. I folded my shoulders as I took each step slowly. The wood creaked underneath us but remained secure.

Dust floated around us. *Dad must not have come down here for a while.*

Well, if he wanted to keep it hidden, he might not have had many opportunities.

Griffin stayed so close that I could feel his body heat on my back. I had a feeling that if he weren't with me, I wouldn't have found the strength to come down here. *Yeah, I wonder if Mom knew about it.* My gut said no. She would've insisted that Dad tell me or would've shared it with me herself. The day I turned eighteen, only a couple of months ago, she'd told me that I was now a woman and that I needed to take my training with Dad more seriously. My excuses wouldn't work any longer.

Unfortunately, you'll probably never know. Remorse poured off him. *But maybe whatever is down here will shed light on everything.*

That was the entire reason I was making myself go through with this.

"Watch your head," Bart said as he turned to the right, ducking.

Killian reached the bottom and laughed dryly. "You weren't kidding about a small room." He glanced at me and winked, but the tension in his shoulders spoke volumes. He was on edge just like Griffin and I were, but he wanted to relax me. He lowered his head and entered the room.

Light flooded the opening as I touched the cement ground and turned toward the room. The rectangular space was around three hundred square feet, which wasn't large, but not as small as Bart had made it sound. The walls were all beige stone, and there was an air vent in the ceiling, so the area was cooled. In the middle sat a large white marble statue of an angel—a man with strong, chiseled features who stood as tall as Bart. His wings fanned behind him, but that wasn't what caught my eye. It was the moon sitting in the palm of his hand.

Griffin and Julius brushed past me, and I tried to move, but my legs were frozen. I stared blankly at the statue. "Why is there an angel in my basement?"

The absurdity of the statement would've made me laugh under normal circumstances...or at least, I thought so.

Hell, I wasn't sure I knew what constituted normal anymore.

"That's one reason you're here." Bart strolled to a desk in the corner of the room where a journal sat with a note on top.

Another damn journal.

Hadn't the last one done enough damage?

Anger fueled me, and my strength returned. I marched to the desk and found my father's neat handwriting once again.

Sterlyn,

If you're finding this, that means that my worst fears have come true. Shadow City has opened the gates once more, and something bad has happened.

Our location has been revealed. I'm working on negotiations for another property, but they aren't finalized. I hope that I'm being paranoid, but if one group found us, that means others could follow. I'm writing this letter in case something happens before I can get us relocated.

I know you must have so many questions, and I hope you never find this. I plan on telling you everything on the new moon. I've been putting it off because when I learned every-thing, I learned it with my brother. How I wish you had someone to rely on like Bart and I had each other, but fate didn't have that in your cards.

None of this matters, but if I don't tell you

this, I know you'll always be curious. Kevin's new mate came from Shadow Ridge, and she told her former alpha about our location, not realizing the severity of our situation. You'll soon read the journal I left behind that will detail what I'm referencing, but just know her mistake wasn't intentional.

So read the journal, and at the very back, I have details on how to contact your uncle for help. Unfortunately, if you're reading this, that means I am dead. Just know that you are a true alpha, and never let any man or woman doubt your capabilities. There is something special in you. Both your mother and I see it. You have a just heart, even more so than most others, and you will be a leader who understands what's best for the entire supernatural race, not just the silver wolves. You are the true embodiment of what a silver wolf is meant to be.

I love you, baby girl. And I will always be watching over you. You deserve to be happy and find a fated mate who will make you even stronger. Please don't be angry with me because everything I've ever done has been out of love.

With all the love of the moon,

Dad

My throat dried as I blinked back tears. I'd read the letter with his deep, vibrating voice in my mind. I *was* angry with him, but he had planned on showing me this room and whatever it contained. He'd died the day he was going to bring me down here.

"Babe?" Griffin asked with concern.

"He was going to tell me." Bart had been shocked that he hadn't, but the explanation was right there in the letter. "The night of the new moon. He died that day."

"Well, at least you got a letter," Julius snapped. His nostrils flared as his nose wrinkled with disgust. "Why are you upset?"

That was the final straw—I couldn't handle his nastiness anymore. "You aren't the only one who gets to hurt." My hands shook as I sneered at the selfish prick. "Just because a witch spelled you and said you were dead doesn't mean that I can't hurt, too. I lost my parents, and you never knew them to feel this kind of sting. And as much as it hurts that you never knew them, I hurt because I *did*. I'm tired of being patient with you. If you can't be civil to me, then you can go run back to whoever the hell took you and left you as a fucking rogue wolf your entire life."

Julius inhaled sharply, but his demeanor didn't change.

"I have a lot to get caught up on, it seems." Bart rubbed the back of his neck. "And if they have a witch working for them, that means other races know about us as well. But if Cyrus didn't connect with another pack, I don't understand how you didn't know he was alive, especially with your twin connection."

"Well, I wasn't alpha, and Dad probably thought he was imagining things." If I were him, that was what I'd think. "He probably didn't want to get Mom's hopes up. When Dad died, I felt, at times, a pack connection, but I thought it was a phantom echo because I'd just lost my pack and I wanted to feel them again." I paused and thought through what he'd said. "What is a twin connection?"

"It's a special bond twins have. You two are only the second ones in the silver wolf line and the first twin alpha heirs. You sense each other more than regular linked pack members do, though it's not as strong as a fated mate bond." Bart paced in front of the angel statue. "How close by was he?"

Julius cleared his throat, obviously done remaining silent. "I was about fifty miles away, holed up by myself."

"Far enough that neither link would be strong." Griffin's head lowered, and he sighed. Then he lifted his head and glared. "But close enough that you could coordinate attacks on Sterlyn."

Bart stilled. "You attacked your sister?"

Though Julius answered Bart's question, he addressed me. "I was told my parents didn't want me and cast me aside. They said that my parents favored you because you were the rightful alpha heir—that they didn't want to keep me around in case I tried to challenge you. That my parents were more concerned about your well-being than anything else. That you were their moon," he said agitatedly. "A woman was hired to take care of me, and some arrogant man said they wanted to help make things right and that they wouldn't harm any of the silver wolves."

"A woman and a man?" That piqued my interest. That was the most I'd gotten from him so far. "Who are they?"

"I...I don't know their names." Julius frowned and tugged at his ear. "I called them Grace and Topper, but I've only seen him a handful of times, and I haven't seen either of them in years. I only get calls now, but Topper promised that we were righting the wrongs done to me."

"Well, clearly they were *so* trustworthy," Killian deadpanned, his irises turning dark chocolate. "Didn't them not accepting you as part of their pack tell you something?"

His words made the question pop into my brain. "Why *didn't* they make you pack?" I asked Julius.

He chewed on his cheek and averted his gaze. "They were going to after my first shift, but..." He trailed off.

"But what?" Griffin growled with impatience.

"He never shifted." Bart chewed on his finger, then dropped his hand.

Griffin blew out his cheeks and released his breath. "How is that possible? His wolf would eventually take over."

I hadn't even considered that. No wonder Julius was so angry—he wasn't in sync with his wolf. He had to be at internal war most of the time. "Because the alpha blesses each wolf cub, and they shift with the pack."

"When they realized I couldn't shift, that's when Topper stopped visiting and resorted to phone calls." Julius's mouth pinched. "And then, a few years ago, they realized that I wasn't the true alpha. That *you* were." He nodded toward me. "So to pay for my keep, he put me in charge of training their guards, since he used so many resources on having me trained from the time I was small."

"That's why all the men hunting us have been fighting with guns more than their animals." Killian spoke slowly. "You couldn't train their animals."

"Yeah. Over the years, I've tried to prove my worth and specialized in weapons. I learned quickly and easily."

Silver wolves were like angels in easily learning the craft of battle.

My blood ran cold.

The angel statue in the room had to explain part of that, and I wasn't quite sure I wanted to know what it was. Or who.

"Well, as soon as we get out of here, we'll get you to shift before we go home," I said. That would most likely be why he was so volatile. His wolf must feel confused, and to make matters worse, trapped. Wolves weren't meant to be contained inside the human form.

"You'd do that for me?" His lips parted as he flinched. "After everything?"

The answer was simple. "Of course. You're family."

Something unreadable crossed his features, but I didn't want to stare at him and make him feel even more uncomfortable.

As much as I hate to ruin this touching moment, we do need to get back soon. Griffin nodded at the leather-bound journal. *Do you want to grab that and head home?*

No. I had a feeling that I'd need Bart to answer questions. *I need to read it here.* But Griffin was right. I needed to stop wasting time.

I sucked in a hasty breath and placed the letter back on the table. I picked up the journal and rubbed my hand over the front. The leather was soft and worn. Gathering my courage, I opened the book, which revealed yellowed pages. I'd expected another of my father's journals, but this wasn't his handwriting. In fact, the first entry was dated 1125.

My eyes scanned the page...and the world seemed to shift. I read the first paragraph over and over again. There was no way I understood the words correctly.

Griffin's anxiety oozed from every pore. *What's wrong?*

The question was simple, but the answer was anything but. The first paragraph had changed everything I'd ever known, and that alone made me afraid to continue. What other truths would be revealed that I'd rather remain oblivious to? By the end of the book, I might not ever understand who we truly were.

You're scaring me. Griffin's body coiled like he was about to fight whatever was bothering me.

But the truth was just that. Truth. Nothing could

change it. I'd read it, and I could never undo it. When Bart had said that the life that I knew would change, he hadn't been kidding.

This changed *everything*.

I cleared my throat. I didn't want to have to repeat the information multiple times, so I might as well get the words out so everyone could hear.

My uncle gave me a sad smile, nodding his head in encouragement.

Now I understood what Dad had wanted, and I was so damn glad Griffin and Killian were here with me. In reality, I was glad Julius was here, too, both of us about to process this new information together. "There is a reason the silver wolves are tied to the moon and stronger than other wolves."

"Okay," Killian said carefully. He tried to sound patient, but I could hear his frustration. "Which is?"

"That guardian angel, Ophaniel, impregnated a wolf who lived in Shadow City." The words sounded foreign to my ears. I'd grown up just accepting we were stronger without questioning why. "She got pregnant, even though it was supposedly impossible. Their offspring was the first silver wolf."

Griffin gasped. "But that actually makes a whole lot of sense. That's why you're tied to the moon and so strong."

"Not to mention warriors." Killian moved closer.

"But that's not all." The next part was the real kicker.

CHAPTER TWELVE

"What is it?" Julius asked, clasping his hands together as if he was trying to prevent himself from yanking the journal from my grasp.

I read the last sentence again, ensuring that nothing had changed. But no, the words glared back at me, mocking me. "This can't be right." My attention flicked to Bart.

I wanted him to tell me this was some sort of elaborate scam or that I'd wake up from this crazy dream. But he gave me a slight nod, confirming something that should've been unfathomable.

"What is Rosemary's mother's name, again?" I was pretty sure she'd mentioned it in passing one day, or maybe I'd seen the name flash on her cell phone.

"Yelahiah," Griffin answered, and he tipped his head back. "Wait...if Ophaniel was the angel that fathered the silver wolves, that means you're related to Rosemary. Yelahiah is Ophaniel's sister. She's refused to talk about her brother ever since his death."

I focused on the most important part of the sentence. "He's dead?" Of course he was.

"Yeah, he died centuries ago." Griffin's forehead wrinkled, and his foot bounced. "I can't remember how."

"It's all in there." Bart pointed at the book. "Keep reading."

I inhaled sharply, steadying myself. I read a few more paragraphs, and something hard landed in my stomach. "Apparently, the angels were angry that he had a child with the wolf. Angels can only reproduce every couple of decades, and Ophaniel had a child born only a decade before the silver wolf was born, so the timing was an anomaly, making it appear as if the silver wolves were destined to be created."

"Things don't happen at random." Bart faced the statue and reached out, touching the moon that the angel held in his palm. "There's a reason for everything, even if it's not apparent at first."

Maybe. I used to believe the exact same thing—that we all had free choice, though fate already knew what our choices would be. Would fate be that cruel?

Surely not.

A slaughtered pack, a kidnapped brother, attacks that rocked my entire world—these should never have been set in stone. Only those who had grown up privileged and never faced the cruelness of the world could think that such horrors were meant to be. When all you'd been given were minor trials and tribulations, it was easy to think something good was in charge. But bad things happened to good people, and communities unraveled or were besieged by terrible events.

The world *had* to be a crapshoot. Just a random series of events that happened, and you either got lucky or not. Your fate could change in an instant, but in my darkness, I'd found light. I'd found a part of me that I didn't know existed.

I'd found my strength, my perseverance, and a new family.

I'd found something I'd never been sure I had inside me, despite Dad's insistence it was there. I finally believed I was meant to be an alpha—the silver wolf alpha—and I'd take down whoever threatened our world.

"Whether silver wolves were destined to be created or not, we're here." Resolve coursed through me. "And they won't kill any more of us. Not if I'm breathing."

"Well, it's not like we have huge numbers anymore." Bart grunted. "There are only eighteen silver wolves left, outside of you and Cyrus, and our pack totals twenty-five."

"Twenty-five?" There were seventeen here now, including Julius and me. "Where are the other eight?"

"Five of us found our mates, and Darrell and I each have one child." He licked his lips. "We left them behind with one of the men as guard."

Of course the children and the mates that weren't silver needed protecting. They were mated to silver wolves, which meant they were regular wolves and not as strong as our kind. The children were full silver wolves—the magic of the moon was dominant and passed to them fully—but they were still young and vulnerable.

"What happens if they're attacked?" We'd thought we were safely hidden here, and we weren't. I'd hate for the others to be ambushed and butchered.

Bart's body became more rigid. "The guard will alert us, and we'll head back as fast as possible. We wanted to check this area out and bring them to meet the pack here if it was all clear. They're all packed and waiting for the nod."

"I wouldn't bring them here—this town is compromised.

But Dad was planning to move us to a new location not too far away that should be safe."

"He told me." Bart rubbed his temples. "That's where I planned on us heading next."

The book grew heavy in my hands, reminding me that I wasn't anywhere near finished. "Good." I flipped to the next page.

The once neat scribbling was now a jumbled mess, the chaotic swirls making my heart pound from whatever secrets they held. "Apparently, the angels weren't thrilled that the male hybrid was able to reproduce and that his child was as powerful as him. But Ophaniel protected his son, his grandchildren, and his great-grandchildren. The wolves were able to reproduce every five to ten years, which angered the angels even more. Apparently, the wolf side of them made it easier to reproduce, and once again, their powers weren't diluted. Each generation angered the angels even more."

"Well, they are kind of elitist." Killian chuckled. "They think highly of themselves, similar to the fae."

I'd never met a fae, though I knew they existed. Most of them stayed in their own realm and rarely crossed over to Earth. If you weren't of fae blood, you couldn't travel to their land.

"What else does it say?" Julius asked as he shuffled to my other side and glanced over my shoulder. He stiffened and blew out a breath. "What the hell?"

"Uh..." I had no clue how to answer him. "No?" That certainly wasn't what the book said. I looked around, trying to figure out what had set him off.

"There are no words on the page." He swiped the book and turned it upside down, making a few pages fall and land on the cement.

"Are you insane?" He had to be. I grabbed the book from him and clutched it to my chest. "You're going to mess it up!"

Griffin squatted and picked up the papers. "Babe. He's right." He stood and held the papers toward me. "There's nothing there."

"This isn't funny." Now wasn't the time for games. The letters seemed even more frantic, but they were legible. It took just a little bit of focus to make out the words. I took the pages from him and placed them back inside the book. I'd figure out where they went later.

"They can't see the writing." Bart smiled sadly as he pivoted toward me. "And this confirms what your father knew all along. Only angels and the true alpha of the silver wolves can read those words."

"Is that why you didn't tell me?" Another stupid-ass test that he needed to perform because he didn't believe a woman could be alpha. "How do you know I'm not pretending?"

"Our father read the entries that day because neither your dad nor I were alphas yet." He kicked at the cement as if he were ashamed. "We had him read the journal to us so many times that I have most of it memorized. You didn't know anything about this room, and your dad's letter confirms that he never told you about it."

"Is it because I'm a woman?" I was going to make him admit it. Dad told me to never back down. Maybe he was preparing me for the first time I met Bart.

"No." He grimaced and lifted a hand. "But I thought maybe the witch lied to your dad when she planned on stealing Cyrus. I just had to make sure."

I guessed that made sense, but it didn't completely settle me. However, the stench of a lie was missing.

"Another thing she gets that I don't," Julius grumbled, sounding jealous.

Maybe I wasn't as safe with him as I'd hoped. He might have alpha aspirations of his own, which meant he could stab me in the back. He'd already done it twice. "Considering how much you whine, you could never handle being in charge." I was done being nice.

Killian snorted while Griffin chuckled.

I waited for a smart-ass retort, but Julius's face only turned red.

Not wanting to keep going down this horrible road, I read some more. "The angels grew disgruntled and tried to overtake the city. The silver wolves realized that the angels had to be stopped, and for more than just their own protection. The angels were trying to control everyone and using the city that had been built for refuge as a place to dominate and control. The silver wolves strategized and got the other supernatural races to work together and overthrow the angels."

A smile spread across my face. "Ophaniel writes that it was the most amazing process to watch. The silver wolves had an even more cunning strategy than the angels because they were able to feel and relate to the pain of the races all around them. They energized an army that stormed the city and demanded justice for all."

Julius bounced on his heels. "What happened next?" He sounded like a kid listening to his favorite bedtime story.

He must have had so many questions growing up as a silver wolf that he was thrilled to get answers. Questions I should've had but didn't because I'd taken things for granted.

"Yelahiah intervened and called a truce, with the majority of the angels backing her, but at a cost." I forced the next words. "Azbogah claimed the silver wolves were an abomination, stating that his judgment was final and that they all needed to die. Ophaniel tried to protect the silver wolves from the angel attack, but all the other angels were afraid to stand up to Azbogah. After all, the angels were forced to stand down to the other races because of Ophaniel's offspring. The angels rallied and attacked, killing five silver wolves. Ophaniel helped the remaining ones flee in the middle of the night." I paused, needing to collect myself. The past seemed like a deadly soap opera. "Who is Azbogah?"

"He's part of the angel council." Griffin frowned. "He's the one who makes decisions for the whole angel community, overriding Yelahiah and her husband. He calls himself the judge and executioner."

"Sounds like a stand-up guy." Pricks like that had huge egos. "I bet he and Dick get along great."

"You know what?" Griffin tilted his head as if something clicked. "They actually do."

"Of course." Killian rolled his eyes. "I've been telling you forever that Dick's an asshole. Assholes stick together."

Hoping to keep the insults from starting, I turned the page to find different handwriting looped across it with a date a few days later. Red-hot anger filled me. "Apparently, after the silver wolves escaped, Azbogah called a meeting of the angels and declared Ophaniel a traitor. He proclaimed the only acceptable penance was death."

"For protecting his family?" Killian sounded shocked.

I nodded, needing a moment before I could continue.

Griffin interlocked his fingers behind his head. "Did someone stand up for him?"

"No. The silver wolves weren't there to help them regain control, so they let the angels proceed." Cowards.

That was what they all were. "Yelahiah says she tried to stop the execution, but it was too late. Azbogah chopped off Ophaniel's head, and Ophaniel didn't even try to fight back, wanting them to take their wrath out on him instead of his family."

"No wonder Azbogah and Yelahiah are at odds." Griffin sounded disgusted.

And I couldn't blame him. For Yelahiah to watch her brother die, knowing she'd done nothing to stop it...I imagined that would make her hate not only Azbogah, but herself, too.

A low growl emanated from Griffin's chest, and he cleared his throat. "I hate to interrupt, but we have a situation."

That was just a variation of us having a problem, and I'd lost count of how many times I'd heard it today. "What's wrong?"

"There's trouble within Shadow City's gates." Griffin pinched the skin at his throat. "We're needed there immediately, along with Killian."

I shut the book. "Then I guess we need to go." I turned to Bart. "How do we contact you?"

"Easily." Bart walked to me and lowered his head, submitting to me. "I am now part of your pack, and you are my alpha, as it should be."

A warm spot popped into my chest, followed by twenty-four more. My heart swelled until I thought it might burst. I could feel not only a connection to them but also their well-being. I hadn't expected him to do that. This must be how my dad had felt every day. I sensed anxiety, worry, and love wafting through each connection, identifying each person's mental state. I couldn't hear their thoughts, but the general gist of their mental states flowed into me. And my uncle pulsed with pride. "You didn't have to do that."

"I know, but I wanted to," he said and closed the distance between us to hug me. "You're even stronger than your dad realized, and I'm so lucky I finally got to meet you and Cyrus." He released me and hugged my brother.

Julius stiffened and patted Bart's back awkwardly, but then he stilled and looked at me. "I can't come with you to Shadow City, or people will see me." He gestured at Bart. "Why don't I stay with him?"

Ugh, he was right, but I didn't want to put that burden on Bart. "We can drop—"

"No, it's fine." Bart tapped his head. "I'll link you and tell you where we land. He can stay with us. In fact, if you bless me, I should be able to help him shift and run for the first time."

"Bless you?" I had no idea what that even meant. "Like sneezing?"

Killian burst out laughing. "I've never heard you sound anything less than smart until this moment."

Nope, I was *not* taking any shade from him. "Then what does it mean, asshole?"

His laughter cut off as his face smoothed. "Um...I'm not sure."

"So I'm not the only idiot." I stuck my tongue out at him. It'd been a while since he and I ragged one another. It felt nice, even though this wasn't the best time.

"But I didn't—"

Bart pinched his lips together like he was trying not to smile and cut off Killian. "Just push some of your alpha will toward me, allowing me to borrow a little bit of your power until the shift is over."

That sounded so simple, but I was clueless about how to do it.

"Let your wolf guide you." Bart encouraged. "She's mixed with your angel side and knows exactly what to do."

"Like an angelic wolf?" Killian asked, wide-eyed. "With wings and all?"

Now I couldn't not give him shit. "And *I* sound like an idiot?"

"Hey." Killian frowned, but there was warmth in his eyes.

Griffin took my hand and chuckled. "She's got you there, man."

I closed my eyes to focus, tuning everyone out. I needed to get this done. I tugged on my connection with Bart...and my wolf pushed a little bit of our magic toward him. *Use this to help Cyrus shift and send it back to me.* Alpha will laced the words, and a small part of me passed to Bart.

"Perfect." Bart squeezed my arm. "Take the book and go. I'll handle everything here."

His sincerity flowed into me, and I turned without hesitation. We had another crisis to face, and the longer we took to get there, the more Dick would take control, which was unacceptable.

CHAPTER THIRTEEN

The five of us ran up the stairs and into my parents' room. As soon as Bart slipped past the door, I pushed the chest of drawers back into place and heard a faint *click*.

I still couldn't believe I'd lived in this house my entire life and had no clue about the secret compartment. Whoever'd thought to build the entrance into furniture was brilliant, and Dad must have taken extra precautions to ensure Mom and I didn't walk in on him whenever he visited downstairs. In fairness, he could've kept the journal in the hidden underwear compartment and rarely ventured down until he feared the rumblings.

"We tell no one about this door," Bart said quietly. "This is meant only for the alpha bloodline to know, so by letting those two down there as well"—he gestured to Killian and Griffin—"I've already broken protocol."

"Because your alpha asked you to." Now that he'd come clean with us and was part of my pack, we owed him the truth. "And I'm sorry, but we're in a rush. Griffin is the alpha of Shadow City. His father was Atticus Bodle, the alpha who contacted my dad about opening the city. And

Killian is the alpha of Shadow Ridge. There's a crisis and we're needed. We can meet up soon, but at least now we can communicate, as long as you all don't venture too far from Shadow Ridge."

"Your mate is the alpha of Shadow City?" he asked, slowly turning toward Griffin. "Are you sure magic wasn't involved in that union? It seems awfully convenient that the Shadow City alpha is mated to you."

"Oh, trust me." Killian snorted. "We know. They hated each other at first, and both he and I had no clue what she was."

Griffin growled as unhappiness pulsed off him. He didn't like the accusation.

Now wasn't storytime, and we didn't have time to waste for them to brawl it out. "I'm positive, and you need to get that thought out of your head." I stared Bart down and continued, "He's my mate, and we've completed our bond. The decision has already been made and is final. That's your one pass. Make sure it doesn't happen again." I touched Griffin's arm, hoping to calm him.

Be glad he's your uncle, or I'd kick his ass. Some of the tension left his body, but a scowl remained. "Since you're worried about her best interests, I'll let it go," he told Bart, then interlaced our fingers, tugging me toward the hallway. "And she's right. We have to get moving. Dick is asking where I am. The guards told him that we left the house."

Of course they did. Granted, we hadn't asked them not to say anything to Dick—that would've raised a lot more flags. We rushed down the hallway with Julius taking up the rear. Once he stepped out the front door, I paused long enough to lock it.

"I'll link you the address to where we're heading. We're still staying close by," Bart said, and pulled me into a small hug. "If you need us, let us know. We won't hesitate to come."

"We need to keep you hidden. For once, we have an ace up our sleeve." My attention landed on my brother, and I allowed my wolf to rise, lacing my next words with alpha will. I wasn't going to chance him ratting us out. Whether he liked it or not, he was both my twin and part of my pack, which was probably why he hadn't gone insane. "You will not communicate in any form with anyone outside our pack with the exception of Griffin, Killian, Rosemary, and Sierra until I state otherwise." I wasn't going to allow him to back-stab us. There was way too much at risk. And if he didn't tell Bart anything that would help us, I would use my alpha will to make him talk. But I wanted him to come clean on his own. I was going to give my uncle a day or two because otherwise, it'd fracture my already broken relationship with Julius.

Julius sneered but kept his witty banter to himself.

Good. He needed to earn his place in my warm regard.

I'll keep an eye on him, Bart assured me. His inside light comforted me. *And I'll try to reach him. Even though I wasn't abandoned like he was, I had to leave my family behind. I can at least relate to his situation. My own father died while I was gone, and I couldn't risk coming back here for the funeral. So I understand what it's like to not get the chance to tell someone goodbye.*

I hadn't even considered the implications of what him leaving the pack had meant. I remember Dad saying something odd the day of Pawpaw's funeral. Something about how he wished that the entire family could be there. It hadn't made sense then, and I thought he'd been feeling regret and turmoil over the death of his father. Now, I understood clearly—he'd meant Bart. *I'm sorry and appre-*

ciate your sacrifice. If you hadn't done it, I might be the only silver wolf standing. Well, me and Julius, but I didn't officially consider him a silver wolf yet. He still had negativity roiling inside him, which didn't fit our kind.

"Let us know if you need anything, too," I said out loud, not wanting to make Julius feel even more alienated. "It goes both ways."

Darrell stalked out of the woods, heading in our direction. His eyes turned to slits when they locked on me.

He must have felt our new connection.

Even though I hadn't replaced Bart as their direct alpha, there was a hierarchy to things, and I would never override Bart's leadership unless I felt it necessary. Maybe Darrell thought I had forced Bart to submit, but I'd let Bart handle this one. The more I got involved, the more he'd believe that had been the case.

I turned, forcing my legs to move to the Navigator. As I opened the passenger door, I called out loudly enough so Rosemary could hear. She was still in the air, keeping a lookout. "Meet us in Shadow City—there's an issue." I climbed into the vehicle and slammed the door. Now we had to focus on getting there.

As we pulled into downtown Shadow Ridge, my gaze landed on the enormous bridge over the Tennessee River that connected this bank to Shadow City. Its immense towers jetted toward the sky, looking graceful and reminding me of the pictures I'd seen of the Golden Gate Bridge, especially with the afternoon sun shining down on it. About a hundred yards from the city's main entrance was the section that could be raised in order to prevent anyone from getting inside.

I'd never been inside the city, nor even on the bridge, so I hadn't thought much about the security and the surrounding protective walls of the city. Probably because what I expected to lie within were corruption and deceit. I wanted to stay far away from it all.

"I've never asked, but there are always humans visiting Shadow Ridge." I glanced at the small two-way road that ran through the heart of downtown, where humans and supernaturals alike loitered along the sidewalks and passed by the picturesque brick buildings that made you feel as if you'd gone back in time. "Why do they not ask about Shadow City?"

"It's spelled from within by the witches." Griffin's finger tapped the steering wheel. He was on edge, and he'd driven faster than he should've to get here. "Only supernaturals can see it. Humans see the Tennessee River flowing through, and the place where the city sits just looks like water to them."

Interesting. I figured it had to be something like that.

He drove to the section of land where the bridge connected and turned onto it. The bridge obviously had been built with care without even a bump, but I shouldn't have been surprised.

Only the best for Shadow City.

The closer we got, the clearer everything came into view. The massive walls stood over one hundred stories high, with the city's emblem carved on them over and over again. The emblem was simple but breathtaking in its own right. The picture must be a skyline view of the city, and hovering over the tallest two skyscrapers was a huge paw print. "Why is there a wolf print on top?" I asked. This was a supernatural city, so it seemed strange that only one race would be represented in its emblem.

"Because of the silver wolves." Griffin's lips smashed together. "That was what Yelahiah demanded when the council was formed in memory of her brother."

No wonder Rosemary had turned out to be such a good ally. I couldn't help but wonder if she knew the story. For some reason, I didn't think she did. But finally, the kinship we felt for each other—which neither of us had understood —made sense.

I glanced at the top of the city, which was covered by a large glass dome so that not even supernaturals who could fly would be able to enter unless the city authorities wanted them to. "I'm assuming the glass is spelled?" Dad had taught me that witches were damn powerful when they worked together. It was both their strength and weakness, as all it took was one turning against the coven to fracture them.

"Yes, they reinforce it with their magic. From what Dad told me, there's been only one occurrence of someone trying to break in, a century or two ago." Griffin nodded toward the top. "Some power-hungry fae dragon king wanted to take over the city. All I remember is that even against fae magic, the dome held tight."

"So only one attack here?" I'd expected several. There was always at least one crazed, power-hungry supernatural alive at any time. Probably more than one, but I chose to think optimistically. Dad always said to prepare for the worst-case scenario, but think positively. Positivity was stronger than anyone realized.

"No, there have been several," Killian said, and he leaned forward, staring out the windshield in awe. "But the last one was during the time when my grandfather had been alpha for only a few years. It was a coordinated shifter attack of a few races that lived in a bordering town. Our pack was able to hold them off, though we lost a lot of lives. Shadow City raised the bridge, and the witches spelled the water to kill the few who got past us when they reached it."

"How many did you lose?" Griffin asked stiffly.

"About half our numbers." Killian sighed. "That's one reason that half our neighborhood is vacant and why you were able to buy the house next to mine. We're still trying to get back to those numbers."

"Dad told me about an attack, but he said the loss was minimal," Griffin said with disgust. "That doesn't sound minimal to me."

"I think there might have been one Shadow City death —one of the city guards in charge of the drawbridge." Killian scratched the back of his neck and smoothed his features, becoming unreadable. "The bridge got stuck, so he had to hang over it to get the rope unhung. The enemy took him out then, and Shadow City gave up on raising it higher. It was up high enough that the shifters couldn't jump to it."

In other words, the Shadow City deaths were minimal. That perspective was yet another example of why we shouldn't be separate packs. "You all have done so much to keep that city safe," I said to Killian. Every time there was an incident, Killian's pack reacted without hesitation. And still, they weren't worthy of being officially invited into the city, only to protect the exterior. To Griffin, I asked, *They came from Shadow City—why are they viewed as outsiders?*

I...I don't know. Griffin squirmed, and regret wafted from him into me. *I never questioned any of this before you arrived. Things had always been that way.*

Now *that* was a sentiment we both shared. We believed in our fathers and hadn't thought to question how and why things were done, or how we were raised.

As children, we'd thought of our parents as heroes. We'd put them on pedestals, but the more we grew and learned, the clearer it became that they were just people. They had strengths and weaknesses and didn't always make the best decisions.

They were flawed.

They were real.

They were the type of people who should lead because a perfect person wouldn't have the empathy to relate to others or the convictions of what was right and wrong. Their imperfections made them better leaders, and I was beginning to understand that. Besides, as I did so, I also realized everything that I'd done wrong along the way.

Questions were meant to be asked. A situation should be looked at from every angle. Supernatural races should work together because we all saw things differently, which could show us that sometimes the way things have always been wasn't the way they should be now.

Things had to change. Each bit of information I learned strengthened my resolve, because Rosemary, Griffin, Killian, and I were going to make it happen. We'd find other allies along the way, but for now, we had a diverse group formed: an angel, the alpha from Shadow Ridge, the alpha from Shadow City, and the alpha silver wolf. Even if I didn't plan to recruit more races for the cause, no one would be able to argue that we didn't have the strength to usher in change.

As we approached a large wooden door that would allow us entry into the city, Griffin slowed. When the car came to a complete stop, he waited, his eyes glowing faintly.

He must be linking with people inside.

Confirming my suspicions, gears ground, and soon, the

door began to lift. The process was slow and loud, as if the weight of the door were too much for its cables.

The city came into view inch by inch...and it was gorgeous. The buildings seemed modern, despite the city being closed off for almost one thousand years, and they filled the skyline. A stucco-like building with a huge, round, purple stained-glass roof stood directly in front. The light shining from the top of the city's dome made a beautiful color streak inside, and it seemed like we had entered a different realm.

"Holy shit," Killian gasped. "It looks unreal. Almost like a drawing from an artist."

That wasn't enough to describe the beauty.

"It has to be beautiful to hide all the snakes inside," Griffin murmured as he drove forward.

When we pulled into the city, the place somehow became even more beautiful. Supernaturals milled through a town square, seeming to have not a care in the world.

Instead of heading toward them, Griffin took a hard right, keeping to the outskirts near the walls where buildings were only on our left side.

"Where are we heading?" I hadn't asked him many questions before now—he'd felt determined but on edge, communicating internally with his pack, and I hadn't wanted to pester him. But now that we were here, I needed a little bit of background.

"To the barrier protection building." Griffin's jaw twitched. "Something bad happened, and they need our assistance."

"Are you going to expand on that, man?" Killian asked, clearly annoyed. "I've followed Sterlyn's lead by not asking you stuff on the way, but now that we're close, why don't you tell us what you know?"

"That's the problem," Griffin said sharply. "I don't know much. All Dick said is there's a problem and he needed to see me immediately."

"Wait. Then why am I here?" Killian sat back, not distracted by the sights any longer. "I thought they wanted me here, too."

"Like I said, there was a protection issue. That's all I know." Griffin licked his lips as he pulled over into a small section of the road that was open and out of potential traffic against the wall. "I figured the two of you should be here because you know security measures better than most everyone else."

Great. That wasn't going to sit well, especially not with the angels.

"Follow me." Griffin climbed out of the car just as Dick ran out of a small building across the street.

"He's here," Dick yelled toward the building he'd left and glared at Griffin. "And this whole thing is his fault."

CHAPTER FOURTEEN

Griffin paused mid-step at the venomous accusation Dick had thrown at him. Alarm and anger poured off him as he stared the man down. "What in the hell are you talking about?"

"Don't act like you don't know," Dick spat. "It's time to come in here and face the music." The soulless man glanced at me and then Killian as a cruel smirk spread.

We'd walked into a trap, and there was no getting out of it. Dick had something up his sleeve, and unfortunately, we were about to find out what it was.

The buildings reminded me of Shadow Ridge's downtown. Hell, most likely, Shadow Ridge was a replica to make Killian's discarded pack feel more at home. In this section, they were smaller, two-story buildings made of brick.

I looked around the street, surprised by the quietness. We hadn't seen or passed one car besides our own. Even in the main part of the city, people had milled around on foot, and for that matter, there was no traffic or even stoplights that I had noticed.

We need to leave. He linked. *Something isn't right.*

Oh, I agreed, but unfortunately, that wasn't in our cards. *He obviously has an audience inside, which means if you leave, it'll work out even less in your favor.* We were in a "damned if you do, and even more damned if you don't" situation. *We have to see what he's done and address it head-on.*

Killian stood next to me, his Adam's apple bobbing. A muscle in his shoulder twitched like he was preparing to fight or flee.

Why do you have to be so logical? Griffin teased dryly, still radiating discomfort.

Needing to be there for him, I held his hand and squeezed gently. *Everything will work out.* It had to.

I hope you're right, he replied, and the two of us walked side by side toward Dick. Killian jogged to catch up and flanked me on the left.

We approached Dick, who stood under the small metal awning, watching with apparent delight. He rubbed his hands together as his irises deepened to the color of coal. Even the pretty pinks, blues, and purples that danced around us from the top of the dome couldn't hide the darkness that oozed off him.

For him to be so gleeful, we had to be walking into something even worse than I'd expected.

Dick opened the door and said loudly, "I'm surprised you didn't run like the coward you truly are." He waved us in, and Griffin straightened his shoulders.

I stepped inside and felt like I'd traveled back in time. The walls and ceilings were dark cherry wood. Matching crown molding covered the corners where they connected with the intricate Shadow City emblem chiseled into the design over and over again. The floor was made of white marble, and in the center of the room, under a large, diamond chandelier, the Shadow City emblem had been incorporated into the design in golden stone.

"He did show." The dark, manly hiss echoed off the walls.

By the center of the far wall, seven people stood in front of a marble fireplace.

The man who had just spoken scowled, his sinister appearance matching his hissing voice. His light brown hair fell over his forehead, emphasizing his fair skin and teak-colored eyes. He stood regally, making him somehow seem taller than his perhaps six-foot frame. His scent, which reminded me of apples, made my mouth water. I remembered that vampires smelled sweet. Handy information I'd picked up from my mate.

"Matthew..." Alex, the vampire prince I'd met at Shadow Ridge Coffee only a few weeks ago, *tsked.* "Calm yourself." He pulled on the collar of his navy button-down shirt, which contrasted with his pale skin and soft blue eyes. He lifted his head, and the chandelier's light reflected off his sun-kissed brown hair as he moved to stand beside Matthew. They were the same height, but Alex had a more syrupy sweet scent mixed with apples.

The vampire prince had intervened, which meant there had to be a catch. We hadn't become friendly, and even though there was no vileness coursing off him, I didn't sense any warm fuzzies, either.

"I'm surprised, too," a man who had to be at least seven feet tall snapped. His spiked caramel hair put even more of an edge on his stoic face, and his all-black attire added to his commanding presence. His pure honeysuckle scent hit me, and I remembered Griffin informing me that angels smelled like flowers. Haunting winter-gray eyes focused on Griffin as the man's nose wrinkled in disgust, which told me everything. He had already determined Griffin was guilty of whatever crap Dick had set up.

Forced laughter pulled my gaze to one of the most beautiful women I'd ever seen. Even with the sneer, her full, blood-red lips were alluring, and her forest-green eyes surrounded by long black lashes flashed at the angel with malice. She was my height and wore a long black dress as if it were a second skin. Her sparkling amber hair shined with her goodness. "Azbogah, you aren't the official judge down here anymore."

That's Rosemary's mother, Griffin linked, keeping me informed.

"Ask the other angels, and see what they say. That is, if you're brave enough," Azbogah bit back. "Just because you don't like my decisions doesn't mean that I don't still get to make them."

Wow. I hadn't expected to meet Yelahiah so soon, but the formal introduction would have to come later. "What is this all about?" I asked.

"I'll tell you what this is about!" A short woman pushed through the two glaring angels, her scarlet-streaked black hair bouncing. She squinted her heavily lined, misty gray eyes in accusation at Griffin. Her body shook with rage as she pointed one long black fingernail at my mate. "You scheduled every single Shadow City guard to attend training, and the spell hiding the city from humans almost failed."

"*What?*" Griffin asked in shock. "Erin, there has to be a misunder—"

"Not only that," Dick interjected. "But you brought outsiders into the city without clearance. Your mistakes keep racking up."

Griffin lifted a hand. "I thought—"

"Oh...you *thought*." Matthew cackled, making my skin crawl. "Maybe that was part of the problem."

My throat prickled with rage, and my wolf slipped close to the surface. If I lost control now, Griffin would look even worse. I took in long, steady breaths, trying to calm the raging storm swirling inside me.

"That's enough," Yelahiah snapped. "Erin was able to restore the barrier, and the guards are on their way back. We can discuss it tomorrow at the emergency council meeting." Authority rolled off her.

Azbogah bristled but remained quiet.

And that put me even more on edge. The hate between the two of them was palpable, and for him not to argue with her made me wonder if he and Dick were planning something together.

That sounded like something they'd do, based on their interactions.

"Well, we can't let him leave—he might not come back." Erin cracked her knuckles like she was preparing for a fight. "So what are we going to do with those two?" She gestured at Killian and me.

"I can escort them back to Shadow Ridge." Dick took a step toward me. "I'd be more than glad to since I need to check on the bar, anyway."

Dick didn't want me to be part of the meeting tomorrow. That had to be why he was so eager to take us back... which made me wonder why.

"If she goes, I go." Griffin's voice was low, bordering on threatening. "She's my fated mate, and I'm here declaring her to make it official and present her to the council. I refuse to be separated from her."

"That's what I thought." Yelahiah nodded at me and smiled. "Rosemary has spoken of you often."

Alex chuckled. "Isn't it kind of awful to have your fated mate working at the coffee shop? Or is that the kind of kink you two are into?" He waggled his eyebrows as he winked.

"Am I the only one who finds this hard to believe? Your *fated mate*?" Azbogah laughed loudly, hurting my ears. He shook his head and gestured at Griffin. "You expect us to believe that you're settling down after the number of women you've run through? I've heard enough stories about them over here; I can only imagine what you've done in Shadow Ridge."

A low growl escaped me before I could stop it. I wasn't stupid. I knew he'd been with other women, but for it to be flaunted in my face like that so maliciously—that was a hard pill to swallow.

Unless that was the point. They wanted me to come off as irrational to prove that not only was Griffin not a good leader, but his fated mate was unhinged. Dad had been right when he'd visited two years ago—corruption was still rampant here.

I had to take control over the situation. I smiled sweetly. "Was it necessary for you to say that?" I'd call his ass out, even though I had a feeling he would take exception. "You're a supernatural, so you know he didn't lie...unless your senses aren't as strong as they once were?"

Azbogah's smile fell from his face, and his hands fisted. "What did you just say?"

"Your senses might be going." I lifted a hand and looked wide-eyed at Killian and then Griffin. "Not only can he not smell, but he's lost his hearing, too." The best way to take control of a situation was to use the same tactic against them. I moved a couple of feet closer to him and cupped my hands around my mouth. I spoke loudly. "I *said—*"

"Oh, I heard you." He breathed raggedly, his nostrils flaring. His jaw clenched as he tried to rein in his anger.

"Good." I patted his shoulder, wanting to push him over the edge. "Dick had such a hard time understanding things the other day at Griffin's house, so I don't want to have to worry about another member on the council losing their edge." I smiled brightly, knowing that the stench of a lie wouldn't come. Dick thought he could threaten me and make me scared. And I'd tried telling him that it wouldn't work, but alas, here we were. He truly hadn't gotten it.

"Now listen here," Dick growled and marched toward me. His face turned red as his anger got the best of him. "I understood exactly what you said, and you don't know who you're up against."

"Up against?" Griffin asked coldly. *Wow, I've been an idiot for so long. He's been conspiring the entire time.* "Are you threatening her?"

"No, he's not." Azbogah jumped back into the conversation and stepped between us and Dick. The dark angel smiled charmingly, but the emotion was absent from his eyes. He was cold, heartless, and power-hungry. "This is all a misunderstanding. Isn't it?" He turned and arched an eyebrow at Dick.

Dick's face turned as red as a tomato.

"I think we're done here," Yelahiah said sternly, but the corners of her lips lifted. "The meeting is tomorrow at nine a.m., and if this woman is Griffin's fated mate, then of course she's welcome to stay here. Fate trumps all laws, as it is predetermined by the divine."

The divine? I'd have to ask Rosemary about that later.

"Well, Killian isn't your fated mate, too, now is he?" Alex beamed at Griffin and placed a hand on his chest. "Because it would kind of make sense if he were. You two are super close, and you even went so far as to buy the house next door to his."

Killian's mouth dropped, and Griffin went as pale as the two vampires in the room.

Laughter bubbled out. This was the first time I'd truly seen Killian speechless, and I kind of loved it.

"No!" Killian jerked his head side to side. "Definitely not. Not that there's anything wrong with that, but we don't swing for the same team."

"What is up with these Earthlings and their sayings?" Yelahiah sighed. "Ever since Rosemary started acclimating to the outside world, she's come back speaking another language."

"We don't agree on much anymore," Azbogah said, "but I feel the same way."

"Thanks, Dick," I interjected before anyone else could step in. "For offering to take Killian home. It means a lot that you care for his well-being." I batted my eyes.

"Actually, I don't need to go back to the bar." Dick cleared his throat as he rolled his shoulders. "I'll get someone to take him home, though. Don't worry."

In other words, he'd wanted me gone, and now that I wasn't leaving, he wanted to stay close by. He must be worried that Griffin had brought me here, but did he expect my mate to leave me behind? Dick didn't have a fated mate, so maybe he truly didn't understand. But the thought of being separated from Griffin after the shit we'd been through the last few days petrified me, especially knowing that an angel was working with Dick to discredit him.

My gut informed me that Dick was making his move. Not only did he want to discredit Griffin, but I was pretty damn sure he wanted to take the alpha title away from him. Instead of challenging him the way our wolves knew and respected, he was fighting dirty. Going behind Griffin's back, trying to gain the council's support.

The only reason I could come up with was that he knew he couldn't win a challenge against Griffin, so he was taking power the one way he knew how.

I refused to let that happen to my mate.

Not now.

Not when he'd decided to step up and continue the plans he and his father had made together to improve things, not only for his own race but for the entire city.

Not when he and I planned to build a future in which all the supernatural races worked together to make things better as a whole.

They wouldn't take that away from us.

Killian glanced at me, seeming unsure how to proceed. At the end of the day, I couldn't force Dick to leave, though I'd love to be able to. Somehow, he'd set Griffin up, and we had to prove it. Griffin would never do something so reckless as to leave the city vulnerable.

I had to assume Killian and Griffin weren't linked because the knowledge of how to link between packs had been lost. One of the things on our first order of business would be to figure this pack bond thing out. Bart had been able to submit to me but still maintain dominance over his pack. I had felt it through our connection. Maybe bridging that gap would result in Killian's pack no longer feeling like second-rate citizens.

"Someone is already here to take him back to Shadow Ridge," Dick said authoritatively. "They just informed me that they pulled up."

They had bypassed Griffin and gone straight to Dick despite my mate being here. That irritated me. Another issue we'd address.

"We'll walk him out, and then I'll take Dove to the alpha home here in the city," Griffin retorted, making the insinuation that he was still the alpha clear.

You're extremely sexy right now. Seeing him take charge warmed my body. He'd been getting like this more and more frequently, and that proved just how much he was changing. *Maybe when we get there, you can show me your bedroom.*

Hell, yeah. He intertwined our fingers and turned so our backs were to the others. The power play was clear: he wasn't worried. However, his next words were equivalent to a cold shower. *Right after you meet Mom.*

Holy shit. I was heading to meet his mother. There was no telling how this was going to go.

CHAPTER FIFTEEN

I'd never met someone's parents before. In fact, Griffin had been all my firsts in every way that mattered. With the way my luck was going, his mom wouldn't like me, which would put even more of a strain on our relationship.

As if we didn't have enough to deal with.

Are you okay? Griffin asked, emanating confusion. *Your emotions were steady the entire time in the building, but now that we're leaving, you seem like a hot mess.*

Thanks. I could count on him to be honest. *That makes me feel so much better.*

We stepped outside, and the assortment of shifting colors made me almost dizzy. The air around me changed constantly, reminding me of the aurora borealis but surrounding me.

A Mercedes SUV waited for Killian at the curb, and the driver rolled down the window, waving him inside. "Let's go."

"Nope." Griffin shook his head. "I already took care of his transportation. Thanks, though."

The driver scoffed but took off, not even bothering to say goodbye.

It was time to get a hold on Griffin's reign before he couldn't take it back. Dick had been working hard against him for them to treat him so disrespectfully.

Killian turned toward us and lowered his voice so only Griffin and I could hear. "Are you sure I shouldn't stay?"

"Honestly, I'm not." Griffin pulled at his bottom lip.

I was. "You can't. That will give them even more ammunition to make Griffin look bad tomorrow." I was so damn tired of the broken link—something had to be done. "You two should try to connect like Bart and I did."

"What do you mean?" Killian asked, his forehead lined with confusion.

"Bart submitted to me back at the house, but he retained his position as alpha of his pack. I'm guessing that the two of you can do the same since Griffin is ultimately the alpha of both Shadow City and Shadow Ridge."

Griffin was stronger than Killian, but neither man had embraced their role in their pack until the past few weeks. "It'll give you both an edge since clearly, your two packs have been at odds. If you can coordinate with each other through the link, that will give us an advantage over Dick. He won't expect a full pack alliance." Most likely, over time, the Shadow Ridge alphas had resented the wolves who were tucked safely behind the tall city walls. As the respect was lost, the relationship between the two packs had deteriorated more and more. At least, that was what I'd gathered during my time here when I'd overheard the grumblings in the coffee shop and from the glimpses I'd caught of Dick's interaction with Griffin, Killian, Sierra, and his own daughter, Luna.

"But we're equals," Griffin said uncomfortably.

"Dude." Killian arched an eyebrow. "We both know that's not true."

Their friendship had been forged after their fathers' and strengthened by neither one wanting to step into their rightful place in their pack. "And because of your friendship, uniting the packs once more would make both packs stronger," I told Killian, then linked with Griffin. *You are stronger than him—you were just sheltered more, and he wasn't. In the past few weeks, you've grown and started to own your strength, but if you don't take your place among your people, Dick will steal it from you.*

Another Mercedes pulled up, but this time, Lars was in the driver's seat. "Here I am, sir, ready to take your friend home."

"One minute," Killian said, then averted his eyes to the ground. I watched his body shake—he obviously didn't want to submit. He was strong in his own right, so for him to willingly stand down, even for his best friend, went against every instinct.

A second later, Killian shifted his body toward me. His voice popped into my head. *You both are my alphas now. Don't make me regret it.* He straightened, and his eyes glowed as his wolf recognized Griffin and me.

My throat closed as yet another warm spot filled my chest. *I didn't mean for you to submit to me.* I hoped he didn't think I was trying to manipulate him into that bond.

He patted my arm and spun around, climbing into the car. *I know, but I never would've been willing to submit to Griffin until you came into the picture. It makes sense that I submit to both of you, as I consider you both my true alphas.*

As soon as the door shut, Lars hit the gas, and the car lurched forward. Griffin and I stood there, watching the vehicle disappear from our sight, heading back toward the gate.

We better go before the council members come out. Griffin walked across the street, not bothering to look both ways. Granted, we would've heard any vehicles coming, but it unnerved me. I'd grown up near a human town where we deliberately looked both ways before crossing the street as part of blending in. But in a strictly supernatural hub, I guessed no one had to pretend to be human. It would take some getting used to.

Following him, I hurried and crossed the street, unable to prevent myself from checking for cars. Some habits would take longer to break.

Wings flapped overhead, and I tilted my head as a familiar rose scent filled the air. Rosemary's mahogany hair flew behind her as she descended and landed next to me. Her twilight-colored irises darkened. "What the hell is going on?"

Honestly, I wasn't sure, so I needed Griffin to help explain things. "Why don't you get in the car? We're trying to get out of here before your mom, Azbogah, Dick, Matthew, Alex, and Erin leave."

"Oh, great," Rosemary groaned as she climbed into the back seat. She sat on the floorboard, hiding so no one would see her if they came out the door. "If those people are the only members involved and they're here, that can't be anything good."

"No." Griffin shut the door and started the car. The composure he'd been maintaining slipped away, revealing his worry. "The crystals almost lost power."

"Impossible." Rosemary crossed her arms and pursed her lips. "That can't happen. The guards would have contacted the witches when the power began to flicker."

"The guards weren't there." Griffin ran his hands through his perfectly gelled hair, causing it to stick up. "And Dick somehow has the council believing that it's my fault." He backed out of the parking spot and turned toward the heart of the city. As we pulled away, the group inside stepped from the building.

We'd left in the nick of time.

Their conversation baffled me. I didn't understand a word of what they were saying, other than the power flickering. "What are the crystals, and how are they important?" I asked. Magic circulating in the air could be powerful, but it was also short-lived, so I didn't understand how a witch could leave if their magic fueled the grid. I hadn't realized how large this city was.

"Crystals." Rosemary blew out her breath. "Varying types of gemstones in different sizes that stabilize the witches' spell to make it last longer and hold the protective shield in place."

"Well, if that's the case, how did the witches not know they were weakening?" Surely they couldn't blame Griffin for that. They should have the replenishments scheduled and not wait for someone to randomly call and ask the witches responsible to come recharge the crystals.

"It's not that simple." Griffin turned back onto the main road and glanced in the rearview mirror. "You can get up now if you want. None of them will be able to see you."

"All this is ridiculous," Rosemary grumbled as she lifted her body into one of the seats.

Griffin chuckled. "Who would've thought you'd become friends with my fated mate and we'd have to keep you hidden?"

"If you would've told me that three months ago, I

would've thought you were insane." Rosemary rolled her eyes. "Not saying that I don't actually think that."

I almost felt like I was listening to Killian and Sierra talk to one another. Rosemary usually stayed on point. "Why didn't the witches know that the barrier was weakening?"

"Because the barrier keeps the city hidden from human eyes, there isn't an exact science to tell how long the spell will last. It depends on how many humans are in the outer towns at any given time." Griffin pulled onto the road that ran parallel to the buzzing metropolis. Even from where I sat in the passenger seat, I could easily see the divide among the races: the angels flew around the city sky in groups; the paler-skinned vampires with their overly sweet smell congregated on the side of the street; shifters were gathered, hanging out in front of a place called Shifters' Dive. Some hairy men who had to be bear shifters were laughing loudly while sipping foaming glasses of what appeared to be beer.

The herbal scent that Griffin had informed me signified witches hovered around a group perusing the wares at a stand that showcased crystals, herbs, and all things needed for spells.

I noticed that whenever two groups of supernaturals passed, neither acknowledged the other's presence, as if the other people didn't exist.

It unsettled me. The lack of regard would mean horrible things in the future if it didn't get taken care of.

I tore my eyes from the beautiful buildings and focused on what had to be fixed first. "So…I'm still not following."

"The more humans who visit, the more magic must be used to keep up the illusion. If there aren't as many humans nearby, the spell will last longer." Rosemary broke the facts down for me. "So we have guards stationed at each gate that leaves Shadow City. The building containing the crystals is guarded by wolves because they had to step in for your ancestors. Someone is always on duty in case something happens or the city is infiltrated, but mainly to keep an eye on the levels. The spell has a signature they're trained to identify, and if it begins to fade, they are to alert Erin that someone needs to come refresh it."

"There are also other magical artifacts in a warehouse near the crystal building that have to be protected." Griffin cleared his throat. "We aren't privy to what, but the witches swear that if the items were to be stolen, there would be severe consequences."

"See, that's my whole point." I felt like a broken record. "The witches don't feel obligated to tell you what's at stake because they see themselves as a separate community. We need to bridge the gap and learn to work together."

"I see your point, but change won't happen overnight." Rosemary sighed. "This is how things have been for centuries."

Dick blamed Griffin, but why? "Why were the guards called off? And how?"

"I have no clue." Griffin tapped a finger on the steering wheel. "I didn't approve anything that would have directed them to leave their stations."

Obviously, the *how* was the leverage Dick had against Griffin, so we had to figure out what the hell it was. "Rosemary, your mom was there. Do you think you could find out from her what Dick told everyone?"

"Yeah, I should be able to do that." Rosemary sighed.

"And are all the guards wolves?" The question kept popping into my brain. "I mean, there are other races, too. Wouldn't they want to protect the city as well?"

"There are vampire guards who protect the vampire side of Shadow City and the bridge that connects the city to

Shadow Terrace, which is on the opposite bank of the river from Shadow Ridge. The vampire gate is also how Shadow City vampires get their blood supply, since humans don't live here," Griffin answered, his voice tight. "And there are Shadow City police, but the force is small and made up mostly of shifters who aren't wolves so that the wolf shifter representatives don't have undue influence in case someone needs to be taken down. There aren't a lot of them, but they protect the artifact warehouse and have a few people on patrol."

That made sense and was great for checks and balances. If wolves protected everything, all Griffin would have to do would be to use his alpha will, and he'd gain access to anything he wanted.

We pulled up to a large golden building with a sign outside that declared it the Elite Wolves' Den with a wolf pawprint underneath. The building had to be forty stories high. Griffin pulled into an attached garage and scanned his badge to open a gate for the lower parking level.

"This is my stop." Rosemary opened the door and climbed out. "I'll get to the council meeting early. Meet me at the coffee stand inside the council building, and try not to act suspicious. I'll tell you everything I know then." The door shut, and she took off so fast that she blurred.

She obviously didn't want to be seen.

Do you think you should've told her that you two are related? Griffin's shoulders relaxed now that we were alone.

That had been the plan. *She left before I could.*

Well, you'll have plenty of time in the future. He pulled into a slot closest to the glass cubicle enclosing the elevator. *Mom is ecstatic to meet you, but she's out with one of her friends right now. Apparently, they're having a girls' night, but she said she'd come home early and ride with us to the council meeting.*

I wished I felt the same way about meeting her, but at least that had bought me a little time. Maybe a good night's sleep would put me in a more confident frame of mind.

He slid his badge against another buzzer, and the cubicle door clicked. He held it open and waved me inside. Once I stepped into the building, I sighed with relief. Inside the building we'd just left and here, the beautiful city lights vanished as if there was something blocking it out on the glass, and I felt more at peace. The lights were gorgeous but overwhelming, much like a nightlight that never turned off and grew so bright that you felt blinded.

Griffin hit the elevator call button, and the silver doors slid open. Once we were inside, he pressed his badge to a sensor and then hit the top floor. Within seconds, the doors slid open again, and my jaw dropped. I'd expected to walk out into a hallway. I wasn't prepared for the doors to open into Griffin's home.

Dark platinum tile floors greeted me with interior walls the color of stratus clouds and all-glass outer walls that overlooked a breathtaking view of the city. White leather couches were placed perpendicular to one another in the living room area with a white coffee table sitting in the center.

One section of the floor-to-ceiling windows had a sliding glass door that led outside to a covered balcony, where the same flooring continued. Two large gold chandeliers hung above several black lounge chairs, and a bar with a black-stone counter sat in one corner.

It was strange to see all the nice furniture outside, but inside the city, there was no horrible weather or wind because of the protection of the dome.

I hadn't realized how wealthy Griffin was. I felt stupid. No wonder Luna had been desperate to get her claws into him. A low growl threatened to escape me from just that simple thought.

Every direction I turned, everything looked almost identical. The same color scheme and style.

Griffin took my hand and tugged me toward the hallway in the middle of the room that led to another section of the apartment. *I know you deserve the tour, but right now, I need some alone time with you.*

That was something I wouldn't argue against. We walked past multiple closed doors until he stopped at the last one on the left. He opened the door, and once again, the gray color scheme stared back at me.

The room was about the same size as his bedroom in Shadow Ridge and featured a king bed against the center of the right wall. Instead of a headboard, pewter squares started at the top of the bed and climbed toward the ceiling. Crisp white sheets that had to have been ironed peeped over the top of a dark gray comforter. The wall overlooking the city was all glass.

Griffin grabbed the edge of the silver-dust-colored curtains and closed them so the view was hidden. "In case anyone flies by." His eyes glowed as he spun in my direction and raced toward me.

His lips crashed onto mine, and his tongue slipped into my mouth. His taste overloaded my senses, and my body heated immediately. Last time, he'd dominated me, teased me, but this time, I needed him hard and fast.

I shoved him onto the bed and straddled him, peeling off my shirt. I didn't know what had come over me, but with all the threats we'd just endured, I *needed* to connect with him in a way that only I ever could going forward. Maybe it was the insinuation of how many girls he'd slept with that fired my urgency, but I needed every single one of them erased from his mind.

My hands grabbed the edges of his shirt, and I yanked it over his head. His hands wrapped around me, unfastening my bra. As soon as he flung it to the floor, his tongue flicked against one nipple, making my skin ignite.

He rolled me onto my back and stood, unfastening my jeans and dragging them and my panties off me. *Damn it, your scent is driving me wild*, he told me, and growled.

I pushed up and yanked his pants and boxers down so hard that the button flew off. My eyes took in every inch of him as I slid up on the bed, spreading my legs wide for him. I was primed and ready, and I didn't want to wait anymore.

With eagerness, he climbed in between my legs and slammed inside me. He knew exactly how I wanted him. He thrust inside me over and over, but I wanted something more...something different. *I want to be on top.*

I'll never complain about that. He chuckled as he flopped on his back, ready for me to lead.

Turning so my back faced him, I slipped him inside me. We'd never done this position before, and he hit inside me at a different angle. I began riding him, and he groaned animalistically, which urged me to move faster. That sound was so damn sexy, and I needed to hear it more.

My legs began to burn from kneeling, but the pressure was building, and I ignored the ache.

He sat up behind me and slipped his hand around my front, rubbing the sensitive spot between my legs that was bringing me closer to the edge. My body moved faster, and he increased the pressure to where it hurt and felt incredible all at the same time.

Within minutes, we both fell over the edge and

climaxed together, our cries of pleasure mingling. Fully sated, I turned and lay against his chest as my breathing slowed and my eyes grew heavy.

Right as my mind began growing foggy, the *ding* of the elevator sounded, followed by a female voice calling out, "Griffin, I decided to come home after all!" Heels tapped on the floor as they approached.

My blood ran cold as realization settled over me.

I was naked in Griffin's room, and his mom was home and heading this way.

CHAPTER SIXTEEN

Attempting to leap out of the bed, I got wrapped up in the sheets and tumbled to the floor. I landed on my shoulders, causing a deep ache to run up my arms as the covers shifted, exposing my bare ass. I'd never felt so clumsy before, and of course, it'd happen now. I didn't want Griffin's mom walking in and seeing me like this.

Sterlyn! Griffin said with concern as his head popped over the side of the bed and he took in the disheveled heap of me on the floor.

This was not a good look for me in so many ways.

He stood up, bare-ass naked, not even pretending to be bothered that his mom was here. *Are you okay?* He squatted next to me and lifted me into his arms.

Yeah, I'm peachy. My cheeks felt as if they were on fire as he sat with me on the bed. *Your mom is here.*

His hazel eyes sparkled with mirth. *Yes, I'm very aware.*

A knock on the door made my stomach do somersaults.

"Griffin, I decided I couldn't wait to meet her, so I wanted to surprise you two." She sounded so happy. "I mean, this is the woman who'll be giving me grandbabies!"

Wow. Even though that statement was true, I hadn't thought that far ahead in our future. With everything we were going through, the farthest I could picture was probably a year's time.

"You didn't think to tell me you were heading here?" he called through the door and chuckled, his face filled with adoration as he watched me.

She huffed. "I thought I'd surprise you two."

"You succeeded," he replied, then laughed outright, making me want to punch him.

The asshole knew why I was freaking out, and he was teasing me. *Not cool.* I bared my teeth at him. Maybe sometime in the near future, I'd find it funny, but not so much now.

"Oh." She sniffed. "I smell that."

Please, someone, kill me and put me out of my misery, I chanted to myself only. Even before I met his mother, she was smelling the scents of our desire from just a short while ago.

"Well, no time like the present to get started on those babies," she said, and giggled. "I'll wait for you in the den." The clatter of her heels grew fainter as she moved away from the door.

I punched him in the arm. *You enjoyed that way too much.* I'd rather hide in here the rest of the night, but she was waiting for us. If I didn't go out there, that would only make seeing her tomorrow even more difficult. I was stuck.

"Ouch." He smiled as he rubbed his arm. "Keep that up, and I'll have to punish you. Mom can wait, after all."

"No way." I stood and hurried across the room to grab my clothes. "That will not be happening. This is embarrassing enough."

"Stop it." He rolled his eyes and pouted. "But I'm serious. If you don't want to see her yet, I can keep your mind occupied."

He might be sexy as hell and able to make my body do things that brought such immense pleasure, but I wouldn't be able to focus on anything but the sound of his mom's shoes for the next little while. "Don't worry, I'll punish you later."

"Later, huh?" he asked and smirked as he watched me dress. "I could get behind that." He waggled his eyebrows, driving the innuendo home.

"Behave." I pulled my shirt over my head and ran my fingers through my hair to at least make it look somewhat tame. I didn't need to walk in there with sex hair since we'd already announced what we'd been doing clearly.

"Fine." He pouted but quickly dressed.

Once we were both somewhat put together, he opened his bedroom door. *Mom has been excited to meet you. I should've realized she might come home early, but the thought of having you in my bed was a little too tempting.*

I wasn't about to complain about the sex. Hell, I was all for it, but had I known there was a possibility of her coming home early, I would've gotten dressed before I started drifting off to sleep.

With each step closer to the den, my heart pounded harder. I hadn't liked nearly every person I'd met from Shadow City. They were pompous and only out for themselves. Rosemary seemed to be the one exception. I feared that Griffin's mom would be the same way, which could cause problems between the two of us. We had enough of those.

Hey, it's going to be okay. Griffin grasped my arm, pulling me to a stop. He cupped my face and looked into my eyes as he continued, *There's nothing to be nervous about.*

That was easy for him to say—she was his mother. *If you were meeting my father, how would you feel?*

His face slipped into a mask of indifference. *Okay, I'd have been nervous, too, but I swear there's no reason to be. There were only two things that my parents wanted for me. The first, and most important, was finding a mate who made me a better man.* He pressed his lips to mine. *And you're even better than that—you're my fated mate.*

I inhaled slowly, calming myself. If that was his parents' first wish, then maybe I was overreacting a tad, and freaking out would make me look bad. Dad had told me to pretend to be confident even if I was the furthest thing from it. Pretending would bleed into truly becoming secure. It was some sort of mind-over-matter trick that he was always teaching me. But he'd been right about almost everything else, so what did I have to lose? *And the second thing?*

Becoming the alpha that Shadow City needed. He shook his head as he dropped his hand. *I always assumed he meant the alpha of the wolves, but I'm beginning to think you and he were more similar than I realized. He wanted to unite the races the same way you do and not have us all be seen as separate beings.*

Be careful who you say that to. I took his hand. *If you aren't careful, Sierra will start accusing you, in some demented way, of sleeping with your father.*

Since she isn't here, you had to go there for her. He wrinkled his nose and booped mine. *But don't worry. That won't prevent me from ravishing your body again when we get back to my room. After all, I did promise you a punishment.*

My body betrayed me, and the spicy scent of arousal wafted from me.

I see you have no complaints. He smiled.

Refusing to give him any more satisfaction, I marched

off in the direction of the living room. I entered the room to find an ash blonde woman standing in the center.

She ran her hands along the sides of her pewter sweater as her light champagne lips formed a warm smile. Her sapphire-blue eyes scanned me, but not in a critical way. Her gaze was more curious. She placed her hands in the back pockets of her dark jeans as she leaned on the high heels of her black shoes. "Sterlyn," she said. "It's so nice to finally put a face with a name."

That was when I realized I didn't know her name. Griffin always referred to her as Mom. "Hi."

"Ulva," Griffin interjected. "Mom's name is Ulva."

"But you can call me Mom, if you'd rather," she said a little too earnestly.

I wasn't sure how to respond. *No, thanks, I already had a mother* would sound too rude, but I didn't feel comfortable calling her that, either.

"Isn't that a little forward?" Griffin asked as he placed an arm around my waist. "You haven't known each other for a minute yet, and you're asking her to call you Mom."

"Ugh, you're right." She tilted her head back and sagged her shoulders. "I'm sorry. It's just...I haven't seen Griffin this happy before."

"Wait." He hadn't gone back to Shadow City since we'd gotten together. "Seen him?"

"Yeah, the night he had to bring Luna here when she was so drunk." Ulva sat on the couch. "I had to come to the gate to let her in since her parents weren't answering their phones. She was ranting that Griffin forced her to take a cab and refused to let her inside his house in Shadow Ridge. That her mother and father wanted them to be together, and why couldn't he just accept that? She deserved to be staying in his house with him. Didn't

Griffin know who she was and what her father was capable of?"

That sounded about right. I'd met Luna only a handful of times, and each time, she'd left a worse impression than the previous one. Granted, she'd tried to kill me on the night Ulva was referencing. Griffin had said he'd gotten her a cab, and obviously, it was true. He'd just left out the part where he'd accompanied her to the gate, but he was right. She wouldn't have gotten in otherwise.

"He told me he was sorry to dump her on me, but he had someone to get back to before he messed things up even more." She looked at her son with a soft expression. "And that's when I realized someone had stolen his heart. When he informed me that you two were fated, that was just the icing on the cake. This was exactly what we'd hoped for him to find."

Kindness radiated off her, confirming her words. I sighed in relief, realizing that she was truly a good person. I needed that; I'd been worried that there weren't many great people in this city. "Well, Griffin thinks the world of you, too."

"Atticus and I were more friends than lovers, but we worked, even to Saga's horror." She chuckled and gestured to Griffin. "That's one reason why we only had one child. The sex was—"

"Mom!" Griffin exclaimed with wide eyes.

"Sorry, you're right." She swatted her hand. "I just meant that we wanted Griffin to find the kind of love that we hadn't been able to find ourselves. It's one part of why Atticus wanted so much to open the city. He wanted our son to find his fated mate. He'd be so happy to see that wish came true."

My heart grew for a man I'd never get to meet. He'd

loved Griffin so much. I'd known that Griffin's mother and father were chosen mates, but I hadn't thought about what that meant.

"So, who's Saga?" I wanted to learn more. I wanted every single detail about Griffin and his family that I could soak up.

"Dick's chosen mate." Ulva smiled. "One of my close friends. The four of us grew up together, and, boy, Saga did everything she could to get Atticus for herself. But he and I were best friends, and he said he trusted only two people in his life—me, most of all, and Dick. I thought that it would cause a wedge between Saga and me, but when Atticus asked for me to be his mate, she surprisingly backed down, and she and Dick realized that they were compatible as well." She smiled sadly. "Atticus was so relieved. He was always wary of her back then, and he protected me, probably a little too much. He was a wonderful man and a good father."

"Mom, I hate to cut this short, but it's late." Griffin made his way over to her and kissed her forehead. "Tomorrow morning is going to be nasty, so we need to get our rest."

"You're right. I'm exhausted." She yawned.

He squeezed her hand and straightened. "You know you don't have to come to the meeting, right?"

"I refuse to let you protect me like your father did." Her face pinched as she shivered. "I wish I'd known that Dick was trying to use you as the scapegoat. You need every person who supports you there. The more people you have behind you, the stronger a leader you'll look, and I want to see who all the traitors are."

That was something my father would say. Despite

Atticus and Ulva being chosen mates, she was strong, which must have been one reason he'd selected her.

"Okay." He nodded. "Fine. I just hate for you to watch someone else you love get hurt."

That was an odd thing to say. *What do you mean?*

She and Dad were at Dick's having dinner when he died. Griffin scowled. *She saw the entire thing.*

They'd been eating at Dick's? That was a little convenient.

"I understand, and I love you for it." Ulva headed toward the hallway, leaving the two of us behind. She spoke quietly, but I was able to hear her with my silver wolf ears. "Maybe if I'd been more involved and paying attention, he wouldn't have died in the first place."

I wanted to ask her what she meant, but I was pretty sure she didn't know I was a silver wolf with extra-sharp hearing. If she had, she probably wouldn't have said the words out loud at all, assuming Atticus had shared with her what he knew about my kind. I bit my tongue, but only because I wanted to protect her. The more she knew, the greater the chance she would be harmed.

"Night, Mom," Griffin called out as he winked at me. "I love you."

"Love you, too," she said with longing in her voice.

Once the door closed behind her, Griffin returned to me with a salacious smile. "Now, let's go have some fun." He bent down and threw me over his shoulder, and took off to his room.

However, I wasn't able to laugh or fully enjoy the moment. My mind kept replaying what Ulva had just said.

Ulva met me in Griffin's bedroom the next morning with a black suit in her hands. "This should work." She placed the clothing on the bed, along with a lavender lace shirt.

The suit bottom was a skirt instead of pants, but I didn't want to complain. I didn't have my own clothes here, so I would graciously borrow whatever she was willing to loan me. "Thank you."

Griffin was on the balcony, waiting on me to finish getting dressed. He'd pouted when I made him leave the room, but after last night, I didn't want to be naked in the bedroom with him while his mom was here. I needed at least a day's buffer before that could happen again.

She turned to leave the room but paused. "I want you to know I meant everything I said last night." She looked over her shoulder, locking gazes with me. "I already see a difference in him. Before you, he never would've been brave enough to face the council like this."

"I'm doing nothing." She must have been able to see that. She didn't need to give me credit for something Griffin was doing on his own. "He didn't even ask if I thought we should run. He's making these choices, not me."

"Oh, I know." She pivoted and tilted her head. "But you helped ground him. He was struggling, messing around, just trying to get by. You stepped into his life and gave him purpose again."

"Maybe, but he's made me a better person, too." I was meant to be a warrior, and that would never change, but he'd made me softer. Not in a weak way, but the opposite. I was able to open up to Rosemary because of him...and see things in the ways that my father had because of him. "I guess that's why we're fated mates."

"They're meant to bring out the best in each other." She nodded. "And being locked in here, the wolves and the other races have lost that way because we were rarely able to find ours anymore. But things are changing, and people fear it. You and Griffin will be an excellent example of a positive change resulting from rejoining the world."

"I have a hunch that the people trying to blame Griffin for the crystals are the ones who want to close the borders again."

She nodded. "You're exactly right. Several council members think we have the strongest supernatural races within these walls, and we shouldn't have to deal with petty problems caused by shifters who weren't worthy to live here to begin with."

"Sterlyn. Mom," Griffin called out. "We've got to go, or we won't get there early enough."

"They'll crucify him if we can't figure a way out of this." Ulva frowned. "We can't let that happen."

I placed a hand on her arm and leaned forward, dropping my voice. "So...there's only one thing we can do." I arched an eyebrow. "We take them down. Are you in?"

CHAPTER SEVENTEEN

The car ride to the council building was made in complete silence. Griffin tried to appear upbeat, but he wasn't fooling either Ulva or me. He drove his Navigator through town, attempting to keep me out of the view of others as much as possible. The fewer people who saw me, the less likely they were to guess my heritage. We passed only one other vehicle, which was heading out of the city.

Griffin's leg bounced the entire way, despite the forced smile he wore.

Fortunately, Ulva and I were in agreement. No matter what, we were going to make sure that Griffin didn't take the blame for the trouble with the crystals. Still, we were working with minimal information, and I prayed that Rosemary had been able to wrangle details out of her parents.

After a few minutes' drive through the heart of downtown Shadow City, the capitol building came into view. It covered an entire block, a white rectangle with a cathedral-like roof. The walls reflected the ever-shifting lights, making it seem as if the building changed colors constantly.

Griffin turned into an uncovered parking lot on the

right side of the building. "Here we are," he said, his voice devoid of emotion.

It's going to be okay. No matter what, I'd make sure we came out of this intact. Even if I had to be the one to take the blame. *Rosemary will have something to tell us, and then we can build our case.*

I hope you're right. He opened his door and climbed out of the car.

His dismissal hurt, but I couldn't be overly sensitive. He was going through a lot, and I couldn't take it personally. I refused to add more worry on top of what he already carried.

I got out of the vehicle, slammed the door, and met him and Ulva in front.

"We need to go in as a united front." I was sure they both knew that, but sometimes stating the obvious helped others feel more in control of a situation. I walked to the other side of Griffin so that he stood between me and his mother.

A few people walked past us, not looking our way. Yesterday, everyone's indifference had bothered me, but today, I was grateful. If anyone tried to talk to us right now, I would likely come off as rude, which might hurt Griffin in their eyes.

We followed the walkway to the building's front entrance. Griffin opened the tall hunter-green door and waved us in. My eyes scanned him as I passed by, enjoying the sight of him in his navy suit. The slacks were tight enough to show off his ass, and I had to restrain myself from pinching it as I brushed by. Now wasn't the time for inappropriate thoughts.

His mom's heels clicked on the beige marble floor, and I cringed as I strolled behind her, making the same type of noise. I hated wearing dress shoes and skirts. They were terrible for fighting, and I was raised to always be prepared for battle. Worst case, I supposed I could try to use the slender heel to pierce the skulls of my enemies.

The entryway was huge and bare, ending with another hunter-green doorway midway through the building. The probably once-white walls were stained yellow from time and wear. On one side of the entryway, a man was sweeping the floor. He walked past us, and a whiff of decay hit me hard, making me gag.

What the hell is that? I'd never smelled anything like it before.

Griffin winced and blew out his nose. *A vampire who's being punished. For him to smell that bad, he's gone without blood for a long time.*

Wait. *They smell sweet, not like that.*

Unless they don't feed, he replied. *I've only ever come across one other person who smelled like that, and it was when Dad took me to see the prison when I was a little boy.* "Hey, Mom." Griffin snagged my hand and nodded to a coffee shop at the right. "Sterlyn and I are going to grab a coffee. Do you want anything?"

"No, I don't think that would be wise." She blew out a breath and adjusted the maroon jacket she was wearing over a matching dress. "I'm on edge enough without the added caffeine. I'll go on in and save Sterlyn a seat."

"I'll be right there." I tried to keep my attention on her, but my gaze flicked over to the small coffee shop. It was a stand built into a corner of the room with no tables. Obviously, people weren't meant to congregate there, which was kind of problematic, as Rosemary was nowhere to be seen. *Maybe we should wait a few minutes.*

We can't, Griffin said in defeat. He wasn't even trying

to hide his despair now that we were alone. *The meeting will likely start a few minutes early in hopes that whoever they're targeting arrives on time. It gives the perception that the accused doesn't care about punctuality. A little tip that Dad shared with me before he died.*

These people were assholes. Someone needed to take them down a notch or two, and there was no time like the present. *Okay. Hey, wait.* I walked beside him as a thought unsettled me. *Does your mom know to call me Dove and not Sterlyn?*

Probably not. His body somehow grew even tenser. *I'll link and tell her now.*

Thank God I'd realized that before it was too late.

We walked up to the cash register and placed our order of two black coffees. I usually got something sweeter, but my stomach was already upset. I didn't want to put too much sugar in it and wind up getting sick.

As the man handed us our drinks, Rosemary's scent drifted in our direction. I turned to find her walking over to us. Her long hair was pulled into a Dutch braid, and she wore a white sundress that made her skin appear to glisten. Her black wings fanned out behind her, contrasting starkly with her outfit and giving her sweet look an edge. Like me, she wore white high heels, but hers barely made a sound. "Hello." She nodded formally as she ordered a coffee of her own.

The older fox shifter manning the coffee counter turned around to make her drink, and she took a step closer, speaking in a soft voice that only Griffin and I could hear. "So, we have a huge problem."

"That's kind of obvious," Griffin bit out, letting his anxiety bleed through.

Babe. I chastised him. *I know you're upset, but being*

rude to her won't get us anywhere. In fact, you could piss her off to where she doesn't tell us anything.

Nah, she loves you too much. Griffin brushed off my concern, but I could feel a little bit of regret through our mate bond connection.

Needing to divert her attention from his rudeness, I tried to refocus the conversation. "Do you have anything specific to help us?"

"Yeah." She scowled at Griffin before ignoring him and focusing on me. "Apparently, Griffin signed an order for the guards to attend additional training in case someone ever tried to attack the buildings."

"That's true." Griffin shrugged his shoulders. "What's the big deal?"

"Because you ordered all of them to go at the same time, leaving the crystals unmonitored." Rosemary lifted a brow and stepped toward the counter, dismissing us as the fox shifter handed her the coffee.

I took a sip of my drink, and the bitter coffee burned my tongue. The pain was a temporary reprieve, giving me something to focus on for a moment. I could feel Griffin practically vibrating beside me.

Slowly, Griffin and I strolled toward the door that must lead into the council meeting room. We moved at a snail's pace as we tried to wait on Rosemary without being too obvious. A tall, commanding figure hovering near the doorway caught my attention.

Yelahiah.

I wasn't too shocked, since Rosemary was getting coffee, but the older woman's attention wasn't on her daughter. She was focused on me. Her eyes narrowed as if she were trying to piece a puzzle together, and even when my eyes met hers, she didn't look away. Instead, her interest seemed to be piqued even more.

Unease filtered through me, and I wanted to run away. I'd never experienced such intense scrutiny before. Normally, I was drawn toward a fight or confrontation, not repelled. That was how silver wolves were wired. But this was different. I didn't know how to explain it.

Remember those papers Dick stopped by to pick up at the house? Griffin sounded miserable, and his body seemed to shrink.

Yeah. I remembered that day clearly. Dick had tried to push me into leaving and had even tried threatening me when he saw that I had every intention of staying. The douchebag had wanted to make me run, and I'd thought it was solely because of his daughter. Luna had been desperate to make Griffin her own. *You didn't read the forms, did you?* I tried not to sound accusatory, but I couldn't help it. Dick had been desperate to have him sign those papers quickly, and now we knew why.

I did. He growled, making the vampire sweeping the floor pause. Griffin didn't even notice and continued with his tirade. *But I didn't know how it would impact the guards' watch schedule. I assumed they'd always keep at least one or two behind.*

Dick had banked on Griffin not scrutinizing the details. The conniving prick. *Did you ask any questions?*

No, it seemed so straightforward. He turned toward me. *I fucked up.*

You trusted the wrong person. That was what this all came down to. *But we'll figure a way out of this.* Dad had taught me not to fret even when there wasn't an obvious strategy. That was what the enemy banked on, and I needed to keep a level head in order to seize the next opportunity to turn things around. *That was you being naive and wanting to see the best in people. You did nothing wrong. Why would you ever think anyone on the council would do something to sabotage the safety of the city?*

I should've done something that day, but instead, I'd let the man go with the papers. I had known something wasn't right and should've followed up on my instincts. Because I hadn't, now my mate could lose his place within his pack and city. All those changes his father and he had dreamed of might remain just that.

A dream.

I was also to blame here. But beating myself up over it would be caving and doing exactly what the asshole wanted.

I was stronger than that.

Griffin and I were more powerful together.

We had to remember that.

Rosemary hung back, most likely due to her mother. We needed to pretend, at least for a little while longer, that we weren't allies. That bit of information needed to be dropped at the perfect time.

"Well, hello there." Yelahiah's musical voice sounded like a lullaby.

There was something pure and raw about her that made me feel safe. But I couldn't tell her who I was. She was angry about what had happened to her brother, but I was very far removed from him, my blood containing only a fraction of his after all these generations. "Hi."

"You seem awfully familiar to me." She arched an eyebrow, reminding me of her daughter. "Have we met before yesterday?"

"No, we haven't." We hadn't even been officially introduced. Instead, I had been an observer to the show.

Griffin took a step closer to me. "She's my mate," he said simply.

"I got that much yesterday." However, her focus stayed on me. "What's your name?"

"I have many." I forced a laugh and hoped that the sound wasn't as crazed as it seemed in my head. "But the one most people call me is Dove." That wasn't a lie. All the customers at Shadow Ridge Coffee Shop on the university campus called me by that name. Only my closest friends and family knew my birth name.

"Dove." She grinned, which made her look more human. The superior angel facade slipped away, if only for a moment. "I like that." She licked her blood-red lips and motioned for her daughter. "Word to the wise—you two better get in there. If I know Azbogah and Richard, they're about to begin the meeting five minutes early."

Griffin's lips parted, revealing his surprise at her support.

"Thank you," I said as I looped my arm through Griffin's, directing him inside. If I didn't know he was gawking at her because she'd helped him, I might have gotten jealous. She could easily pass for mid-thirties, despite being centuries old. Angels were immortal.

As we entered the room, I scanned the area, looking for Ulva. I spotted her sitting next to a dark-haired woman on the end of a row of chairs against the wall close to the door we'd walked through. More chairs were set around a rectangular table with a cut-out section that faced the door. Twelve people sat around the table, which I'd expected: three angels, three witches, three vampires, and the wolf shifters, representing the shifters as a whole.

Dick stood in the middle of the table facing the door, with Azbogah on his right and Alex on his left. Erin's deep brown eyes darkened even more as she glared at my mate from next to Azbogah, and the red in her hair seemed to emphasize her anger. Then each council member's seat rotated between the supernatural races. Based on what Griffin taught me, I was able to sniff out each one. The only two vacant seats were the ones closest to Ulva.

The wolves represent all shifters, Griffin explained as he ushered me to the seat beside his mom. *The original council refused to let every shifter have a representative because then that general race would have the most say. They wanted it balanced, and the one race every shifter trusted was the silver wolf, so a vote was cast that silver wolves would be the shifter representatives. After all, they'd been the ones to organize the civil war against the angels. The silver wolves left before the first council meeting, but the decision couldn't be undone, per the other council members, so the strongest alpha wolf took that spot instead.*

I wondered if Yelahiah had hoped that the silver wolves would come back for her brother.

Griffin led me to Ulva with a frown now marring his face as his mother and the woman next to her looked up at us.

"Is this the girl that you were telling me about?" The lady's hair was twisted into a bun, and her icy blue eyes scanned me. Her skin was a light olive that highlighted her beauty.

"Oh, yes." Ulva gestured to me. "This is...Dove. Dove, this is Dick Harding's wife, Saga."

I stilled. From the way people spoke about Dick's wife, I'd expected her to have a weak persona, but there was strength and determination in those eyes. And I could read nothing from her. "Hello."

"Luna's told me all about you." Her mauve lips pressed

together in displeasure. "We all thought that Luna and Griffin would wind up chosen mates since we got pregnant near the same time and they grew up together. It's a shame what all you've put her through."

Her words were meant to rattle me, but I couldn't get past the fact that I couldn't get a read on her essence. It was like it was neither good nor bad...or it was hidden.

"She didn't do a damn thing to your daughter," Griffin growled, getting riled up enough for the both of us.

Dick heard his voice and spun around. "Griffin, you're here—" he started.

Azbogah cut him off. "Right on time. Almost late, in fact."

My body tensed, and I readied myself to defend Griffin, when he kissed my cheek and linked, *Calm down.* He held my gaze an extra beat and then made his way calmly to one of the last two spots at the table.

Shit. If he had to remind me, then I was closer to losing it than I realized. Taking a deep breath, I calmed myself and sat next to Ulva. Rosemary entered the room and took the vacant seat beside me, while her mom went to the last spot next to Griffin.

I wondered if Azbogah had done that on purpose, but it didn't matter. Yelahiah wasn't on trial. Griffin was.

"So we're here to agree that Griffin is guilty of circumventing an all-council approval and ordering our guards to take additional weapons training." Azbogah jumped right to the point. "All those in favor of removing him as the top wolf representative of Shadow City, say aye."

"Aye," Erin said, jumping to her feet with Dick following right after. Matthew agreed without batting an eye.

They weren't even going to give him a chance to defend

himself. Dick's grin morphed into a smirk when Alex confirmed.

Five of the eleven voting members had now agreed to remove Griffin, making it clear that there was only one thing that could prevent Dick from taking control.

I jumped to my feet. "He can't be stripped of that title. I'm the rightful wolf representative of Shadow City, and I'm here to take back my position as upheld by the divine."

CHAPTER EIGHTEEN

Azbogah glared at me as he stood next to Dick and said, "We're in the middle of a vote. Sit *down*."

No. If I budged, they'd finish the vote, and then I'd have to try to reclaim the title from Dick. Staying firm and asserting myself before Griffin lost the role was my best strategy. "But he isn't the rightful representative," I repeated loudly. The more confident I acted, the more inclined at least a few of the other representatives would be in hearing from me.

"Sit *down*," Dick said through clenched teeth. "This doesn't involve you."

"But it does." I took a step forward.

Rosemary turned in my direction and shook her head marginally.

I didn't need a pack link with her to understand what she was telling me—sit down and shut up.

What are you doing? Griffin's fingers trembled on his pant legs under the table. *You can't tell them what you are.*

Luckily, no one but Saga, Rosemary, Ulva, and I could

see him shaking. His face remained confident as he pretended to not be fazed—like any real leader would do.

Maybe. I had to admit that I hadn't thought this through, but something had to be done.

"I said"—Dick spat the words as his face twisted in disgust—"*sit. Down.* You aren't part of this."

"Actually, she's the current Shadow City alpha's fated mate. Weren't you planning on presenting her to seal your relationship in front of the council, and thus, the Divine?" Yelahiah lifted a hand in my direction.

Warmth flowed through our bond as Griffin stood and looked at me. "She is, and effective immediately, she's the alpha mate of Shadow City."

"You do realize you're about to lose that position?" Dick gloated.

"I wouldn't be so certain." Yelahiah motioned for me to come forward as she continued, "Technically, this is supposed to be an open environment where anyone can speak their piece. Is there a reason you don't want her to state her case?"

"Why would you ask such a question?" Dick placed a hand on his chest. "We were just in the middle of a vote. She can speak at a later time." The evil inside him swirled so thick that there was a faint mist around him.

I'd never been able to see it before. Usually, I could feel ill intent only within my soul like a coldness and ickiness that radiated off a person.

"I, for one, want to hear what she has to say before casting my vote." Yelahiah walked over to me and stopped at my side.

We faced the council down together, and the third wolf shifter representative's sea-green eyes sparkled with interest, contrasting against his olive skin. He was only a couple of years older than Griffin, with sable brown hair that fell naturally against his face. It wasn't gelled back like Dick's or Griffin's. He seemed more like a wolf shifter who lived outside of the snobbish city. But like several of the other council members, there wasn't anything notable about his essence—as if he were neither good nor bad. "I would like to hear what she has to say, too."

"Ezra," Dick hissed. "I said we don't need to hear her." His eyes glowed faintly like he was trying to force the younger shifter into submission.

So that was how Dick had managed to take the wolf vote by the balls. He bullied this representative into doing whatever he wanted, and Griffin had been so wrapped up in his grief from losing his father that he'd handed the control right to him. "Are you seriously trying to force him to take back what he said?" I would call Dick out on it if no one else would. "Everybody is here and can see you doing it!"

Dick's face turned pink as his nostrils flared. He was losing his composure yet again. He straightened his shoulders. "I'm merely looking out for his best interests. If you're able to sway these intelligent people with whatever insane story you're trying to weave, he would be the one kicked off the council, seeing as he is the weakest of the three current members."

"I wouldn't be so sure about that." I filled my lungs, making sure my voice remained steady. I wanted to give him pause and drive him crazy. "After all, you admitted that this council is intelligent, so why would you even try to prevent them from stating that they'd like to hear my very *interesting* story."

A smirk spread across Yelahiah's face as she rocked back

on her heels like she was enjoying the show. "She has a point. Wouldn't you agree, Azbogah?"

Azbogah scowled at us, but he nodded. "Sure. Whatever she has to say, I'm sure it'll be a waste of time, but we can see if anyone else would like to hear her story." He gestured at Ezra. "So one person has agreed to hear her story. Would anyone else like to express interest?"

"I would." A thin man leaned forward in his chair, and his peony scent told me he was an angel. His white feathered wings spread behind him, almost blending in with the white suit he wore. The only color on him was his butterscotch-blonde hair and piercing sky-blue eyes. One of the purest essences I'd ever encountered warmed me inside.

"Of course you would, Pahaliah." Azbogah shuddered and pressed a hand to his stomach. "You wouldn't want your precious wife to be mad at you."

So this was Rosemary's father. He looked nothing like I'd expected him to. With her darker complexion, Rosemary definitely took after her mom.

"What about you, Gwen?" Dick puffed his chest as his arrogance fell quickly back in place while his attention landed on a gorgeous woman who sat between Ezra and Pahaliah.

Gwen tapped her four-inch burgundy nails on the table as hate flashed through her chestnut-brown eyes. "I don't want to even hear from the wolves who are already part of this council, so that's an easy decision for me." She licked her cranberry lips, stopping to emphasize her sharp teeth, which screamed vampire, and ran a hand through her messy, shoulder-length ivory hair. "In other words, that's a no."

We had two yeses and one no. If they did a majority rule type of thing, we'd at least be at a draw, and then I'd share my story, even if they didn't want me to. I'd respect this little game they wanted to play since it was buying time from them all betraying Griffin.

The witch who sat between Pahaliah and Alex flipped her waist-length, deep forest-brown hair over her shoulder and leaned back in her chair. She ran a finger along her black-stained lip as her coffee-shaded eyes lit with mischievousness. "You know what? I'm in. I could use a good laugh."

"Breena," Erin scolded the younger witch. "We have a lot of stuff that needs to get done back at the coven. Why are you wasting our time?"

"What if she does have a story worth hearing?" The dark-headed witch shrugged. "I don't want to be too hasty."

"Don't worry, Priestess." A maroon-haired witch chimed from the end directly opposite Griffin. "I understand the importance of getting our work done, so I don't want to waste precious time on some desperate girl who's willing to throw herself under the bus for her mate." Her ebony eyes matched her soul. "It's kind of pathetic."

"See, you should be more like your sister." Erin chastised Breena once again and smiled sweetly at the redhead. "Diana, you always make me proud."

"Anyone else?" Azbogah asked, avoiding looking at Yelahiah. "I'm assuming Griffin is a yes, so all it would take is two more to hang the council."

"Then I'm all ears." Alex leaned forward, placing his elbows on the table. "I'm hoping Matthew will agree with me." His eyes sparkled with mischief.

"Fine," Matthew huffed. "I will humor you this one time, but it'll cost you."

"Do I even need to ask how you're going to vote?" Azbogah's head flinched back, and his gaze clouded as he glanced at the female angel.

Yelahiah batted her eyes, smiling victoriously. "You've never wanted to break protocol before, so why start now?" She touched my shoulder. "Yes, I'd like to hear the girl's story, especially since you and Dick seem almost desperate that we don't."

"Not desperate." Azbogah waved his hand at me, gesturing for me to take the floor. "Just trying to be efficient, but please, proceed. Delight us with your carefully crafted tale."

Oh, how kind of the prick. Anger tightened inside of me, but I couldn't let it take hold. All that would do would allow me to miscalculate and mess up this chance. "There is something that everyone here should know," I said the words slowly and deliberately, buying time so my pulse settled and my mind cleared once more. "You see, one of the wolf council members does need to step aside."

"Those are some bold words without backing them up, *girl*," Azbogah barked.

All my life, I'd been taught to hide my heritage. That being a silver wolf put a target on my back, and boy, had I learned it was true. Not only had my brother been kidnapped and my entire pack massacred, but someone was desperately trying to capture me. Yet, maybe staying hidden had given away part of our power. Instead of standing to fight and keep our place in this society, we ran and hid, allowing corruption to take an even stronger hold in those we'd left behind.

Sterlyn, what are you doing? Griffin sounded scared. *Don't sacrifice your safety because of me. We can figure something out without throwing ourselves on the mercy of the council.*

I'm doing what we should've done all those years ago. Maybe I was being stupid, but with Yelahiah standing behind me, I became even more certain. *I'm taking back our place in the world.* Proudly, I said, "I'm Sterlyn Knight, the alpha of the silver wolves, and the shifters voted centuries ago that my race should be the council's shifter representatives."

Yelahiah inhaled sharply, and her hand tightened on my arm.

I wanted to check on her, but I refused to avert my gaze from Dick's. He'd take it as cowardice, and probably many of the others here would, too. I lifted my chin, making it clear that I'd stand my ground.

"A silver wolf?" Alex gasped as he pounded the table. "That's not possible."

"But it is." I urged my wolf forward, feeling the tingle along my skin. I removed my suit jacket so they could see my bare arms as silver fur sprouted. Then I pulled back on my wolf, not letting her go any further. A partial shift was hard to hold, but the full moon was close.

"Oh, my God." Ezra's breath caught. "She is."

"This is impossible." Azbogah's hands fisted as he turned to Dick. "Did you know about this?"

"I..." Dick stuttered. "I didn't." The stench of rotten eggs poured off Dick, alerting everyone that he'd lied.

Murmurs filled the room as Azbogah closed his eyes and pinched the bridge of his nose.

"You *knew* about her?" Griffin rasped as his feeling of betrayal rushed into me. "For how long?"

"I don't answer to you." Dick scanned the room as if in search of an exit.

Dick had known about me all along. This couldn't be a coincidence. Even though I was relieved that my instincts had been right, I couldn't help but feel horrible for Griffin. He'd trusted this man for so long, and to find out that he'd not only been sabotaging him, but hunting me, made him feel responsible.

The way to right the wrong was to address it head-on. *Make him submit to you.* I could do it, but this was something Griffin had to do for himself. He needed to realize the strength he held inside him. Not just that, but he'd command respect from the others in the room. Griffin needed to do this for himself. If I took care of it for him, I'd insult him on so many levels.

I refused to be that kind of mate. He and I needed to support one another and make each other stronger, not try to outshine each other.

"Actually, you do." Griffin jumped to his feet and marched around the table toward the older man. "You aren't fit to lead the wolves or be any sort of representative for the shifters. You're selfish and conniving."

"I've sacrificed everything to earn this position," Dick said as he pointed in Griffin's face. "I made the hard calls while you screwed your latest conquest or got drunk with that pathetic alpha who was supposed to be in charge of guarding the city."

"I'm going to college to get the kind of education I can use to help this city grow," Griffin countered. "If my dad were still alive, he'd have been leading the city while I was away."

"Exactly," Dick snarled. "If he was still alive. He isn't, so you should've stepped up, but you were too weak."

"You *told* me to go to college." Griffin's eyes glowed faintly as his anger took control. "You practically pushed me out the gate, telling me I needed to set an example for others and attend the university so more supernaturals would come."

Once again, Dick had been manipulating him for who knows how long. There was no telling what kind of deceit he'd fed everyone, and though I hated to see Griffin spiral in front of the council, this confrontation had to happen. It was long overdue, and hopefully, the damage wouldn't be too terrible.

"Let's not forget how you dropped off the paperwork at my house for what you've put me on trial for, telling me you'd be back soon to get the signed documents. Paperwork *you* created." Griffin spread his arms out. "You risked letting the city be revealed to humans just to put me in this position so that you could take over as alpha of my own city. This stops now. You're no longer part of the pack, and you need to go."

"What? I did not." Dick stumbled back as the sulfuric smell assaulted our noses yet again. "You can't do that. We're about to vote you out. Besides, no one believes you."

"But he's not voted out yet." I put my jacket back on as I moved to stand next to my mate, showing my support for him. He and I would always be a package deal, and no one would ever take that away. "And everyone believes him. Or did you forget that supernaturals can tell when someone lies?"

Dick's face turned pale, and his attention shifted behind me, I assumed to his mate.

I wanted to turn around to see her reaction, but I had to remain focused, especially now. We already had a ton of stuff against us—Griffin with his flippant lifestyle before he'd met me, and the silver wolves running away, leaving the other races behind. They had to believe that we were different and would change the tides.

"She's right." Yelahiah took her spot back at the table. "We haven't voted, and it's clear that Griffin isn't the one who should be on trial. So the previous vote is now void, and a new one will begin. Isn't that right, Azbogah?" She beamed at the dark angel who had been in alliance with Dick just moments ago.

If he said no, he'd be discredited completely. His reputation was already partially ruined.

"Yes, a new vote shall be taken." Azbogah nodded.

"*What?*" Dick's shoulders slumped as if he'd been deflated. "But—"

"Who is in agreement that Dick should be removed from the council, effective immediately, and replaced by the silver wolf standing before us as decreed by the divine?"

One by one, each council member said "aye" until only Griffin remained.

My mate locked eyes with the man who had once been like a father to him, and magic pulled inside him as he called his alpha will. He bellowed, "You are no longer part of this council nor part of Sterlyn's and my pack. You have until tomorrow to get your affairs in order and leave."

Despite Dick being part of Griffin's pack, it was clear that he didn't respect my mate as alpha. He hadn't challenged him...yet. I was so proud of my mate for making the douchebag submit to him before he could cause any additional problems.

Dick bared his teeth as he averted his gaze and vowed, "You haven't seen the last of me," before stomping out the door.

"So what does that mean for us?" Saga asked from the back, not even bothering to follow her husband. "Does that go for me and Luna, too?"

"Yes." Griffin spoke low but clearly, and he didn't

bother to turn around. "Your daughter tried to kill my mate. You all must leave, too."

"Fine," she whimpered, and the door slammed behind her, leaving the gawking council's attention on the two of us.

CHAPTER NINETEEN

The silence in the room almost overwhelmed me. I hated being the center of attention, but in this unfortunate situation, that was exactly what we had to be. It was important for the others to know we had the guts to lead, to prove that we were serious and would take down any adversary.

We needed to portray confidence and solidarity.

Griffin took my hand as we stared down the council together, practically daring them to challenge us.

I will die to protect you, he linked with me before adding Killian to our bond. *Kill, Sterlyn just informed the council who she is.*

Of course, she did, Killian deadpanned. *I thought we were keeping that shit secret.*

Secrets never stay buried, I told him. The truth could take centuries to come out, but eventually, it always caught back up to people. This was something I'd come to learn ever since Dad passed. *And by hiding, we were giving our enemies exactly what they wanted. Leverage. Control. The only two things that could make Dick hard.*

Obviously, his mate didn't give a shit about him. She would've happily stayed here while Dick roamed the world outside.

I'd been so stupid. I should've shouted my heritage from the rooftops instead of keeping the secret guarded.

Killian burst into laughter through our bond. *Damn, I'm so glad I can link to you two. Sterlyn has a way of making me smile that no one else can.*

Everyone but Rosemary. I'd seen the way they looked at each other, but both of them were too damn stubborn to admit their feelings.

Watch it. Griffin growled, teasing, but it fell flat because of the severity of the situation.

Whatever, man. Killian sighed exasperatedly. *She's my sister. Let me know if you need me. You coming back today?*

No, it'll be tomorrow. We had to stay here and make sure that Dick actually left. If we left the city ourselves, it could make us look weak, even though that wasn't the case.

"That was unexpected." Alex chuckled, bringing me back to the present. He sat back in his seat as he steepled his fingers and looked at me. "And silver wolves are still alive. Who would've ever guessed that?"

A murkiness swirled inside the vampire prince. He considered me as if he were at a crossroads where he could go evil or good. Most of the council members had corruption rolling off them—all except for Rosemary's parents, Ezra, and Alex. Each member was out to get something for their race or perhaps even for their own personal gain.

"Definitely not me." Erin's nose wrinkled with disgust. "We've done just fine without them. There's no need for them to return now."

"I have to agree." Azbogah sneered. "But at least her coming here has helped accomplish something. I can finally finish what we started all those years ago. My judgment still stands that the silver wolves should die."

"Not so fast." Yelahiah moved partially in front of me with a wide stance. "When you came to Earth, you forfeited being the judge, which means that your opinions don't carry weight anymore."

There was so much tension and hatred brewing between the two of them. Even if I hadn't known the history, it was clear that something had happened in the past.

I couldn't help but wonder if everyone knew why Azbogah wanted us dead. He knew we contained the power to rally the races and ensure the angels never gained control again. But this was a piece of information that could hurt us if shared. We needed more alliances before the members got nervous, thinking whatever plans they had would be thwarted. These people didn't want to unite the land—they just wanted to gain power of their own.

"Opinions?" Azbogah's jaw twitched. "What I say is the law."

"No, it's not." Pahaliah shook his head as he pushed his seat back. "Your influence has been fracturing, and the whole point of this council is for everyone to have a voice. I agree with Yelahiah. No harm can come to Sterlyn."

Griffin's hand tightened on mine. *We need to get out of here before things get worse. You being here is going to make others act irrationally out of fear.*

That didn't make sense. Why would they fear me? I was here to make things better. *We can't.* That wasn't how an alpha handled problems. Everyone needed to take a step back and think things through. "Why is it so important to kill us all? We've been living for centuries, and now that you learned we survived, you're determined for us to die again?"

I wanted Azbogah to admit to everyone that we were part angel. It seemed that our heritage had always remained a mystery, and there had to be a reason. But I was already rocking the boat enough. I'd leave it alone...for now.

"Wolves aren't meant to have powers beyond that of any shifter." Azbogah shook his fist at me. "The fact that you do means that something got perverted. Your kind should never have been created in the first place. The only way to purge the world of silver wolves is to kill each and every one of you." A scary grin flitted across his face as if he relished the thought.

My stomach revolted. Could he have partnered with Dick and planned my pack's slaughter? But if that was the case, then he couldn't have known that they had meant to spare me and use me to breed more of my kind. He wouldn't have been okay with that if he believed everything he said. And I hadn't smelled a lie.

"Well, there's only one way to make that call, because the council was formed for situations like this." Yelahiah scanned every member of the council as she continued. "A vote on whether the silver wolves should be protected."

"Are you fucking serious?" Griffin spat as he spun toward her and glared. He growled as he took a menacing step in her direction. "My mate's life depends on a vote?"

Be careful, I warned. I didn't like it either, but this was how Shadow City operated. The last thing we needed to do was piss them off even more—they'd be out to kill Griffin as well. I had to trust that Yelahiah knew what she was doing. *Don't insult them, or we'll be on even more dangerous ground.*

This is your life, Sterlyn. Griffin's shoulders bunched. *Not some vote on what movie we're watching tonight.*

I almost smiled despite the seriousness of our situation.

Sierra always made us vote on what to watch because there were three women to two men. Needless to say, she got to watch whatever she wanted each night because Rosemary and I didn't want to hear her whine about girl solidarity.

I get that, but if you act out now, they won't keep Dick out of the city. Even worse, they'll probably put him back on the council. He'll pretend to play by their rules. I hoped I wasn't making a mistake, but regardless, the suggestion was out there, and I could already tell that Azbogah approved by the corner of his lips tipping upward. *If they agree to kill me, we'll go from there.* We couldn't think about the worst-case scenario and be defensive until we knew we needed to be. Otherwise, we'd be creating a problem that might not exist.

"Fine." Azbogah pressed his lips into a line and nodded. "That is an excellent idea. All of those in favor of killing the silver wolves, say aye."

"Aye!" Erin shouted with such enthusiasm.

Wow, that was eager. I had no clue what we'd ever done to her, but she was going on my *keep an eye out for* list. Maybe Griffin had been right, but it was too late now.

Diana raised her hand. "Aye."

"Agreed." Gwen rolled her eyes and crossed her arms. "No way in hell am I talking like that."

Azbogah scowled but didn't say anything. Most likely because she'd voted in his favor.

Then silence descended, which didn't make sense. I figured the vampires would jump at the chance, too, but both men glanced at the floor as if they would rather be anywhere but here.

"What the..." Erin leaned over the table in Breena's direction. "Girl, if you don't—"

"Fine." She blew out a breath, making her bangs puff out of her eyes. "Aye."

"Wait." Rosemary jumped to her feet, not able to remain silent any longer. "Does that even count? She got bullied."

"Rosemary, shush," Yelahiah scolded. "We're in the middle of a count."

"Who else?" Azbogah asked through gritted teeth. "Including me, that's five in favor. Only two more votes needed for a majority."

No one made a noise beyond their breathing.

"Only two more votes are needed." Azbogah rubbed his fingers together and tapped a foot on the ground. "You have to say aye for it to count."

When everyone remained quiet again, I was ready for the dark angel to throw a tantrum. Maybe roll around on the floor like a toddler. Given how his face twisted, that might not have been a crazy possibility.

"I'm thinking the final tallies are in." Yelahiah beamed as she patted my arm. "Which means Sterlyn and her wolves are protected."

"For the time being," Azbogah retorted.

Thank God. Griffin wrapped an arm around my waist. "I think we've done enough for today, don't you agree?"

"For once, I agree with the pup." Alex twirled a finger. "I second that. The meeting is adjourned."

Everyone got out of their chairs and segregated into their own races except for Azbogah and Ezra.

I glanced at the other wolf shifter, who seemed to avoid my gaze.

Odd.

Let's get out of here. Griffin placed his hand on the small of my back, leading me toward the door. *The longer we hang around here, the greater the chance Azbogah will try to pull something.*

He didn't have to encourage me—I wanted to get out of there just as much as he did. *Should we talk to Ezra?*

No. Griffin didn't even bother looking back. *He likes to hang out after these things. I'll catch up with him later.*

Ulva opened the door, waving us through. Her irises had deepened to more of a cobalt, revealing her own worry.

I brushed past her, and the three of us rushed through the lobby with three sets of footsteps following behind us. Someone was hurrying to catch up, which meant that another argument or threats wouldn't be far behind.

My body was prepared for battle, but the scents of Rosemary and her family put my anxiety at ease.

"Sterlyn," Rosemary called as wings flapped, and soon, she landed right in front of us. Her black wings feathered out behind her, giving her an unearthly beauty. She continued, "We *all* need to talk, but not here."

Ulva glanced over her shoulder, back at the council room doors.

"Tomorrow, we'll be at Griffin's," I replied. "That probably would be the safest place to meet. "Talk then?"

She nodded. "Sounds good. "

Griffin marched past her, waving both Ulva and me on.

He wanted to get back to his apartment before someone tried pulling something on me again. The farther away we got from the council, the safer I'd be.

Supposedly.

Not with Dick still out there, but one thing at a time. I made sure my back was straight and walked out of the building like I didn't have a care in the world.

My dad's words echoed in my mind. *Fake it if you have to.*

THE REST of the day remained tense. Saga called Ulva over and over again, begging her to do something about their family's banishment. As if she could, or would, even want to attempt to talk her son out of Dick's punishment. At first, Ulva had tried to be nice, but it didn't take long before she made the situation perfectly clear: Dick had tried to sabotage her son, and she had no interest in helping him or the rest of his family.

Something was off about the woman, but I couldn't imagine what it would be like to be married to a man like that, someone so heartless and power-hungry. He probably stepped all over Saga and Luna, trying to use them to climb his way to the top. Perhaps that was why Luna had been so desperate to claim Griffin as her own.

Griffin snored gently next to me in his bed. It was close to two in the morning, and he'd just dozed off. His mom had been pacing the apartment for hours, adding to our anxiety. When she finally went to her room, he'd calmed down enough to fall asleep.

However, my wolf stirred inside me. She was on edge and continued to surface, making my skin tingle faintly. I heard nothing out of the ordinary in here, but maybe if I checked the entire apartment, she'd finally calm enough to sleep.

Given Azbogah's push to murder me, I didn't blame her for being on edge. The angel more than hated me. Actually...hate was too mild an emotion.

He *loathed* me.

Or rather, the silver wolves.

I was pretty sure it wasn't personal, just my genetics.

That didn't sound much better.

Slowly and quietly, so as not to wake Griffin, I untangled myself from his arms. He grunted and tried to pull me close again, but I rolled far enough away that he flopped over on his side and resumed his gentle snoring once more.

Whew. I didn't want to wake him. The day had been traumatic, and even though he now hated Dick, tomorrow would still be hard on him. He'd grown up with Dick as a constant presence in his life, and I hated to consider all the possible ways that Dick had screwed Griffin's family over. In fact, it was safer if I didn't consider it.

I inched the door open just wide enough to slip through and padded down the hall. I tapped into my wolf, helping me to remain silent. It was strange being in Shadow City because the moon's pull seemed to be a little stronger inside. Maybe the glass dome somehow magnified the magic. That made sense to me.

As I entered the den, nothing seemed out of place. My eyes were slowly scanning the area when hands grabbed the balcony wall outside.

I ducked behind the couch and crept over to the edge so I could peek without being seen. I could have rushed out there, but I wanted to see how many intruders there were, and how the hell they'd gotten up here.

The person grunted as they lifted their body over the side. All it would take was a finger slipping for the person to hurtle to their death unless they had wings. But if they had wings, I doubted they'd be dangling like that.

Salt and pepper hair peeked over the top, informing me of who it was.

Dick.

A memory of Griffin mentioning that Dick's family lived next door and how he would sometimes hear him and Saga scream at each other filtered through my mind.

The asshole had somehow gotten from his balcony to

Griffin's. He threw his legs over the side and tipped onto the balcony floor on his ass.

He grimaced and slowly climbed to his feet. He tiptoed to the glass door and pulled out a set of keys. Taking hold of one, he slipped it into the lock and turned. A faint *click* confirmed that he'd unlocked it.

Did Griffin know Dick had the keys to his home?

The door opened, and he removed his shoes. Once he stepped inside, he pulled a knife from its sheath.

He was here to hunt, but little did he know, he was now the hunted.

CHAPTER TWENTY

My pulse quickened under my skin. No wonder my wolf had gotten antsy. Both my animal and human sides knew that Dick wouldn't just give up and walk away from all of this. He'd have to try something.

I'd expected him to try to frame Griffin again, or maybe cash in some favors with other council members.

Not murder.

Although, if he was, in fact, the man who wanted me for breeding, I shouldn't be surprised. Still, even if he didn't have a problem with ordering death, being the one to inflict it was a whole different story.

I knew it all too well. Every person I'd killed haunted my dreams, breaking my heart all over again. Yes, every single one of them had been trying to hurt me, and I'd killed in self-defense, but each life was precious. Taking someone's life wasn't something to relish or reminisce about. It festered inside you, and in some ways, I remembered those people better than even my own parents' faces.

That was telling in itself.

Dick scanned the den. However, his attention never

went behind the couch or to the walls. He was too busy looking in the corners to check places someone would actually hide.

Dick had no clue what the hell he was doing.

A desperate gleam filled his eyes, and he began to shake. The moonlight reflected off the edge of the knife, casting diamond-like patterns across the room.

Rashness was both a blessing and a curse. Dick was willing to do whatever it took to stay in the city, but his foolishness had clouded his judgment.

His breathing was short and shallow, which informed me that his mind was unfocused. Taking him down should be easy, but I knew that underestimating your opponent made you cocky and arrogant. I had to prepare for the worst-case scenario in which he would be a formidable enemy.

"This will be over soon," he breathed. "Kill the girl, then Griffin, and it'll all go away."

If I were a normal wolf, I wouldn't have been able to hear the words, but he'd confirmed my suspicions about his intent.

He wouldn't be getting close to my mate.

"Are you sure about that?" I asked, staying crouched.

My voice faintly echoed around the room, making it so he couldn't nail down my location.

"Sterlyn?" He startled and sniffed. "Is that you?" He took a step deeper into the room, where he should have been able to pick up my scent now that he was indoors.

"Nope." I wanted to infuriate him. "It's the boogeyman."

He placed his knife back in its sheath as if he didn't think I saw it. "I just had something I needed to get off my chest and knew Griffin wouldn't answer my calls or open the door."

At least this time, he was being careful with what he said. There was no stench of a lie. "Is that so? What do you need to get off your chest?" I wanted to see how far he'd go. What all he would be willing to say. "I'm all ears."

"Funny." He chuckled lightly as he took a few steps closer to me. He was sniffing me out but trying to pretend like he wasn't. "You aren't a man, so I find telling you hardly worthy of my time."

Did he think I was stupid because I was a female? Like he thought that I would just believe whatever he had to say. Wanting to throw him off-kilter, I stood, revealing my exact location. "You're right. I'm so glad you brought that to my attention. Now my boobs and vagina make *so* much more sense."

"Do you think your smart mouth makes you appear strong?" He faced me and frowned. "I don't understand why Griffin and Killian dote on you. You're just a woman trying to live in a man's world. Pathetic."

Pathetic.

That was what he had the gall to call me.

"Me? Pathetic?" Rage brushed against me, but I let it simmer. We weren't fighting yet, and there was so much I had to say. It was about damn time I got some things off *my* chest. "You're the one who tried to set up Griffin so you could steal his power instead of challenging him like a real alpha would do. You're the one who lives in this city, afraid to go outside the walls for too long because God knows why. You're the one who pushed his daughter to try to lock down a man who had no interest in being with her. And you're the one who will let others fight but isn't willing to risk your own neck in those battles. You're a coward, and now no one respects you."

He straightened his back as he marched closer to me, stopping in front of the couch I stood behind it. He sneered. "A true leader realizes that staying safe is the only thing that makes sense. Why should I be fighting the battles when I can pull the strings?"

"Because you should never ask someone to do something that you wouldn't do yourself." Dad had taught me that, too. He'd taught me so much that I'd taken for granted. My heart ached since I would never be able to thank him, but now wasn't the time for mourning. "A true alpha leads by example. If every one of the people who looked up to you followed your lead, nothing would get done. They'd be hiding out in their homes, waiting for someone else to do the very things they're too scared to do themselves."

"Don't act like you know me." His voice grew louder. "You don't know shit. You're just some alpha wannabe who landed Griffin for what he could get you. The only thing you're good for is breeding, but the angels won't let you live long enough for that to happen. You screwed yourself by coming out."

Maybe.

I had a feeling that a war was coming, but right now, the imminent threat was Dick. "You're just upset that they found out about me when you wanted to keep my existence hidden. Why exactly was that?" I wanted him to admit it. I needed to hear him say everything he'd done, not only to me, but to my former pack.

"Just like a woman, thinking I have to explain myself to you." His hand went back to where his knife hid under his polo shirt. "I don't owe you anything."

He was getting ready to attack. At least we were away

from Griffin. There would be no risk of my mate becoming injured. I tensed and inhaled deeply, clearing my mind.

Just as I expected, he pulled his knife and jumped at me. His wide eyes locked on my heart, telling me exactly where he was aiming.

He had no training whatsoever. He'd been sheltered his entire life and had never practiced battling another wolf because of his position. His cockiness would be the death of him because I refused to let him live after this.

He'd had my brother kidnapped, slaughtered my family and pack, had me hunted, and now wanted to kill me and my mate. He put everyone I loved at risk with each breath.

I bent and rolled out of the way, making him land awkwardly. Standing to face him, I found the front half of his body slumped over the back of the couch. He'd expected the knife to lodge into my chest, keeping him upright.

Struggling, he tried to straighten, but before he could get off the couch, I punched him in the face. As I pulled back, he sliced my arm with the knife, and my blood spattered onto the couch. The metallic scent almost made me gag, but I breathed through my mouth, lessening the impact.

"You stupid bitch," he bellowed.

Sterlyn? Griffin's voice popped into my mind. *What the fuck is going on?*

Shit, I'd hoped we wouldn't wake him, but that had obviously been stupid. Dick wasn't leaving without killing us, so it wasn't like Griffin would sleep through it all. *Dick is here and attacking us.*

"I've been wanting to hurt you since the first day I laid eyes on you." Dick rubbed his jaw as he got back on his feet and stalked around the couch toward me. "I should've had you killed that day. It's one of the biggest regrets of my life."

One. Wow, the fact that he admitted he had regrets kind

of shocked me. He seemed like the kind of guy who thought his shit didn't stink when everyone around him could smell it. "Well, you won't be living much longer to dwell on it."

"You think you're going to win?" He laughed maniacally. "You have no idea who you're up against."

"Oh, but I do." I knew exactly who he was. "A man desperate for power who's willing to sacrifice everything to get to the top. Maybe even kill his best friend so the man's son would spiral and he could swoop in and be the hero."

He laughed darkly. "You think I killed Atticus? I would never have done that."

I expected the stench of a lie, but it never came. I'd been so certain that he'd been involved, given that Ulva and Atticus had been at the Hardings' house for dinner. Atticus's death had led Dick into a stronger position, but maybe I did have that part wrong, which didn't sit well with me. "And yet, you set up his son? Doesn't that kind of counter the argument?"

"You stupid bitch." He held up the knife, making it clear what his next move would be. "I'm not telling you anything."

He lunged at me, the knife aiming for my shoulder, and I ducked the blow. I kneed him in the stomach, causing him to stumble back several steps.

Griffin's footsteps pounded down the hallway toward us, which made Dick's nostrils flare.

"You ruin everything." Hate filled each one of his words. "This was supposed to be easy, and yet, here we are again."

"You still have a chance to cut your losses and climb back over the railing to your own balcony." Ugh, I knew I needed to kill him, but I had to give him one last chance. People could be redeemed if they wanted it themselves.

Maybe this was his rock bottom, but I doubted it. Darkness circled him like a plague.

"I can't." He sighed, and his face lined with regret or worry. "This is all I have left."

He attacked again, this time not using the weight of his body. Instead of aiming to kill, his intent was now to injure. He swung the knife around crazily, making it so I couldn't get near him.

I'm coming in from the other side, Griffin linked. *Just stay safe, I'll handle him.*

Well, that was easier said than done. Dick had completely lost his marbles. At this point, he wanted only to inflict pain, and he didn't give a damn about himself, which made me sad. Was power that important to him that he'd rather die and leave his family behind than be disgraced? What kind of mate and father did that make him? If anything, it put him in an even poorer light. I almost felt bad for Luna. There was no telling the kind of hell she'd been raised in. No wonder she was a psycho, too.

He picked up his pace as he rushed me, his face contorting as if fighting his alpha's call. With each step he advanced, I countered, looking for something to help me. My wolf surged forward, and fur sprouted along my body. Griffin was close, and I didn't want him to get hurt, which was quite possible with the way Dick was acting.

My bones cracked as my body shifted into wolf form. Before I was on all fours, Dick grazed my wolf in the shoulder, struggling to continue the fight as Griffin growled. At least it wasn't an injury that I couldn't bounce back from. I bit into his wrist, and the knife clattered to the floor. Then I lowered my head and steamrolled Dick into the wall.

"No!" he yelled as his fingers dug into my fur. His nails bit into my skin, but his hand loosened of its own accord.

The alpha will was finally taking hold.

Griffin flashed past me, running to the spot where Dick and I had been moments ago, but I had to stay focused on Dick.

I took a step back, snarling and baring my teeth at the older man. Now that Griffin was here, there was no way he could win.

"You need to stop right now," Griffin rasped from behind me. "Leave Sterlyn alone and get the fuck out of my house."

"Do you think it's that easy?" Dick snorted as he held his arms wide. "That you can cast me and my family out and we'll just go all obediently? You aren't meant to be the alpha here. I am."

I wished I could talk sense into him, but you couldn't rationalize with someone who'd lost their damn mind.

"Dick, please," Griffin begged. "Don't make it come to this. All you have to do is stand down. You can find another pack. It's not like this is the end of the world."

"But it *is* the end of the world." He breathed raggedly. "And I have to do whatever it takes to right the wrong." He reached for my neck, and I growled, ready to bite him.

"Damn it," Griffin bellowed as he appeared beside me with Dick's knife in hand. He plunged it into Dick's heart, and the older man gasped. His hands dropped to his sides as his back fell against the wall and he slowly slid to his ass.

My heart hurt that my mate had been put in this position. He'd loved this man at one time, and I'd never wanted him to have to live through this guilt and pain.

Ulva's footsteps came running down the hall, and they stopped when they came into the room.

I couldn't tear my eyes away from Dick until he was dead, so I couldn't check on her.

"You actually did it," Dick sputtered and glanced at the knife protruding from his chest. "I...I didn't think you had the balls."

"When it comes to protecting those I love, I've learned that I'm willing to do whatever it takes." Griffin ran his fingers through my fur as he kept his gaze on the man. "And you've made it clear that you have no problem hurting anyone as long as you get what you want."

"Ahhh, if only you knew everything." Dick chuckled as blood trickled from the corner of his mouth onto his shirt. "You think you have all the answers, but you have no fucking clue."

My blood ran cold at the implications.

"What do you mean?" Griffin tensed as he squatted to be on eye level with the man. "What don't I know?"

The question hung over us like a cloud as Dick coughed, splattering the blood now pouring from his mouth. His heartbeat was slowing, and he wouldn't be alive too much longer.

I urged Griffin to find out what he knew before it was too late. I growled, wishing I were still in human form now that his mother was here.

"Dick, please." Griffin sounded almost broken. "What do you mean? At least tell me that."

"I want you to know that I loved your father," Dick whispered as his black eyes lightened. The hate that was always present began to disappear. "When he died, I lost a part of myself, too."

Sincerity dripped from his words, and some of the darkness that swirled inside him began to dissipate, which didn't make sense to me.

"Okay, but what did you mean?" Griffin asked desperately. "Do you want to leave Luna and Saga behind with secrets hanging over their heads?"

Dick flinched and took a shallow breath as death settled over him. "You will never win." Then his heart stopped beating.

"Damn it!" Griffin yelled as he pounded his hand against Dick's chest. "Tell me what I need to know."

But there was no point. Dick couldn't answer him any longer.

I nuzzled Griffin's side, trying to comfort him, but my mate wasn't here with me. He continued beating on the dead man's chest, screaming for an answer.

Ulva gasped, and I turned to find her in the hallway in a pale blue nightgown. Her mouth dropped in horror as she watched her son in his frenzied state.

This whole situation was a clusterfuck, and I couldn't do a damn thing in wolf form. I hated leaving Griffin like this, but the thought of shifting back into human form in front of his mother didn't sit well with me. I could shift and return within a minute.

I rushed back to Griffin's room, passing his mother. She stood there, frozen, her hand on her throat, watching her son lose control. Her being unable to feel his devastation was a good thing. That was all on me, and it broke my heart. His feelings of hatred, love, and betrayal mixed together as he came to grips with the knowledge that even in death, Dick hadn't tried to help him.

When I entered the bedroom, I shifted back into human form, then quickly grabbed one of Griffin's long shirts and some boxers and threw them on.

Within seconds, I was back in the living room.

As I passed Ulva, she grabbed my arm and begged,

"Please help him. You're the only one who can get through to him right now."

I nodded and patted her arm as I reassured her, "That's the plan."

"Of course it is." She waved a hand in front of her face like she was trying to dry tears before they fell. "You already knew that."

Giving her a sad smile, I walked past her and hurried to my mate. His face was the color of a tomato as his fingers, coated with Dick's blood, tugged at the edges of his hair. "No." Tears dripped down his face, causing sections of his gray shirt to darken. "He was supposed to leave in the morning. Not die."

My heart broke for him, and I took some of his pain into myself. "Hey." I placed a hand on his shoulder, hoping my touch and voice would at least pull him out of his current state. I continued, wanting him to know that I was here. "I'm sorry."

"You're sorry?" Griffin repeated as he shook his head. He looked at me and inhaled sharply. "You've done absolutely nothing wrong. He forced our hand."

"He did." I wanted him to know that I agreed with that. Sometimes it was easy to doubt our decisions. "I just wished I had killed him, not you."

"I won't lie." He reached out to cup my face but stopped when he saw his fingers coated with blood. He blew out a breath and dropped his hand back to his side. "He was determined to kill you. I would do it all over again because keeping you safe is my top priority." His love bled through our bond, so much stronger than the pain of losing Dick. "Your life will always come before anyone else's."

My life wasn't worth more than any other person's, but I

knew that he'd disagree. So I said the only thing that made sense: "I love you."

"I love you, too." He kissed my lips. "And at least this is over."

"But is it?" Dick's last words haunted me. "He made it sound like he wasn't working alone."

"We know Azbogah is involved." He frowned. "So that's not shocking information. Dick was just trying to unnerve us."

That could be it, but I wasn't sure. Either way, we still had to deal with Dick's death.

"You two go get cleaned up," Ulva said as she appeared beside us. "I'll call some guards to take care of the body. Maybe we can get some decent rest now that this asshole is gone."

I wanted to argue, but my mate needed to get clean. The sooner he washed off the blood and got into fresh clothes, the better his mental state would become. For now, fortunately, the battle was over.

CHAPTER TWENTY-ONE

After the restless night at the apartment, which included the Shadow City police getting involved since Dick had died in the alpha wolf's home, I almost cried in relief when we pulled into Killian's pack neighborhood and I saw our house.

Just getting out of the city and away from all the politics put me more at ease...almost.

"Do you think when Julius and Bart get here that your brother might be willing to tell us information now?" Griffin growled. "I mean, he could've helped us before now."

Part of me wanted to take up for my resurrected brother, but Griffin was right. I understood that Julius didn't trust us, especially with how he was raised. However, I was done being patient. We had to make sure both he and I were safe.

I linked with Bart, *We're back at the house. How much longer until you two get here?*

We're walking into your backyard now, he answered. *Just know he's nervous.*

Oh, I knew that. I could feel it through our connection,

but I worked to lock it down. I couldn't let Julius influence me. I'd been so concerned with his feelings and well-being that I'd put Griffin and myself at risk. That time was over. I just hoped that Dick had been the person in charge of hunting me and my pack. *Doesn't matter. Do you think he'll tell us anything?*

Yes, I think he's ready to come clean. Bart paused. *Hearing that you were attacked again bothered him.*

Well, there was that.

When we pulled into the garage, I opened the door, eager to get the conversation going. "I'm going to let them in. They're in the backyard now."

"Okay, but Sterlyn..." Griffin grabbed my hand. *If he doesn't cooperate, we've got—*

I cut him off, not wanting to hear it. *I get it. The games are over. He puts everything on the table, or I'll have to figure out a way to punish him without him feeling like we're turning our backs on him.* He was family and a silver wolf, after all.

Appeased, he let me go, and I marched straight for the door. When I opened it, Bart and Julius were standing right there, their floral, musky scent invading my nose.

Julius averted his eyes to the ground, not even attempting to challenge me, and his usual animosity was absent.

My concern for him coiled inside me, and I had to make a conscious decision to push it down. "Thanks for coming so quickly. Please come in."

"I'm glad you're safe and well." Bart hugged me and kissed the side of my head. "But you are the alpha of our kind, so I'm also not surprised."

Being around him was nice. He reminded me of my

father and had the same temperament. The association was bittersweet, but I clung to it.

I stepped out of the way, not wanting too many of the guards outside to take notice of them. Griffin had talked with the guards who were watching the back, but the fewer who knew about Bart and Julius, the better. They entered the house, heading directly to the living room, where Griffin waited, as tense as if he were preparing for a fight.

I hoped it didn't come to that, but I couldn't blame my mate for his demeanor. The best course of action was to get everything in the open and let things fall into place. That was something Mom taught me when having candid conversations with Dad. She'd say, "Men aren't mind readers, and they aren't very intuitive about certain things. Be assertive with them, and remember that it does not, in fact, make you a bitch or aggressive. Those are terms that men who aren't as confident as your father call women when women act the same as they do."

I pulled out a picture Ulva had given me of her, Atticus, Dick, and Saga, taken a few weeks before Atticus died. "Was this the man who gave the order to kidnap me?" I asked my brother.

His eyes flicked to the picture, and he grew pale. "Yes, that's Topper."

"I wish you'd known his real name." I tried keeping my voice even, but a little frustration leaked through as my throat tightened. "This is the man who was trying to steal Shadow City away from *my mate*."

"I didn't know that." Julius lifted his hand. "The way he talked and acted, I thought he didn't even live in the city."

"Wait." Griffin's hands clenched. "Dick wanted to *breed* with my mate?"

"No!" Julius shook his head, then paused. "At least, I

don't think so. When he was talking about it on the phone, it sounded as if she was intended for someone else. Topper said that person was weak, but he needed an ally. That was almost two years ago. I haven't seen him since then."

My stomach dropped. He *did* have an accomplice. "Who was he working with?"

"I...I don't know." Julius sighed and walked over to the windows to look out. "I grew up with a woman who was disinterested in me, who made sure I had the bare necessities and trained hard each day with instructors they brought over with any sort of combat skills a non-shifting wolf could use. When he first met me at sixteen, Topper—Dick," he amended—"didn't seem comfortable with me and didn't want to be around me more than he had to. Almost as if he'd just found out about me. When he talked to some woman on the phone—I never met her, just heard her voice—she pointed out that Topper was meant to lead, and that some man named Atticus being dead was a blessing for everyone."

Heartbreak slammed into me as my mate heard how Dick had regarded his father. He'd already been through so much. I wished I could take this hurt away, but unfortunately, this was the world we lived in.

I wished, at least, that Julius knew more so we could take down every single asshole who'd caused our families pain. "Who sent all the people you trained?"

"Once again, they just showed up." Julius shrugged. "You have to understand, I was just trying to survive. All I knew was that Grace said that the people who saved me wanted me to train all those men because I had a natural talent for battle strategy, and if I didn't train them, they would kick me out. I had nowhere to go and no one to turn to."

I sighed, nearly over the conversation. The one thing we'd learned was that Dick was the contact, but there was someone else out there. "Where did you grow up?"

"In the house you were taken to." Julius pursed his lips. "I lived there my entire life, and two years ago, Grace left, right before Topp—Dick showed up. I've been on my own since then."

Most likely because they didn't want the lady to see Dick. Just another clue that there were so many more people involved than we'd originally thought. "How did you get your orders?"

"At first, Grace was the one who talked to whomever—until the day Dick appeared." Julius growled in frustration. "After that, he'd call me and tell me when people were coming, where to send people, and what training needed to be accomplished. They kept me out of the loop for the most part."

It was as if every time I felt like we were getting closer to the truth, we took several steps back.

I hated to keep pushing, but we needed answers. "I've seen at least two guys take their own life instead of being captured. You trained them—why did they do that?"

"Because if they're captured, their families will die." Julius grimaced. "It's for safety measures so no identities get released. I was willing to run because I didn't have anyone to risk."

His words hit hard. He was that alone.

"Look, he's telling the truth." Bart sighed. "We all know it. At least part of his hellacious past is gone."

Yeah, maybe. But I hadn't gotten much closer to the truth other than realizing that someone else was still out there. A woman—which didn't make sense, as Dick had such a problem with people of that gender being in charge.

"Look, I'm sorry, but...I need some time." Julius ran his hands through his hair, and his pain pulsed through me. "I... I just..." He turned and walked out the back door, rushing toward the woods.

I took a step to go after him, but Bart grabbed my arm. "It's best if you let him go for now. He's been on his own a long time, and has to process things his way."

"I hate that I caused him pain, but we've got to get some answers." The longer we stayed in the dark, the more death and chaos might result.

Bart patted my arm. "I know. But now he's connected with his wolf. He's mellowing out, though it's going to take a little time. Don't push too hard, or he might shut down again. Let me go run with him, and I'll connect with you later."

"Okay," I sighed as Bart hurried after him.

Still, I couldn't help but think that maybe this would've all been over if Julius had told us everything to begin with.

A FEW WEEKS LATER, Sierra entered Griffin's Shadow Ridge kitchen and yawned, placing several bags of food from Dick's Bar on the table. "So, what are we doing tonight?"

I'd hoped that they would change the establishment's name, but Saga had moved into the back of the restaurant in Dick's office and insisted on keeping it the same. Almost as if it would serve as a reminder of what we'd done to them.

I wanted Sierra to quit, but she was insistent that the tips made it all worthwhile. I finally relented when she promised she'd let us know if something went wrong or if anyone shady showed up.

"We?" Griffin arched an eyebrow and placed some canned drinks on the table. He sat in the seat closest to me and pointed at one of my best friends. "Why does she always assume that she's hanging out with us?"

"Because she's part of the group." I winked at Sierra and settled back, feeling the happiest I'd felt in forever.

Rosemary sat on the other side of me with Killian next to her. We had one open seat that Sierra had dubbed hers since the first night we'd all piled in here together.

"And I always feed you." Sierra pulled out a styrofoam box that had *Griffin* written on it. "But I mean, if I've overstayed my welcome, I can take this and the rest of the food back to my house."

"*Your* house?" Killian snorted. "Can you even still claim it? You're still staying here with the rest of us."

"Speaking of which, why are we all still staying together?" Griffin glared at everyone. "I mean, maybe Sterlyn and I could get acclimated to our *own* space."

"Sorry, but I want to spend more time with my distant cousin and be here, since this whole predicament isn't over." Rosemary snatched the container with her name. "We have a lot of catching up to do, and Mom thinks it would be wise for me to stay out of the city while things are so tense with the angels. She's afraid a civil war could break out at any second."

When I'd told Rosemary the truth about my heritage, her face had lit up with surprise and relief. She'd felt a strange connection with me that she hadn't understood, since I was all wolf. But the revelation of our real relationship explained our familial pull toward each other and mine to Yehaliah when I'd seen her in the council room. Apparently, it was my angel genes recognizing our family.

After Dick died and Luna and Saga were banished, the

mood in Shadow City had darkened. The angels were beginning to divide, either siding with Rosemary's parents or Azbogah. Of course, the other races weren't thrilled about Dick being kicked out of the city and his subsequent death, but there was no denying that Dick had broken into Griffin's house. However, Griffin killing Dick had elevated his alpha status within the shifter community. The change was good, but I hated that it had taken that for the shifters to actually look at him as their leader.

A leader should inspire confidence, not instill fear, and I had a feeling that Griffin's acceptance was due to the latter at the moment.

Our best bet was to let things calm down and go back into the city in the next couple of weeks for the first council meeting after the entire debacle. We'd been gone for a few weeks now, and the tension was still at a boiling point. We weren't hiding, but we didn't want to stir up more drama by just being seen.

Yelahiah had visited us a few nights after we'd returned to Griffin's Shadow Ridge home and told me her side of the story. She'd shared with me her guilt and regret for not standing firm with her brother. She'd never thought it would go that far, but when she'd realized that his death was imminent, she'd taken a stand beside him.

By then, it had been too late.

She'd carried the guilt with her for so long, but she wanted to have a relationship with me and the rest of the silver wolves. She said that we were family and that our angel side was just as strong as it had been all those centuries ago. Angel magic didn't dilute even when they mated with other races—rather, the power manifested over generations and remained just as strong. That was why, when Griffin and I finally had a child, they'd be a full-blooded silver wolf, too, and the oldest would be the future true alpha heir of both packs with our second child being the spare.

"Speaking of tense, how're Julius and Bart?" Sierra asked as she plopped into her seat. "I figured we'd have seen more of them by now."

"We met with them yesterday." For now, they were staying out of sight. Until things were settled with Shadow City, I didn't want to make it easy for anyone to find the remainder of the silver wolves. I didn't want to risk them being slaughtered, too. "They're at the new location Dad was developing. Apparently, a few houses have been finished, so they're staying there."

"Is Julius still being ornery?" Killian asked, leaning toward Rosemary.

"Actually, he isn't." He didn't stare at me with outright contempt anymore. He'd finally shifted and was more settled with his wolf, which hopefully changed things. "He wasn't overly friendly, either, but he confirmed that Dick was who he'd been working with."

"I still don't trust him." Griffin took a bite of his hamburger and talked around the food. "He went against his own race and family once—he could be biding his time to do it again."

This was something he and I had agreed to disagree on. I couldn't blame him for feeling that way because if the shoe were on the other foot and someone had tried to kidnap Griffin, I wouldn't have been too forgiving, either.

"Okay, enough depressing talk." Sierra clapped her hands. "It's movie night. Now, show of hands, who wants to watch *Mean Girls*? Majority wins."

"Is there even a point to this?" Griffin sighed and shook his head.

Killian shook his head. "Nope, but we need to find another guy to hang out with us so it's a split vote. I swear, my pecs are softening from the amount of estrogen we're around nightly."

"Hey." Sierra jumped to her feet and grabbed her box of food. "Rules are rules, so deal with it."

GRIFFIN SHUT the door to our bedroom, then grabbed my waist and pulled me against his chest. He linked, *I swear, Sierra better be glad you enjoy those movies, or I'd throw a fit.*

I wrapped my arms around his shoulders and grinned. *Is there anything that you wouldn't do for me?*

Nothing, he replied, kissing me.

His tongue brushed my lips, and I opened my mouth, letting him inside. Every touch and time we were together was better than the last. Each day, I fell more madly in love with him, to the point that it was almost scary, but I wouldn't have it any other way.

The last week had been some of the best times we'd ever had. The fact that my secret was out was freeing. Our group had been able to run together without fear of someone finding out what I was. Despite the alpha duties we were attending to, we got a lot more alone time, and without a constant threat hovering over us.

You taste so good. He growled. *Better than any dessert.*

Really, now? I teased as my hand brushed down his chest and below.

He was hard and ready, and I was a very willing partici-pant. I unfastened his jeans, ready to see him in all his naked glory. His body was perfect, and I couldn't wait for it to be all over me.

God, I love you so damn much. He pulled back and removed all of his clothes. His hazel eyes darkened to almost liquid gold as he advanced toward me. He stalked me like I was his prey, and I loved it.

He was the only person I'd ever been thrilled to feel that way with.

My body warmed just at the promise, and I was beyond ready for him. The back of my knees hit the side of the bed, and I fell onto the mattress, leaving my silver hair fanning out around me.

"You are so beautiful." He paused, studying me, his face filled with adoration. "I don't know what I've ever done to deserve you, but there are definitely no take-backs."

"Are you sure?" I teased. "I mean, maybe I could find—"

He covered my body with his and nipped my lips. *You finish that sentence, and you'll have to be punished.*

Promises, promises.

The scent of our arousal hung heavy around us, and his breath caught. He grabbed the collar of my shirt and ripped the material away from my body.

I gasped with surprise but also with need. He'd never done something like that before, and the possessiveness and desperation were the perfect aphrodisiacs. His hand unfastened my bra as his mouth captured my nipple.

My body arched against him, already wanting him inside me. *Griffin.*

He tensed as I slipped my hand between us, touching him. I stroked him, and his body coiled on top of me.

Oh, God. He moaned as he rolled to the side of me. He pulled back to yank down my yoga pants and growled. *No panties.*

I thought you might like that. I quickened my pace, enjoying the control I had over him.

Hell, yeah. His fingers slipped between my legs, and the two of us rubbed one another, bringing each other close to the edge.

The pressure built inside me, and I grabbed his hand, yanking it aside. I straddled him, guiding him inside me, and then rode him hard.

There was no gentle build to it, as close as I already was to the edge. He bucked against me while his fingers dug into my waist, turning me on even more. I spread my legs further apart, letting him slide in as deep as he could go.

Our bodies slicked with sweat as pleasure rocked through us. Our feelings merged together, making our orgasms even more intense as our bodies convulsed in pleasure.

"Holy shit," he rasped, raising himself to kiss me once more. *That was amazing.*

Yes, it was.

A loud knock sounded on the door, and Killian said, "We've got a huge problem. Two of the guards have disappeared, and their connection has gone cold."

The implication rang clear. "You think they're dead?" I asked.

"Yes," he said tensely. "And whoever is behind it all is here."

CHAPTER TWENTY-TWO

The moment of solitude and pleasure vanished. My body tensed as I hurriedly dressed again.

Both of us rushed, desperate to get outside and see what we were facing. Each moment we were blind to the threat meant the attackers had longer to get into prime position.

Dick said we had no clue who we were up against. That was what I'd been worried about when we returned home a week ago, but when nothing happened in those first few days. I should've known that our unknown enemies would wait long enough for us to let our guard drop.

He'd told the truth, and there was someone else after us.

Do you think it's Azbogah and his followers? Griffin asked as he buttoned his jeans.

I slipped my shirt over my head. *No, I don't. Azbogah is an in-your-face type of person. He wouldn't do a sneak attack. He wants a production to make himself feel more powerful. This is whoever was working with Dick...or whoever Dick was working for.*

Maybe Julius knew this was going to happen, Griffin growled, watching me put my jeans back on.

Thinking the worst of my brother was easy. We hadn't gotten off on the right foot with him trying to attack me and all, but he hadn't known that Dick had my pack slaughtered. *When he said Dick was the main person, he wasn't lying. You know that.* There had been no signs, neither smell or physical tells like a racing heart, of a lie.

More guards are being attacked. Killian connected with us again using the pack links we now shared. *The enemy is surrounding us.*

Any clue who it is? Griffin asked as he opened the bedroom door.

No, but they're all shifters, Killian said as worry pulsed through our pack bond. *I'm shifting and joining the fight now.*

We entered the living room just as Killian opened the back door, with Sierra and Rosemary right behind him.

"I'm going to fly around and see what I can see. I wish Mom and Dad could help, but they have their hands full in the city with all the problems Azbogah is creating." Rosemary looked at me. "From the sound of it, you need to get Bart and the silver wolves over here to fight."

I hated to do that, but the sounds of howls and screams wailed outside. Whoever was attacking us was pulling out all the stops, and the heartbreak pouring from Killian informed me that it was worse than I had initially understood. We needed backup, and it would take Bart and his pack at least ten minutes to get to us. Every second could mean another life, which was unacceptable.

Are you and the others able to get here quickly? I linked to Bart, not bothering to beat around the bush. I allowed my alarm to penetrate the bond. He needed to realize how bad of a situation we were in.

Of course. Bart answered immediately. *What's wrong?*

Whoever was working with Dick is here.

Shit. Bart sighed. *I'll get Cyrus and the pack, and we'll be there shortly.*

I hated to be that person, but I had to ask. *Are you sure bringing Julius is the right thing? If he knows the attacker...* I trailed off, trying not to say too much. However, my lack of words probably spoke volumes.

The one time I'd called my brother by his birth name, he'd flipped out on me. Yet, Bart had been calling him Cyrus since we'd first met him at my old house. I tried not to let it bother me, but I was slightly jealous that they'd gotten closer while my twin didn't seem to want much to do with me.

Look, I know things are strained between the two of you, but he's changing. Bart's voice softened. *I promise, if I see any hint of him going out of line, I'll deal with him. He still hasn't been able to control his emotions and thoughts very well when situations get intense, so I'll know.*

Even though I wanted to push the conversation further, we didn't have time to argue. The longer we took to spring into action, the more people would get hurt. *Fine, just...be careful getting here.*

We'll take the woods, Bart replied. *I'll let you know when we're near.* He ended the connection between us.

The new land Dad had purchased for us was even closer to Shadow Ridge than my hometown was. I couldn't help but wonder if Dad had thought the same thing I did when we were found—hiding wouldn't get us far. The closer proximity made me think that he had, that he was working on a strategic plan to announce our presence.

The best way to fight an enemy was to come out of hiding. That had taken me a moment to realize, given we were being attacked right now. But at least it was all coming to a head instead of the small attacks they'd been focusing solely on me.

I linked with Killian and Griffin, *They're on their way*. I ran outside after Killian with Griffin cursing behind me.

My steps slowed as I took in the horror. At least twenty enemies were trying to get to the house. Killian was fighting a sandy brown wolf who appeared to be almost as strong as he was.

I scanned the area, trying to determine who needed the most help. Two bears shifters were in animal form, fighting four guards in human form, while the rest of the fighters were wolves. A few of our guards had shifted, and the ones who had remained human were using their guns to fend off the bears.

My wolf surged forward, and my clothes ripped from my body as I landed on four legs.

Damn it, Sterlyn, Griffin said angrily. *This has to end.* His bones cracked as he followed suit, shifting into his animal form.

We should've taken Dick's warning more seriously. This was partially my fault, but remorse could be felt later. Right now, I had to focus on the matter at hand—kicking ass.

Sierra shrieked as a sable wolf attacked her mid-shift, the wolf taking advantage of her moment of weakness.

I'll help her. Griffin ran in her direction.

That was for the best because I wanted to help the human guards with the bears, who were large and not the easiest to injure. Only two other races were harder to fight, which were angels and dragons. However, Dad told me that the fae dragons kept to their realm, and the few that had moved to Earth had disappeared a long time ago, even before the birth of silver wolves.

Pushing off my paws, I reached our guards in record

time. All of the enemy wolves were engaged in battle, and our people seemed to be holding their own.

A black bear threw his head back and roared as he stood on his back feet. The four guards paid attention to him, as he sounded like he was going to attack. But as they raised their guns to fire at him, the brown grizzly charged forward, using the other bear as a distraction.

The grizzly used its speed as its biggest asset.

The moon was near full again, and I tapped into my moon powers, tugging on them harder than ever before. My wolf raced across the small clearing, and I reached the grizzly just a few feet from his target. I bit into his shoulder as his head swung in my direction.

"Sterlyn!" the tallest guard yelled, aware of what was happening. He pivoted his gun toward the grizzly, but sharp teeth slashed into my side before he fired.

I whimpered, and my jaw slackened of its own accord. White-hot pain stole my breath, forcing my mind race.

The bear released me, but his dark, soulless eyes stayed locked on me. Blood dripped from his mouth as he raised a paw to claw at my other side. He was purposely not going for kill shots, which petrified me.

Whoever was leading them still wanted me alive. I could only imagine why, and every possible thought churned my stomach.

A gun fired, and a bullet plunged right between the bear's eyes. The grizzly stumbled as the realization of what had happened settled over him. He crashed to the ground, causing the earth to shake. My side throbbed, but I didn't have time to focus on that. There were still so many shifters left to fight, and I could hear more battles farther away, which meant more enemies were coming.

The tall guard who had just protected me yelled to his

friends, "The black bear is charging. Get a tranq and shoot him."

I climbed back to my feet and turned in time to watch the black bear sink its teeth into the thinnest guard's arm. The guard's blood-curdling scream churned my stomach.

"Not happening!" the shortest of the four yelled as he shot at the black bear, but the tranq whizzed past, missing its mark.

"Get back," the thickest guard yelled as he shot two consecutive rounds. The first bullet lodged into the black bear's front right leg, and the second nailed the chest. However, the chest wound wasn't fatal, and the bear didn't appear fazed. He jerked his head, thrashing the guard's arm. Crimson blood poured from the wound, soaking the grass.

The metallic stench turned my stomach, but I breathed through my mouth. I hurriedly limped toward the bear, desperate to injure him enough that he couldn't cause any additional damage. Each time I breathed or moved, my own throbbing side almost knocked me down, but I pushed through, focusing on the air moving in and out of my lungs.

"You asshole," the thick guard yelled, and he lifted his gun to fire more. His rage was getting the best of him; he wasn't paying attention to his surroundings.

A cream wolf ran through the trees, its focus entirely on that guard. Just as the guard fired, the wolf lunged, aiming for the guard's neck.

Crouching down, I pushed hard, leaping farther than ever before. I collided with the cream wolf in midair, and my acceleration offset his forward motion, causing him to fall backward. He hit the ground with a loud thud, and I landed on top. I ripped out his throat, reducing our enemy count by one.

Gunfire continued, and I rolled off the dead wolf and

faced the guards once more. This time, the remaining three uninjured guards shot at the black bear one by one. Each hit caused blood to trickle from the wounds. The bear tried to retreat, but the guards countered each move.

Now that the guards had it handled and could help the injured one, I needed to move on and help someone else. It would've been nice if I had inherited angel healing powers so I could help the short guard and myself, but that wasn't part of the silver wolf package.

Another wolf ran from the woods, stopping me in my tracks. The golden-bronze fur and overly perfumed musk told me exactly who it was—Luna.

Her Caribbean-blue eyes sparked with loathing as she slowed and stopped.

What the hell was she doing here? I linked with both Griffin and Killian, *Luna's here.*

Fuck me, Griffin bellowed. *I should've killed the whole family. Banishment wasn't enough.*

The darkness I felt from her before was nothing compared to this moment; evil swirled around her like a tornado. She bared her teeth at me and growled, making her message clear.

She wanted me dead, and she knew I was injured.

But that wouldn't stop me from kicking her ass, so I howled in warning. I wanted her to know this place was mine and she needed to get out.

Luna gave me a wolfy smile that somehow made her look more sinister than dopey. She trotted a few steps toward me, refusing to step back and cower.

I expected nothing less.

A snapping branch to the right made me fully aware of what she was doing. She was distracting me, the same way the black bear had the guards. However, I wouldn't allow them to get the jump on me. I pretended not to hear a thing and bared my teeth. I needed them to think that my hatred had blinded my senses.

Bart's voice popped into my mind. *We're almost there. How are you all holding up?*

Not wonderfully, but telling him that would make his pack more frantic and desperate. In other words—vulnerable. I needed them on top of their game and fully engaged with their surroundings. *We're managing, but I won't lie. Knowing you're close thrills me.* Hopefully, the others wouldn't be prepared for a group of silver wolves to join us. Dick must have thought that Julius and I were the only ones left alive. This had to give us an edge, or at least I had to believe that it did.

While I kept feigning that Luna had my entire focus, in my peripheral vision, I could see a black wolf trying to sneak toward me. The animal hovered close to the tree line, his coat nearly the color of the night. However, my eyes could make out each strand of fur, and his yellow eyes seemed as bright as flashlights to me.

Luna pawed the ground, stirring up dirt and grass. She danced around as if she were considering attacking me. If I hadn't been alerted to the black wolf, which was now only about ten feet away, her peculiar actions would have alerted me to something. She had no intention of fighting me, or she would've charged by now.

The black wolf dove toward me, looking to take out one of my paws and not going for a kill shot. That was actually smart, seeing as I was injured on that side already.

I jumped, and my injured muscles burned like they were being ripped apart. However, I managed to make the black wolf miss me completely and crash to the ground.

Extending my claws, I slashed the black wolf's fur and

skin as I landed on top of him. He whimpered and tried to roll away, allowing my claws to rip across his neck and twist his head. His neck cracked from the momentum, and he fell limply to the side.

A snarl from Luna forced my gaze away from yet another person I'd killed and back on her as she retreated into the woods. Now she was running scared.

Oh, *hell*, no. That bitch wasn't getting away. Not this time.

CHAPTER TWENTY-THREE

Not willing to let her disappear, I linked with Griffin and Killian, *I'm going after Luna. She just tried to distract me while another wolf attacked me.*

Are you okay? Griffin asked with concern. *Are you injured?*

I'll be fine. I couldn't lie because he could feel the pain through our bond. But if I told him the extent of my wounds, he would be even more upset about me going after Luna, and worse, he'd be distracted. *Nothing that won't heal.* In fact, my magic was already kicking in, and the pain was beginning to lessen as the moon rose higher in the sky.

Maybe one of us should go with you. Killian wasn't thrilled with my actions, either.

No, you're all engaged in battle as is. If one of them went with me, that would expose another of our guards to additional attack. Right now, looking around, it seemed that we were evenly matched, and I felt bad leaving them. But I had a feeling Luna was the key to figuring out who the hell was behind this mess. Saga must have contacted the person

Dick had been working with. *Besides, I'm already in the woods.*

Damn it, Sterlyn. Griffin growled. *Couldn't you have waited for one of us since you're hurt? Wait for me, please.*

Annoyance flared through me, but I took a deep, calming breath and kept my eyes locked on Luna running ahead. Griffin wasn't being controlling or possessive; he just hated that I was doing this alone. It had nothing to do with my fighting capabilities. *I would, but remember that last time, they had a boat. I don't want to chance her getting away.* If Luna thought we were winning, I could see her zooming off and leaving her allies behind. She was that kind of a narcissistic asshole. *Look, Bart is close by. I'll get him to join me. Does that work?*

Fine. Griffin sighed. *But the first sign that you might be in trouble, please promise me that you'll retreat.*

Now *that* was an easy promise to make. *I promise. You can't get rid of me that easily.*

Do I need to still be part of this conversation? Killian groaned. *I mean, I'm glad that my brother and sister are together—it makes family events so much easier—but I'd rather not hear the mushiness. It's going to distract me from my fight because if it gets much worse, I'll have to vomit.*

Wow, you have been hanging out with Sierra. Griffin snorted. *You've grown so dramatic.*

You know what? You can kiss my ass, Killian retorted.

Nope, sorry, man. Griffin's voice grew proud. *There's only one ass I kiss, and yours is definitely not it.*

See! Killian's voice grew higher. *I don't want to hear that shit.*

The trees flew past me as I kept my pace, despite their banter. *Let me know if you two need me. I'm going to contact Bart like I promised.*

I love you. Griffin's tone grew serious. *Call if you get in trouble. I'll get there as soon as I can.*

Be safe, sis, Killian said.

Love you both, I said before shutting down the connection.

Luna cut left, heading in the direction of the water, as I'd feared. That must have been how they'd arrived. Boats putted down the river so regularly, it wouldn't have alerted the guards. We were going to have to include a river watch in the future. Our enemies must have surveyed us long enough to know the extent of the perimeter we kept an eye on.

One of the key strategies Dad had pounded into me and driven into the other pack members' heads was to be unpredictable. If you had a set schedule, your enemy could easily identify holes in your defenses, leading to attacks that could take out a chunk of your manpower. That was likely what had happened here, and even though Killian and the guards were amazing, it showed that they didn't have the training that the silver wolves did. It was time to break down the divide and for all wolves to work together, because at the end of the day, we were on the same team.

To ensure that I didn't close the distance between Luna and me, I had to constantly adjust my pace. I didn't want to gain on her but rather to play up my injury and make her overconfident. The water's trickling grew louder. Time to link with Bart. *Hey, where are you?*

About a half a mile away from Griffin's backyard, Bart answered immediately, including all the other silver wolf pack members into our connection. *What's the status? It sounds like the battle is still going strong.*

I hadn't been part of a group pack link like this in a month. My heart warmed as the connections flared inside me—which gave me an idea. Why were we still operating in silos? All three of our packs could talk and strategize at once. I linked Killian and Griffin into the conversation so we could all hear one another. *I was there a few minutes ago, and it seemed like we were on equal footing. I'm thinking it wouldn't hurt to have a few of the silver wolves help fight by the house and a few join me.*

But right now, the focus needs to be on backing up Sterlyn, Griffin jumped in, ready to lead alongside me. *She's running after Dick's daughter, and we should assume she's being led into a trap.*

Where are you? Bart asked, concern wafting through the bond.

Heading to the river. We were slowly approaching the area of our first large battle, only weeks ago. Blood from both sides had coated the ground already. We didn't need more blood spilled, and yet, here we were. *There's a small cutout where a boat can anchor and have easy access to the woods while keeping passengers relatively dry when they disembark. We're about a quarter-mile from it.*

The closer I got, the more scents I smelled. There had to be at least eleven other people there, one of whom was Saga. *Dick's mate is here, too. I smell her.*

I picked up your scent, Julius linked. *On my way.*

That's not comforting, Griffin growled, not thrilled with my brother being the one to come help me.

The truth was, I didn't like it, either. Dick was the person who'd worked with him, but being around people who might remind Julius of that didn't sit well with me. For all I knew, he could decide to switch sides again.

You come here and help the guards near the house, Killian said, siding with Griffin. *Griffin and I will go after*

Sterlyn. We just can't leave, or our people will be slaughtered.

No, that will take more time. Let the silver wolves join me. I appreciated how loyal Killian and Griffin were to me, but we couldn't afford to toss strategy aside and let our emotions get in the way. *They're closer, so stand your ground. This is the best way to end it all.*

Shadow City reinforcements are en route, too, Griffin informed us. *They should be here in the next few minutes. I alerted them as soon as we knew of the attack.*

That was good. We needed all the guards we could get. There could be more enemy shifters coming, but if Saga and Luna were here, that probably meant every one of Dick's fighters were here, too, or they wouldn't have risked coming. They'd assumed that they would take us out, which solidified that they didn't know about Bart and the other silver wolves.

The river came into view between the trees, and Luna increased her pace. Three boats floated in the water with several people in each one of them, poised as if they were ready to take off at any time. *There are three large boats here.*

Darrell and I will go with Cyrus to help Sterlyn, Bart said. *That should be enough to get us by, and the rest of the pack will come help Griffin and Killian until more guards arrive.*

Fine, but if Julius betrays us, Griffin linked, allowing his feelings of distrust to be felt by all, *then I'll kill him.*

I'm on your side, Julius tried to reassure him, but it fell flat. Things always seemed to fall flat when it came to his interactions with any of us, which made Griffin not trust him even more.

He won't, Bart reassured. *We're near Sterlyn now.*

I slowed my pace a few feet from the tree line of the

river, not stepping into clear view. The three motorboats were in front of me, and Saga walked to the side of the middle boat with a hate-filled smirk as Luna raced toward it.

She cooed, "Good job, Luna. You actually managed to do something right, for once, unlike your father."

Her hateful, mocking tone sent a chill down my spine. Her once hidden soul swarmed with an evil that I'd ever seen before. It coated her so thickly that her skin took on a demonic reddish glow.

"And you got the silver wolf I wanted all alone." Saga lifted her arms outward as her eyes locked on me. "She's injured, which will make things easier for us. We still have big plans for her." She snapped her fingers, and three men walked up behind her while six more—three in each of the other boats—turned their attention to me.

Her words rang inside my ears.

She still had big plans for me. She'd been in on this with Dick.

My stomach revolted at what the original plan had been for me. A fucking breeder. But with whom?

Honestly, not knowing the answer was probably best.

Luna had purposely led me here, but I'd expected that. What I hadn't expected was for these people to seriously be listening to Saga, though the darkness clinging to her told me enough. She must have had someone help hide her true self inside Shadow City, which was why I hadn't felt either good or bad from her—a witch must have aided her, similarly to how my brother had been spelled to appear dead.

Maybe it was the same witch.

Saga laughed heartily and placed a hand on her chest. "Even in animal form, I can see your confusion. You thought you had this all figured out, but you know nothing."

The man on Saga's right, who had a long scar down one

cheek, moved as if to get off the boat. Saga lifted a hand and commanded, "Don't use the real guns. Get the tranq ones. We can't chance killing her."

He obeyed immediately, rushing off to do as he was told, but five others stayed, leaving their rifles pointed at me.

Holy shit, there was no hesitation. He thought of her as his superior. But Dick had been so against women leading.

Realization washed over me, making dread weigh down my body. This whole time, she'd been in charge, not Dick.

Rosemary landed next to me, the purple of her eyes glowing in the moonlight as she stared down Saga. "What would good ol' Dick say about you taking charge?"

Hope sparked in my chest. Out of everyone due to arrive, Rosemary could not have been timelier. She and I thought similarly. Even though we didn't have the mind-linking ability, she'd asked the exact question I'd been thinking.

"Who do you think has been in charge since the beginning?" Saga retorted. "In fact, it was easy getting his attention, but I had to play the submissive role. After all, Shadow City wolves don't take female alphas seriously. You didn't even suspect me." She frowned and gracefully climbed out of the boat. She walked past Luna and toward me, not even acknowledging her daughter's presence.

That was why she'd wanted to mate with Atticus. She was an alpha forced to play down her own power, so she had to get the strongest wolf possible to pick her for a chosen mate. She'd been working this angle for longer than Griffin and I had been alive. This had been a cold and calculated plan—no wonder we'd felt like we were behind for so long.

Julius overhearing a woman on the phone say Atticus being dead was a good thing made sense. Saga had somehow gotten pregnant soon after Ulva, to try to come into power that way, and had used Dick to strong-arm Griffin, using his grief against him.

"You got pregnant on purpose, didn't you, right after Ulva did? Luna is only a few months younger than Griffin," Rosemary said with a sneer.

Her eyes glazed over like she was going back in time. "Yes, when Ulva got pregnant and we learned it was a boy, I got my backup plan in place." She gestured at her daughter.

How the hell was that possible? She couldn't have known she was going to have a girl...unless a witch helped her.

Rosemary shook her head, and her eyes widened. "You wouldn't use magic—"

"Yes, I would. I have witch friends—" She paused, pursed her lips for a second, and giggled. "Okay, 'friends' is a stretch. Nonetheless, I have witches who will do my bidding because I have leverage over them, but that's a whole different story."

I stayed still, afraid to move. Her ramblings were filling in some serious holes and giving Bart and the others time to get closer before I had to fight. Silver wolves were strong, but I couldn't take on nine men by myself, especially when they were armed.

"God, this feels so good." She strolled closer to me, placing a hand on her chest. "I mean...despite all the bullshit, here I stand, in charge like I should've been all along. Dick wanted to work with Azbogah, but I should be the real leader of Shadow City. I can do things no man could do."

Tilting my head, I tried to look fascinated to encourage her to keep going. It wasn't like I could ask her questions in animal form.

"You're crazier than your mate." Rosemary snorted.

"Was it the same witch who found the silver wolves that stole Sterlyn's brother?"

"Yes, I stumbled upon her granddaughter and used her as leverage. To get her granddaughter back, she had to steal the alpha heir. He was meant to be Luna's breeding partner so we could take over the entire wolf race, but your dumbass brother couldn't shift," she said, turning her attention to me. She sighed and rolled her eyes as if it had been a mere nuisance. Like he'd put her out instead of her actions trapping him in his human body. "And I couldn't risk your pack desperately searching for their alive, kidnapped alpha heir. So I killed them, making sure I could start over with you."

The woman was insane. The way she talked about my pack's death as if it were nothing and why she'd pushed Luna so hard at Griffin. Since she couldn't breed with the silver wolf, she needed to get her child angled as alpha mate.

The guard with a scar appeared beside her with the tranq gun in hand.

Shit, the others should be there at any second.

Rosemary's eyes flicked toward me, and she nodded slightly. She was trying to buy time for the others to catch up to us. "But then why kill Atticus and Sterlyn's pack?"

"I pushed Luna toward Griffin and used Julius to train my warriors. When Griffin hit puberty, his attention strayed to every other girl but her." She pointed at Luna and sneered. "She obviously needed a helping hand, so I invited Atticus and Ulva over for dinner one night and poisoned Atticus's food. I was nervous that someone would figure out that his death was abnormal, but the herbs the witch gave me weren't detected, so his death was documented as natural causes. Just an abnormality." Her nose wrinkled, and she glared at her daughter, who whined and cringed back. "And yet, Luna *still* couldn't capture the attention of a man mourning his father."

Luna whimpered and pawed at the ground.

She'd killed Atticus so that Griffin would be stricken with grief, allowing her daughter to finally lock him down. All the hate I felt for the girl was now replaced with pity.

But after Atticus died, Dick was also spiraling, and Saga was able to get him involved in her plan. A growl escaped before I could clamp it down. I had never hated anyone as much as I did her.

"Oh, shush. You've caused a lot of problems." Saga shook her head. "If it weren't for you, Griffin would still be an unfocused mess, and Dick would still be alive, but I guess it's all worth it now. I found someone who still wants you and will make an excellent mating partner for you." She pursed her lips and tilted her head. "Well, time's up." She glanced over at the guards. "Catch her now, and kill the angel. It's time to go."

The man with a scar lifted his gun, aiming at my shoulder. It wasn't a kill shot—they wanted to injure me so I couldn't fight.

No, I had to figure a way out of this.

CHAPTER TWENTY-FOUR

My heart pounded so loudly that my ears rang. I didn't see an escape. I tore my gaze from the guards and scanned the area for anything that could help me out of this mess. Bart, Julius, and Darrell were so close that I could smell their floral musky scents, but I was on my own.

Every bad situation I'd experienced had been caused by this bitch, and I let the pain and rage build inside me. Normally, I would attempt to calm the beast, but I needed to channel her strength to get myself out of this situation. Even if I had only a nebulous idea of what that solution might look like—at the moment, nothing was coming to me.

Rosemary took to the sky, spinning round and round like a tornado as I glanced frantically from side to side, knowing that the seconds were counting down. If I even wanted a slight chance of coming out of this unscathed, I had to make a move.

A few trees covered me, but the men ran from the boats. I couldn't turn my back on them or run off because they could stumble upon the silver wolves that would be here at any moment. I needed to buy time. I tried scooting backward, deeper into thicker trees, but a bullet could travel faster than I could move.

Still, I couldn't just stand there and do nothing.

I refused to give up. I wouldn't give Saga that pleasure. It would make her victory that much sweeter, knowing she'd broken me. I'd go down fighting, even if it was futile.

My side twinged with pain, but I'd take it. The sharp throbbing had diminished to an ache, which made it easier to move...for now. Unless I was injured again.

As I leaped for the protection of the tree, I heard the cock of the tranq gun Scarface prepared to fire. A sinister chuckle escaped him. Assholes like him enjoyed being the predator with its rush of power. Unfortunately, my life was in his hands.

"Do *not* kill her," Saga commanded, obviously picking up on the guy's intent. "You have the tranq gun for a reason."

It would have been nice if she'd said that because she cared, but she didn't. She wanted me for something worse than death, and I'd do everything I could to escape or die trying. Being her captive wasn't an option for me.

Dying would be the better alternative.

At least in death, I would find peace. But the thought of leaving Griffin behind gutted me. I *had* to make it out of this, for him. For *us*. We deserved to be with each other and make a life together. We couldn't let them take that away.

I slunk deeper into the green leaves, desperate to hide behind the trunk. Maybe I'd be able to use the tree as cover after all.

The asshole fired, and the crack of the gunshot mocked that thought.

There was no getting out of this alive. The dart would hit my left side just as I reached the tree. I braced for impact, but something black flashed across the sky and sacked me.

Rosemary's floral scent hit my nose as she wrapped her large wings around me. Then the sound of flapping wings reached us, disorienting me. She must have broken the sound barrier to reach me in time.

The *clink* of the dart bouncing off her wings amazed me once more. For her feathers to look so soft, they were stronger than anything I'd ever seen.

"Damn it, why do these angels keep getting involved?" Saga growled. "Get your asses out of the boat and kill the angel. Your guns won't work on her." She stomped her feet and glowered. "Ugh, this angel has caused enough trouble, especially since she and her parents decided to align with them instead of me."

Yeah, she was completely irrational. How had she managed to keep up the act for so long? Maybe Dick dying and her being cast out was the final straw.

We're here, Bart said as Rosemary lowered her wings, staring at the nine guards who were now climbing off the boat to get us.

Thank God. We needed more people, but we should be able to get by until the others could reach us. I linked with all three men. *There are four of us and eleven of them. Each one of you take three while I go for Luna and Saga.* I was being selfish, wanting to handle those two on my own, but they had caused so much suffering. I had the right to want justice.

As if Rosemary were part of the pack link, she turned toward the guards. "I'll take the big burly one and the other two with guns. You focus on the ones who aren't armed."

Aren't armed was a stretch. The other six had knives, but at least they had to be much closer to us to strike. *Follow her lead.* When I nodded my head, Rosemary took off flying directly at the others with Julius, Darrell, and Bart racing after her.

I focused on Saga. Luna stayed at the riverbank, avoiding eye contact like she would rather be anywhere but here. Granted, her submissive stance could be an act, so I kept an eye on her anyway.

Shots fired, and I sighed with relief as I watched Rosemary twirl around, fending off the bullets. The guards were desperate to injure her since she was the most durable one there. If they didn't focus on her, she'd kill them with her strength and wings, so their hands were kind of tied.

Good, let them sweat.

"Just because you have her on your side doesn't mean you'll win." Saga bared her teeth at me, reminding me of a vampire. Usually, wolves did that only in animal form.

She kept talking as if I cared what she said or she could somehow intimidate me. But that wasn't how this was going to work. Her running her mouth only made me more determined to kill her since she had absolutely no remorse. Instead, she sounded proud, as if I should be in awe of her.

She was the worst kind of coward. She hid behind everyone else to try to get what she wanted. She wasn't willing to fight her own war, even now. She watched as the guards fought on her behalf, and she tried to psych me out with her words.

I took long steady strides toward her. I wanted her to feel like prey...to feel weak and worthless. Killing her quickly would be too nice. She deserved to suffer for every life that she'd stolen, including Dick's.

"It's in your best interest to stop." She took a step back, revealing some of the nervousness she had attempted to hide. "The more you fight, the harder this will be on your friends and even yourself. If you come willingly, then all the hurt and injury can be spared. We won't even tranq you." The rancid stench of her lie almost made me choke. Even outside, it didn't appear to dissipate, which told me everything.

She wanted to hurt us all. No one was off the table.

Luna whimpered and rubbed a paw against her nose.

For once, I sympathized with her. She couldn't handle her mother's stench, either.

I growled and crouched, letting her know that I didn't believe a damn word that she said. For someone so strategic, she sure hadn't thought through the whole lie.

"Fine, you caught me." She lifted her head and smirked. "Every single one of your friends and family will die, including your bastard brother. I thought I killed them all, but I won't make that mistake again."

My self-control snapped, and I jumped at the lady, wanting to rip her throat out.

Her eyes widened, and she stumbled back. "Luna, attack now!"

I'd expected her to want someone else to fight her battles for her, so when Luna charged toward me, I fell to the ground and rolled, causing her to miss.

I jumped back up on all fours and snarled. I wanted this all over.

Luna's eyes deepened to navy as she turned to face me. Her breathing was quick and shallow, revealing the state she was in. She wasn't thinking clearly.

I took deep breaths, letting the adrenaline flow through my body. Most people thought being upset was the best way to get your body buzzing, but it wasn't. Adrenaline pumped through you when there was a threat in front of you. You didn't have to be a hot mess to get it to come, and channeling it appropriately could give you an edge over your opponent. Thankfully, the pain from my injury vanished as the hormone took control.

Luna lowered her head, telegraphing her next move. She wanted to bulldoze me on my injured side. I had to give her props for critical thinking, but she was clearly untrained, always broadcasting her next move. When she charged, I waited a few seconds before moving out of the way.

"Look up, you idiot," Saga yelled. "She's moved. You're going to run past her again."

If I were in human form, I would've retorted for her to come fight me herself if she could do so much better. No wonder Luna was so angry and full of hate—her mother had probably talked to her like that her entire childhood. That kind of emotional abuse could crumble even the strongest person.

A whimper left Luna as she stopped and lifted her head to find me. Her eyes locked on my shoulder, once again informing me of her next move.

There was no way this girl could ever win a fight. Obviously, neither Saga nor Dick had bothered to train their daughter in combat, yet here she was, expected to fight a silver wolf.

She attacked, and I waited until she was right on me to stand on my hind legs. Since I wasn't there to offset the impact, she propelled past me, and her face rammed into the ground. I jumped on her back, digging my claws into her skin.

However, I couldn't bring myself to kill her. It didn't seem right, seeing as Luna had suffered more than I could ever imagine. No wonder she'd been desperate to lock in

Griffin with a mother like that constantly whispering in her ear.

Luna whimpered and jerked underneath me, making my claws go deeper. Damn it, she had no clue how to fight me off from this angle, and everything about this just felt wrong.

I took the opportunity to check on my packmates and friend and realized that they all had taken down at least one of their opponents. But every time I thought we were getting the edge, another surprise knocked us back on our asses. I feared that maybe Saga had another trick up her sleeve.

Warm blood trickled under my paws, and I detached myself from Luna and stepped to the side.

"How pathetic!" Saga yelled as her face twisted with disgust. "She doesn't even want to finish you off, that's how pathetic you are."

Luna tried to stand, but she couldn't. She stayed still, not even bothering to attempt to protect herself any longer.

Pain rocketed through me, and panic clamped my throat as someone from my pack got hurt. At first, I thought it was Griffin, but when I dug deeper, I realized it was Julius.

My brother.

I pivoted in his direction to find him crumpled in a heap with blood pooling underneath him. I couldn't tell where he was hurt, but the two guards standing over him smiled. The guard with the unibrow held a knife that dripped with blood and cooed, "Hell, yeah. I took down a fucking silver wolf."

Rosemary, Bart, and Darrell were still engaged in battle, but Bart and Darrell kept throwing glances at my brother. His link was still there, which was the only reason I wasn't losing my mind.

Focus on your fight, I linked with Bart and Darrell. I could come back to Saga later. She was too scared to do much of anything. *I'll take care of them.* I jumped, thrusting my legs against the ground, drawing power from the moon. My body buzzed as I snarled and charged the men.

Griffin's voice popped into my mind. *What's wrong? Are you injured?*

No. Julius is hurt, and I don't know how bad.

I'll be there soon. Griffin sounded funny for a second. *We got some reinforcements, and some are heading your way now. Just please be careful.*

I will. It was time to bring this to an end before anyone else got hurt.

Unibrow's eyes flicked to me before bulging. "Holy shit. Sean, get ready. She's coming."

"What?" Sean was smiling as he turned to glance at me, but his mouth dropped in pure terror. "That's what we get for trusting Luna to handle her."

Those assholes had expected an untrained wolf to take me down? I wasn't sure if I should be insulted or not. They were obviously idiots, which spoke volumes more about them than me.

The image of their smiles flicked through my mind, and I leaped at Unibrow. He was the one who'd hurt Julius, so he'd be the one I took care of first.

Unibrow lifted his knife, but his movement was too damn slow. The fact that Julius got hurt by this jackass blew my mind, but the proof was right before my eyes. Bart and I needed to work with him in wolf form.

I sank my teeth into Unibrow's wrist, causing him to drop the knife. He howled, which only made me chomp harder. I wanted him to feel the pain before I ended it for him.

"Don't worry, I got you," Sean cried, informing me that he was making a move. He was almost as bad as Luna.

I released Unibrow and spun just in time to see Sean swing downward. He was aiming for my back, and I moved away, leaving him to catch air. I sprang forward and slashed my teeth through his neck. Blood poured down his chest, and he tried to speak, but he only gargled words formed as he released the knife and clasped both hands around his neck.

"Sean!" Unibrow whispered as he watched his friend, and then his body coiled. He faced me, rage evident on his face.

This was the part I'd come to hate most. The inevitable deaths. But these people would never leave us alone. I prepared myself for the attack, which I welcomed, because I was *over* this entire thing. A certain cold-hearted bitch deserved some of my attention.

But instead of striking me, he kicked Julius. When he moved to kick him a second time, I swiped at his leg with my claws and lifted upward, causing him to fall on his back. Then I slashed through his neck, not wanting to taste any more blood and needing to end this.

"You stupid bitch! You keep ruining everything." Saga bent and removed a gun from around her ankle. "I don't need you." She stood and aimed at my heart.

CHAPTER TWENTY-FIVE

I'd gotten out of one precarious situation just to land in another. What was it with people pointing guns at me? At some point, I'd like to not have the constant threat of someone trying to kill me. Being bored was underrated and exactly what I wanted.

Saga was maybe fifty feet away, and there were no trees close by. The best I could do was use Sean or Unibrow as a shield. They were already dead, so they wouldn't feel the pain, but something felt wrong about it.

I'm on my way, Bart linked with me as he fought off two men. He kept glancing at me, not paying attention to his own battle.

She fired, and I rolled out of the way, channeling the moon. I dodged the bullet by barely an inch.

Focus on your opponents, I told Bart. He wouldn't be able to reach me any faster, and instead of talking with him, I needed to determine a solution. If I didn't do something, I'd be lying dead right next to them.

As if Rosemary could hear my thoughts, she glanced in my direction. She paused, which allowed one of her opponents to stab her in the stomach with a knife. She clutched the knife, stumbling back as blood trickled down her stomach, coating her black shirt. She hissed, "You dumbass mutt."

A deep, threatening snarl escaped me. No. This couldn't happen. Rosemary was part of my family, and none of us were going down.

What's wrong? Griffin linked, including Killian in the bond. *Are you hurt?*

No, I said. *Rosemary's been stabbed.*

Killian's anger rang thick through the bond. *Son of a bitch. I'll kill the bastard.*

Not if I get him first, I vowed. I wanted to hurt every single person who had inflicted any sort of pain on my people.

"It ends now!" Saga yelled, and her finger tightened on the trigger.

Sterlyn! Julius shouted through the bond. The amount of pain he felt washed over me. I dove to the ground and shoved myself under Unibrow's body as best as I could.

His dead weight almost stole my breath as I crawled underneath him, and his body jerked from the impact of a bullet, making a few thick drops of his now congealing blood fall on my face.

Holy shit. That worked. I couldn't comprehend how I'd pulled that off. With me in animal form, I'd figured there was no way his body would shield me completely, just maybe prevent her from landing a kill shot.

"How do you keep doing that?" Saga screamed, and her footsteps grew louder. "You keep messing everything up!" Her anger propelled her toward me.

The closer she got, the better I'd be able to protect

myself. When she was too far away, I was at the mercy of the firearm with limited ability to strike back.

I stayed still, wanting her to get as close to me as she dared. If I moved, she might stop and shoot again. I linked with my brother, feeling his pain exploding through our bond. *Julius, how badly are you hurt?* I couldn't lose him like this. There was too much we hadn't said, and we hadn't spent any time together. He was my twin, for God's sake, and I had hoped that we had time to get some sort of relationship established. He and Bart were the only two people from my parents' side left alive.

Please call me Cyrus, he rasped, even through our bond. *I should've asked you to do that days ago.*

Stop. Fear coiled inside me, and I refused to acknowledge why. *You cannot die. I won't allow it. We have so much time to make up for.*

But it was like he hadn't heard me as he continued. *I blamed you, which is so fucked up, but you were the only one I could. Bart kept telling me that I had to stop, but I didn't want to listen. I have so much anger inside, and even though shifting has helped, it's still heavy in me. What I'm trying to say is—*

Do not *apologize to me now.* He was saying goodbye, and I wouldn't let him die on me. I didn't care what it took— Cyrus was going to live. *We're making it out of this, and you're going to take me somewhere nice and apologize to me there. Got it?*

I— He started.

Got it? I pushed as Saga's footsteps grew closer. She was beginning to slow but still moving forward. I held my breath to remain still, hoping she thought I was injured. *This is not our end, I promise.*

He snorted then groaned in pain. *Ugh, don't make me laugh.*

Then tell me you understand. Even in this horrible situation, the corners of my wolf's lips tipped upward. I hadn't realized the extent of how badly I wanted a relationship with him, and now that it was possible, I felt happy, despite the horrible current situation. *Or I will be forced to make you laugh.*

I don't plan on going anywhere, he reassured me just as Saga stopped.

She breathed in loud, short gasps, making it easy to determine that she was standing at Unibrow's feet.

My head and chest were lodged under Unibrow's back, but if she moved to my right, she could hit my back or my side. Either option wouldn't kill me, most likely, but it would hurt like a son of a bitch. However, if I moved, she could get an even better shot.

As if she read my mind, she fired, but I burrowed under him to the best of my ability. She must have been so angry that her hands shook, causing her aim to be off.

Keeping my head clear was hard with a dead man on top of me. The scent of his blood was overwhelming. His skin was already cooling, making his death harder to ignore. Damn it, I wanted her to come right up to me.

"Get up. You're coming with me," she spat. "Hiding under a body won't prevent what's going to happen."

I'm on my way, Bart linked as his paws hit the ground, moving closer to me.

No one else needed to get hurt on account of me. *Focus on your fight.*

Don't worry, he replied. *I took both of them down.*

Thank God. With his help, the fight would be over soon. From the sounds of it, they were getting things settled back at the house. I connected with all the silver wolves, as well as Killian and Griffin, and felt them begin to celebrate victory, but the fight wasn't finished. *Don't get overconfident. We might be winning at the moment, but that also means they'll grow desperate.* I repeated the words my father had beaten into my head. *Desperation makes people crazed. They'll do whatever they can to take down whoever they can.* In rare cases, their desperation could even give them leverage to come back on top, but I didn't want to worry the others more than I already was.

Got it, Killian said. *We'll be careful, but with the vampires here, hopefully we'll end this soon.*

Vampires? Really?

Yeah. Griffin sounded even less thrilled than me. *It was a shock. The vampire king, vampire prince, and a handful of their own guards showed up with the Shadow City wolves to help. They stayed back and watched until we were obviously winning before stepping in, but we weren't in a position to turn down help in case something went awry or we risked insulting them.*

That was true. *No, I get it.*

I'm on my way to you now, Griffin promised. *Things are under control, and Alex and Matthew are also heading your way. They have speed that could come in handy with guns.*

Those words would normally comfort me, but not now. I didn't want him to get here and be hurt, but if I tried to dissuade him, that would only get him to come faster.

"You do realize that you won't make it out of this alive," Saga continued, and her footsteps shuffled over, I assumed so she could shoot me in the back.

My body tensed of its own accord, bracing for impact.

Bart growled.

"What? No!" Saga screamed, and a gun fired.

Something crashed hard on the ground. I pushed the corpse off of me and scrambled to my feet. What I saw would forever scar me as Bart's pain washed over me.

Saga stood over my uncle and fired another shot between his eyes. Tears burned my eyes as hysteria licked throughout me. While she was distracted, I pounced on her back, forcing her to fall on top of my freshly dead uncle.

This bitch had taken so much from me. She'd not only kidnapped my brother but slaughtered my family members. If Cyrus didn't make it, I didn't know what the hell I would do.

"Get off me," she screamed as she tried to roll away from my uncle. I chomped down on her right arm, the very one she used for the gun. If I ripped her arm off, she'd never shoot anyone again.

For the first time, I didn't mind the taste of blood. In fact, I relished it. This woman deserved to bleed for every damn thing she'd done to us. My mind grew hazy with so much hate and anger that I felt like someone else.

Sterlyn, watch out! Cyrus yelled through the bond, snapping me out of whatever warped reality I'd been in.

I stumbled back and let go of the wretched woman, realizing I was acting just like she had—crazed with the desire to kill.

The other wolf! he screamed again.

Shit, I hadn't kept an eye on Luna like I'd planned. I pivoted to find her jumping toward me, her eyes locked on my neck.

I didn't have time to move.

Something flashed between us, sacking Luna mid-pounce. I blinked several times as Luna slammed against the tree and the vampire prince came into view.

Alex had saved me.

She snapped at him, trying to bite his arms, but he held her head firmly. Vampires had strength that normal wolf shifters lacked.

"Will you stop it?" he huffed. "You aren't going to get out of this. Hell, you're weaker than any wolf I've ever fought before."

"What are you doing here?" Saga bit out the words. "Haven't you interfered enough? Leave us the fuck alone!" She climbed to her feet as she held her wounded arm close to her body. Blood poured from it, and if she didn't slow the flow, she would definitely get dizzy.

"Do you want to die?" Alex asked with a chuckle as Rosemary landed next to him with a wince.

Matthew strolled into the clearing with Griffin on his trail. Griffin's hazel eyes found mine, and he raced toward me.

I inhaled sharply as Saga lifted her left arm.

No. Not again.

Her hand shook as she aimed the gun at Griffin. A cruel smirk filled her face.

Magic like I'd never felt before bolted through me, making the blood rush through my veins with incomparable power. My body propelled itself toward the woman with a speed almost as great as that of Rosemary and the vampires. I reached her within milliseconds, this time sinking my teeth into her neck.

"Imposs—" she started, but my teeth cut off her words as I severed her throat. Her body fell limply to the ground as I landed back on my feet, watching her. I tensed as I kept my gaze on her, waiting for her to move. Every time I thought we defeated our enemies, they surprised us again. At this point, if she'd popped up even missing half her neck, it wouldn't shock me.

Baby, Griffin said softly as he trotted up next to me. *It's okay.*

No, nothing is okay. My chest constricted, and air wheezed through my lungs. Once again, I might have lost my entire family. A family I had just found. I'd hoped to get to know Bart, but that had been taken away from me. *Cyrus.* My gaze flicked to him, and I found Rosemary standing over him, her hands glowing white as she healed him.

I should've felt better, but a huge part of me was just numb. I kept my body tense as I surveyed the area. Every enemy was now dead except for Luna.

Darrell's heartbroken howl pierced my soul as he leaned over his dead alpha. He lowered his head to Bart's body and cried once more.

Once again, the silver wolf pack had been torn apart, and this time, I'd be expected to put it back together. But I couldn't abandon Shadow City, either, since I'd demanded my spot on the council. I wasn't sure how I was going to handle both situations, but I didn't have a choice.

"Why don't you go home and shift back into human form, and we can figure things out from there," Alex suggested. "Matthew and I can handle this one." He nodded toward Luna, who had stopped fighting as her eyes latched onto her dead mother.

Regret flitted through me. Even though Saga was a horrible person, she *was* Luna's mother. In less than two weeks, Luna had lost both her parents at mine and Griffin's hands.

Griffin nuzzled my neck, trying to bring me comfort. *Let's go back and shift so we can take care of everything.*

He was right. I didn't have the luxury of staying here and breaking down, so I turned and slowly walked home.

When Griffin, Killian, Cyrus, Sierra, and I left our house again to deal with the consequences, my heart was still heavy. Dead bodies littered the ground, although this time, they were mostly Saga's allies. But there was still at least a dozen of our own down with them. There was so much to do, and the first order of business we had to contend with was Luna.

Rosemary was pacing the back patio. "Mom has asked for you, Griffin, and me to head back to Shadow City to meet with the council. We have to deal with the fallout of Dick's and Saga's betrayal and decide how to handle Luna."

"I have to help my pack. They just lost my un—uncle." My voice broke on the last word.

"Let me be here for them," Cyrus said softly as he touched my arm. "Lean on me, and let me take care of them for you."

The sincerity flowing through our bond warmed my heart, making me feel a little bit more like myself. "Okay. But if you need me..."

"I'll let you know," he promised.

"One wrong move—" Griffin growled.

And Cyrus nodded. "I know. How about Killian stays with me and keeps an eye out?"

Griffin's shoulders slackened like the wind had been let out of his sails. "Uh...yeah. That sounds good."

I hated that it had taken *this* to get Cyrus and me heading in the right direction concerning our relationship, but at least we were finally getting there. "Is that okay with you, Killian?" I hated not to at least ask, since Killian had his own pack duties to contend with.

"It's fine." Killian hugged me. "Honestly, at this point, we all need to work together, right? Just one large pack."

"That's right." He understood what I'd always wanted. Just because we were technically three packs didn't mean we couldn't work closely together.

Snarling came from the woods, and Alex walked out carrying Luna. Her eyes locked on me, and she thrashed, trying to get free and foaming at the mouth with desperation.

She still wanted to kill me.

CHAPTER TWENTY-SIX

"Don't worry." Alex beamed at me. "She'll ride with us. She won't harm you."

Luna twisted and writhed some more, but he didn't even seem bothered by her efforts. She could have been a baby doll for the amount of concern he gave her, which seemed to infuriate her more.

Of course, Alex and Matthew would be heading back to the city with us. They were two of the vampire representatives, after all. There couldn't be a council meeting without them, or at least not an official one, from what Erin had said before.

"Thank God." Rosemary sneered. "If I had to ride in the back seat with her, I'd wind up slicing her to make things even."

"You do realize she didn't injure you, right?" Sierra arched an eyebrow and wrinkled her nose. "Ignore that. I have no clue why I'm taking up for her. Slice the bitch."

"Because you enjoy arguing with me about everything." Rosemary sighed.

"To the point of siding with a psycho," Killian jumped

in, taking up for Rosemary. He took a step closer to the angel while *tsk*ing at Sierra. "Maybe you'll reconsider in the future."

"Yeah, do you think that will actually work?" Sierra stood tall as if she were proud of having no filter. "I say what I think, and there are times when even I'm surprised by what falls out of my mouth, which is saying something."

You guys are weird. Cyrus chuckled through the link, though not using the mocking tone I'd grown accustomed to hearing from him. *It's like no matter what gets thrown at you, you all bounce back together...like family.* He sighed, and sadness trickled to me. *I'm jealous of that.*

Well, I have a feeling that you'll fit right in soon enough, I replied. The truth of the matter was that I wanted him to be part of our team. He was important to me and the only immediate blood family I had left. *If you're open to it.*

The image of Bart's body flashed into my mind, making my smile fall.

"We'd better go before Erin and Azbogah get tired of waiting." Griffin took my hand and turned, opening the door again to head back inside the house.

A council meeting seemed like a terrible way to end the night, but if we didn't show up, it would cause more drama. Things were already tense between Griffin and me and most of the others on the council. That was probably why they wanted to talk to us.

"You guys go. We'll take it from here," Killian said as he patted Cyrus's shoulder. "We'll get the packs handled and bury the dead while you're gone."

"We're leaving," Matthew said as he pulled the keys from his pocket. "And we'll meet you there." The corner of his mouth tipped upward like he was up to something.

Alex winked at me as he followed his brother, clamping his hand over Luna's mouth to keep her quiet.

Not even bothering to give the prince a reaction, I focused on my friends. "Let me know if you need anything." My voice sounded thick with emotion. I wanted to help pay my respects to everyone who'd given or risked their lives for us tonight, especially Bart.

"We will." Sierra hugged me tightly. "Just go take care of things. This will all still be here when you return."

My side had mostly healed, so her touch didn't hurt, and I was able to hug her back before stepping past Griffin. She was right. It would take time to heal and mourn the dead.

Rosemary's breath caught as she turned, once again reminding me of her injury.

"Why don't you heal yourself?" I asked and paused inside, waiting for her and Griffin to walk through. "Or can you not do that?"

"I can, but it takes even more magic." She gently touched her chest just above her stomach, and the clean shirt she'd changed into clung to her from fresh blood. "I need to recover from healing Cyrus, but I'll be able to do it closer to Shadow City."

At least there was that.

I glanced over my shoulder, watching as Cyrus, Killian, and Sierra headed over to several men who were already working on moving the dead. The men listened and looked at Killian and then Cyrus with respect as each man spoke, so I knew things would be okay. Cyrus was ready to learn to be a strong beta. The role he was always meant to play.

Forcing myself to move forward, I faced the front again and headed to the car.

Rosemary groaned as we hit the bump where the land and the bridge that led to Shadow City connected. "Pull over."

"Now?" Griffin asked as he slowed the vehicle. "We just got on the bridge, and we need to get to the council."

"I know that," Rosemary snapped. "But stop. I need a minute."

She hadn't healed herself yet, and her attitude worried me. "I thought you said—" I began, but my words died off as a bright light started to glow from the back.

The light grew brighter, and as I turned to check on her, the whole back seat lit up brighter than the sun. All I could do was close my eyes, hoping that my retinas hadn't been burned to a crisp.

"Damn it!" Griffin bellowed as he slammed on the brakes, making the car lurch forward. "A little warning would've been nice."

I faced forward, stretching out my arms to brace myself on the dashboard. The seatbelt caught, causing my body to jerk. The light in the back seat ebbed.

"I did warn you." Rosemary's voice was clear now, without any evidence of pain. "I told you to stop the car."

"She's right." I blinked a few times, trying to stop seeing spots. "Are you going to light up again, or are we safe?"

She huffed. "I'm healed, and I couldn't do that again right away, even if I wanted to."

"Are you still hurt?" I looked at her and realized that her skin was a shade darker than normal. She still looked beautiful, but she looked tan. How the hell was that possible?

She shook her head. "No, I'm not, but it took a lot out of me to heal myself." She lifted her arms and examined her skin. "My magic is almost depleted. It's going to take some time for it to recharge."

Griffin glanced in the rearview mirror. "Is that why you look different?"

"Yeah, our power inside projects outwardly more than it does in other races." She rubbed her fingers together. "You can easily see our essence, though only angels can sense it."

Her words settled over me. "Wait, are angels able to see the intent of others, too?"

"Yeah, we are. That's one reason why I warmed up to you so quickly." Rosemary shifted around, stretching out her arms. "Your light was pure like Mom's, and of course, I felt the familial bond, though I didn't quite understand that since it was different with your wolf and all."

She'd warmed up to me *quickly*? The first time I'd met Rosemary, she was complaining about not being waited on fast enough, which I hadn't tolerated. When I'd pushed back, I'd somehow gained her respect, despite Carter bitching about how I shouldn't have told her off. But I wouldn't have called her reaction...*warm*.

"So I can see intent, too." I ran my fingers through my hair, pulling it away from my face. "That's why I don't trust certain people, especially the ones negativity clings to, like Luna, Azbogah, Saga, and Dick."

"Yeah, the wickedness around them is probably the worst I've ever seen, too. Granted, I haven't been around much in the world outside of the city." Rosemary blew out a breath. "God, it feels good to be able to move and breathe without hurting."

"I'm glad you're okay." I leaned over and touched her arm. "Seeing you get hurt..." I trailed off as my throat dried. I'd lost so many people I loved.

"Hey, I'm not going anywhere." She patted my hand

awkwardly, clearly still uncomfortable with intense emotion. "So we're good."

A chuckle left my throat as I slumped in my seat. Rosemary being back to her awkward self comforted me.

Griffin pressed the gas, and the car accelerated toward the large gate. "Why didn't you do that back at the house before we got into the Navigator?"

"Because I wasn't strong enough yet, and I didn't want to do it in the Ridge in case any humans were close by. They didn't need to see the light." Rosemary cleared her throat and crossed her arms. "I waited until the witches' spell hid us."

The gate opened without Griffin even having to get out, just like the last time we came. "Should we be worried?"

"No, there isn't a threat inside, so someone was watching for us," Rosemary answered. "Mom probably put out the word to the guards on duty."

We pulled into the city, and within minutes, we were at the council building. The lights were on, making it clear that people were already inside.

"Alex and Matthew aren't here yet," Griffin growled as he parked. "Good, I wanted to beat them."

"They left before us." Rosemary opened her door and climbed out. "That's actually not a good sign."

Damn it, I hate to admit it, but she's right, Griffin complained as he got out of the car. *What if they don't show up? They'll say the wolves are siding with me because I'm their alpha.*

I tried to smile like I wasn't concerned, but the trepidation through my bond spoke volumes. It had been a shit night, and the vampires unnerved me. They weren't known for being helpful, and they hadn't asked for anything in return.

Rosemary marched to the front door, with Griffin and me following close behind. The city's ever-changing colors were more muted in the darkness. They didn't demand my attention quite like they did during the day and almost reminded me of lightning bugs in the fields in summer.

The front door opened, revealing Yelahiah. Her gaze landed on Rosemary and then me, and her body relaxed. "Ever since I learned you all were under attack, I've been so worried. But we couldn't chance leaving with Azbogah being the only angel in charge, so we mentioned the war to Alex and Matthew. Are any of you harmed?"

"No, we're good," Rosemary answered quickly. "I got hurt, but I'm fine now."

She glossed over her injury like it was nothing, which I found intriguing.

Now's my chance to get her back. Griffin smirked as he opened his mouth to rat Rosemary out, but I intervened.

If Rosemary didn't want to go into detail over her injury with her mom, then we didn't need to waste time. "Saga was the one coordinating the attacks. We had to kill her, and Alex and Matthew are bringing Luna here."

"They aren't here yet, and they have the one girl that can prove your innocence?" A muscle in Yelahiah's jaw twitched. "Azbogah is trying to paint you two as the culprits behind Dick's death and the attacks tonight, saying you're the common denominator. If you can prove that Luna and Saga were involved, that should satisfy the other council members who would side with you."

Great, we were back on trial. I shouldn't have been surprised. Azbogah would do anything in his power to get in a position to kill me and the others of my kind.

The door to the council room opened, and Pahaliah poked his head out. "Are you ready?" He gave his wife a sideways glance. "They're waiting for Griffin, Sterlyn, Alex, and Matthew."

Yelahiah replied sweetly, "We're on our way."

"Good." He gave Rosemary a solemn gaze before closing the door once more.

"Uh...what did I just miss?" I asked. Pahaliah's visuals had been a clue of some kind, but I wasn't sure what.

The older angel straightened her shoulders. "Azbogah has already begun working the room. That's one reason you all needed to get here as soon as possible. The longer he has to sway people, the harder it'll be to keep those in your favor."

I took a deep breath. I was so tired of having to prove ourselves, but there wasn't a better alternative. The only other option was letting Azbogah weave more control through the council. I wouldn't give the jackass the satisfaction.

"You two go first, since I'm not officially on the council." Rosemary motioned in front of her. "Let's get in there before the others get here." She nodded in the direction of the parking lot.

She's right. Griffin placed a hand at the small of my back and led me toward the council doors. *Who knows what those two vampire idiots will say? Let's at least say our piece first.*

I had a feeling that if the vampires sided with Azbogah, it wouldn't matter, but this was our best shot. We had to take it.

The four of us entered the council room. Everyone sat in the same seats as before, but each one glowered at us, clearly not happy to be there at this late hour. Ezra's hair was messy from either sleep or stress, but the witches and vampires were all made up, proving they enjoyed the nighttime.

Is Ezra okay? In all the commotion, I hadn't even considered the other council representative.

Griffin blew out a breath. *I don't know. When we were attacked, I couldn't get ahold of him. Maybe he was asleep. I had to coordinate the guards, which was one reason I needed to stay close to the house and be there when they came.*

I wasn't sure how I felt about the shifter.

"*There* are the troublemakers," Azbogah spat as he stood and pulled at his oddly crumpled button-down shirt. "It's odd that you all blamed Dick for your troubles, and yet, within weeks of his death, another deadly battle occurs with you two at the center. Maybe you were behind all of these supposed attacks and set the whole thing up for Dick and Saga to take the fall."

Hell, he jumped right to the point, making his assumptions sound like facts. No wonder Yelahiah wanted us to get here so quickly.

"We are innocent." Griffin tensed, his anger already bleeding through.

We needed to hold ourselves together, not come off as unhinged or easily upset. That would make us look guilty even if our words and actions rang true. We had to remain calm and purposeful. I looped my arm through his, showing our solidarity as we walked closer to the council.

Erin slammed her hands on the table, making her breasts bounce under a low-cut shirt that left little to the imagination. She leaned over the table, and I wasn't sure how they didn't spill out of the top. "That's what everyone says. Now let's vote that these two are the problem so I can get back to my date."

Yeah, *date* had to be a far stretch of the word, but I forced my lips to stay shut. The woman already hated me enough. "Well, at least two of the vampire representatives are missing, so shouldn't we wait for them?" This was a risky move, but there had to be something we could find to prove that we hadn't been the people involved.

"If the majority here votes to get rid of the two of you, then we don't need their votes." Azbogah smirked cockily. He appeared so confident that this would go the way that he wanted. "So everyone who agrees to remove both Griffin and the silver wolf from the council, say aye. We don't need people who cause this kind of drama representing the city. Gwen?"

The ivory-haired vampire flipped her hair over her shoulder, and her eyes sparkled with maliciousness. "Aye."

Diana fluffed her hair. "Aye."

"Aye!" Erin yelled gleefully and then glared at the dark-headed witch, who seemed to like to cause problems for her. "Now, Breena, tell them aye."

My heart sank when I realized that if Breena and Ezra voted in favor of Azbogah, we would be removed from the council, and then the dark angel would come after me. Strong wolves always wanted a higher rank, so if Ezra were the one who could make the final decision, I wasn't sure what he'd decide. No wonder the witch put Breena on the spot.

The young witch sighed dramatically and leaned back in her chair. She opened her mouth to cast her vote just as the chamber's double doors crashed open.

Alex cruised into the room with his hand clutching a now human Luna's arm. Matthew trailed in after them, wearing a smug look on his face.

"I can't believe you started without us," Alex chuckled, but there was a glint in his eye. "The whole council wasn't present, so I don't understand what's going on."

"We have your sister here," Azbogah explained,

pointing to Gwen, "And if six people here want Griffin and Sterlyn removed, then your two votes wouldn't matter. It's not like you would vote for these wolves. You know better than that."

"Actually, we vote in favor of Griffin and Sterlyn staying," Alex said as he jerked the wolf toward him. "Luna and her mother attacked them in their very own home."

"Are you serious?" Diana hissed. "You're going to side with shifters?"

"No, I'm siding with the truth." Alex shrugged. "I mean, Azbogah seems a little too eager to get the wolves off the council. To me, it sounds like he has a vested interest in discrediting Sterlyn, maybe for his own selfish reasons."

"Hey, now!" Azbogah growled. "I'm for all races having representation. I have worked across races for centuries now."

"Yeah, you're a saint." Matthew shoved his hands into his pockets and stood on the other side of Luna. "But we can prove that Luna and her mother were the aggressors. Tell them, Luna."

She jerked her head, refusing to say a word.

"Well, then we will," Alex said, and winked at me. "We saw the fight, and actually, I'm the reason Sterlyn is standing here. I saved her from Saga, who was about to shoot her to death to avenge her husband. Dick and his family have been causing all the problems in the city and outside its gates, and Luna here can't say otherwise because we'd all know it was a lie."

"Tell them the truth," Rosemary hissed at Luna. "Tell them what happened. Remember what happens to those who need to be forced. We can torture it out of you. I wouldn't feel bad about it at all. One of your men stabbed me."

"No, you wouldn't." Luna's bottom lip quivered, and she shook her head back and forth.

Yelahiah played the part with her daughter. "We're angels. We're willing to do whatever it takes for the truth to be set free. If you're honest, you know the punishment won't be nearly as bad."

Luna swallowed hard.

"Now listen here, you don't get to threaten people," Azbogah shouted.

But Luna nodded her head. "It's true. Mom organized the attacks. All of them. Even the ones outside of Shadow City, with shifters fighting each other. She wanted to make Griffin look weak so Dad could take control. They had plans to take over the entire city."

"What?" Pahaliah said in shock. "Then that settles it. If she were lying, we'd all know it, and that means these two aren't guilty of anything."

Azbogah's face dropped in such disappointment it was almost comical. "Fine. Then what do we do with her?" He jerked a hand at Luna.

There was only one option that would work. It was the option that would hurt her the most. "Put her in jail and let her live out her days in solitude," I said.

"What?" Luna jerked her head toward me. "No. You don't get to make that call."

"I second the motion," Yelahiah stated, followed by Pahaliah, Griffin, Alex, Matthew, and then Ezra, even though the wolf shifter didn't seem too thrilled with that decision.

But that didn't matter right now because we managed to get the majority.

Before anyone else spoke, I stepped in, wanting to drive

the knife deeper into Azbogah's chest. "That's seven votes right there, a majority rule."

The dark angel scowled at me as Luna screamed, "You bitch. I'm going to kill you. You wait and see!"

"Ugh. Take her to the prison." Erin waved her off. "Now I'm going back to my date."

"And we're going to head back to our packs to help bury our dead," Griffin said tightly. *Azbogah and Erin hadn't counted on a real council meeting. They wanted the vote done quickly, thinking there was no way we could come out of this ahead.*

I know. They had made that clear.

As we walked past Alex, he whispered just loudly enough for me to hear, "That's three favors now, silver wolf. Remember that."

My stomach dropped at the implication.

CHAPTER TWENTY-SEVEN

Though I wanted to ask what the vampire meant, I refused to give him the satisfaction of letting him know that his statement bothered me. He could try to turn this around on us, but at the end of the day, the damage was done. Even if he tried to take back his support, he'd obviously still claim that I owed him for the time they'd voted to hear me out when Griffin had been on trial by Dick, and then for helping us fight Saga. What was one more favor at this point?

Forcing my legs to continue to move without faltering, I pretended the prince hadn't said anything. If he saw that his words affected me, there was no telling what he'd do.

Vampires enjoyed manipulating and messing with their victims.

And the king and prince were just like all the other vampires I'd met or heard stories about, which had been my fear. I should've known that they weren't any different and would want something in return for their help.

Rosemary rushed after me and touched my arm, making

me still. She said softly, "I'll fly back over there. You two go on without me."

"Okay, be safe." I nodded. She'd been spending most of her time with us, so I understood. "Let me know if you need us."

"I will." She patted my arm awkwardly, then headed back to her mother.

It might be better if she didn't try to be affectionate. Griffin chuckled as we stepped into the lobby. *I think she feels more uncomfortable trying than just being her stand-offish self.*

Do not *say anything to her.* For her to want to connect with me in a more human way meant so much to me. It emphasized how important I was to her, and she probably didn't even realize it. I tried not to push her too hard, either, because even though I was more affectionate to her, I understood not wanting to be too touchy-feely. I was only comfortable hugging those who were close to me.

Griffin rolled his eyes but kissed my cheek. *Fine, but only because you enjoy it.*

When we stepped outside, the sky was still dark, but I wasn't tired at all. Adrenaline still pumped through me.

The sickly sweet scent of vampires hit my nose from where the king and prince had walked in moments ago. The unease I'd felt flooded back.

Griffin walked to my door and opened it. *Hey, are you okay?* His concern washed over me like a wave against the sand.

I'm just ready to go home and have you hold me. I'd tell him about the vampires, just not tonight. We'd already endured too much. All I knew was that with Griffin by my side and with our packs and friends, we could get through anything.

We had to.

I climbed into the car and tried to smile, but my mate studied me. He pressed. *You avoided the question, so that worries me. What happened?* He stood there, not budging.

He wasn't going to let it go, so I filled him in on what Alex had said on our way out.

Damn bloodsuckers, he growled as he slammed the door and marched over to the driver's side. *Let's get the hell out of this forsaken place.* He jumped in the car and had us heading back to Shadow Ridge within seconds.

Shadow City was supposed to be this glorious place that people coveted, but the harsh reality was that it was cruel and the opposite of what it should be. Something had to change, but it wasn't going to happen overnight. It would take time and, unfortunately, political strategy.

But until we could change things, I felt exactly like Griffin—I didn't want to stay here any longer than we had to. All we seemed to have inside were enemies within the different races. Hell, even the shifters were segregated. We were supposed to represent the bears, birds, cats, and everyone else, but the only interactions I'd had were with the ones who had attacked us.

As soon as we pulled back onto the bridge heading to Shadow Ridge, some of the tension left my body. I hadn't even realized how stressed I'd been until that moment.

The moon was high in the sky, and as we drove through the dark and bare downtown, it almost felt like Griffin and I were the only ones awake. I closed my eyes and enjoyed the warmth of his hand on my thigh.

There was no telling what we'd be walking into once we reached the house, so I took advantage of the peace of the moment.

This is how it should always be. Griffin's voice practically purred in my head. *I don't think I've ever felt you this relaxed before.*

Relaxed was pushing it—there was still so much churning inside me—but I actually felt like I could breathe for once. *I'm just trying to enjoy a moment of peace before walking back into that nightmare.* I hated that the woods surrounding our home were now full of bad memories. There should be good ones there of us all hanging out and running in the woods together. Maybe day by day, we'd make more good memories to help drown out the bad.

The rest of the car ride passed in silence, and when we took the sharp turn into our neighborhood, I sat upright. We passed by several Craftsman-style homes before turning into Griffin's driveway.

When we walked in through the garage, I was surprised to find Killian, Sierra, and Cyrus already there. Cyrus stood next to the living room window, looking outside, while Killian and Sierra sat on the couch.

"Is everything okay?" My body tensed, but I managed to remain calm because the three of them didn't seem to be alarmed.

"We just finished burying the dead." Killian yawned.

"Already?" Griffin asked with surprise. "There were so many."

"With the silver wolves, the Shadow City guards, and my pack working together, we managed to get everything accomplished in record time," Killian said, and pointed at Cyrus. "And that man is a natural leader."

That I already knew. He'd trained all those guards, and none of them would've listened to him if he hadn't earned their respect. He was born to be a leader even if he wasn't the alpha. A lot of wolves thought you had to be an alpha to lead, but that wasn't true. An alpha couldn't oversee every-thing at all times—that was setting a pack up for failure. An alpha was only as strong as the rest of the pack. "I'm not surprised." I walked to Cyrus and squeezed his arm. "He reminds me of our father in a lot of ways."

"Really?" His silver eyes lightened to almost white.

"You'd know if I were lying." I dropped my hand, not wanting him to feel uncomfortable. We were finally moving in the right direction, so I didn't want to push too hard and fast and ruin it. "Where are the other silver wolves?" I glanced outside to find a bare backyard.

"They went back to the houses that our father had purchased to move to." Cyrus chewed on his bottom lip. "They want to head home in the morning to get the rest of the pack. They're tired of being split up."

I wasn't sure I could afford to leave right now when things were so unstable. If we ran, Azbogah and his angel followers could come after us. "Like permanently back?"

"No." Cyrus ran a hand through his hair. "They're moving to the new land...Dad was working on. They...*we* want to stay close to you. They only went home to get their stuff for the move. We all want this pack to stay together, and we understand now that Shadow City needs us, too. We're stronger together than apart."

I had to agree with that. "I don't know if I can leave right now."

"Then let me do it," Cyrus said eagerly. "Let me help you. I've done so much to hurt you—I want to make it up to you and be there for our people. Losing Bart and almost dying, it puts a lot of things into perspective."

"Okay." I nodded and smiled. "If that's what you want, then I'm okay with you taking over Bart's role."

Babe, Griffin asked with concern, *are you sure that's a good idea? I mean, he does seem different, but—*

He is. I can feel it. Our twin bond hummed with a new kind of energy that didn't seem tarnished. The darkness that had surrounded him was gone, as if things were finally clear to him for the first time.

Then I can't argue with that. Griffin's worry lessened, though it didn't completely vanish. *I just want our packs in good hands.*

Our packs. I'd never heard him say that, and honestly, I hadn't said it, either, but I liked the sound of it. He was completely right. We were mated, and our packs needed both of us. *And I love you for it.*

"You want me to take over as their leader?" Cyrus beamed. "Are you sure?"

"I'm positive." It made sense for him to lead and report to me when I couldn't be in two places at once. "I think Bart would like that, too." My heart ached at the thought of my uncle, whom I hadn't gotten to know nearly well enough. "Where is he buried?"

"Close by, between here and the new pack neighborhood." Cyrus nodded toward the woods. "Under a large, strong tree. I talked to our cousin—Bart's daughter—and she wanted him buried where she could visit his grave when they get here."

That sounded perfect. Bart was tall and strong, so he should be buried in a place that mirrored him. "Will you take me in the morning?" I wanted to leave flowers and say goodbye.

"Right before the rest of the silver wolves and I head out to get the rest of the pack." Cyrus nodded.

"Guys, I'm not trying to whine here, but..." Sierra started.

"You're gonna?" Killian jabbed.

Sierra stuck her tongue out at him. "Oh, you think you're funny stuff, don't you?"

"Well..." Killian patted his chest. "When you're as good as me—"

"Oh, God." Sierra gagged and pretended to dry heave. "Please don't make me vomit."

"You better not throw up on our rug." Griffin's face twisted in disgust. "If you vomit, your ass is going to be buying Sterlyn and me a new one."

Cyrus chuckled beside me, making me grin.

"Anyway." Sierra sighed. "I'm too amped up to go to bed, so I say it's television time."

"Yes, and we're going to watch *Die Hard*," Killian said and pointed at Griffin. "Am I right?"

"Hell, yeah." Griffin sat on the loveseat and looked at me while he patted the open spot beside him. "It's our turn."

"We haven't voted." Sierra's mouth dropped. "Where's Rosemary?"

"Not here yet." Griffin chuckled. "So three guys to two girls. We win. Turn that shit on."

"Cyrus, don't you wanna watch *How To Lose A Guy In Ten Days*?" Sierra pouted like she thought that would make him agree.

"Uh, that's a huge no." Cyrus leaned against the wall and arched an eyebrow. "I'm with them. *Die Hard*."

"Maybe you're all right after all," Griffin said, and smiled at my brother.

At my mate's approving words, Cyrus's happiness flowed into me. I linked with Griffin, *Thank you. That made his day.*

I meant it. Griffin patted the spot next to him once more. *And I need you here now.*

Not wanting to waste another second away from him, I hurried across the room and sat as he slipped his arm around my shoulder.

"It's about damn time." Killian grabbed the remote and turned on the television and movie.

"This is not fair." Sierra crossed her arms and leaned back in the chair. "This was not how it was supposed to go."

"Oh, stop." I had to give Killian and Griffin credit. They'd been watching a ton of movies they didn't want to see. It was time they had their turn.

The sound of flapping wings rose outside the back door. Cyrus jumped up and ran to open it, and Rosemary came walking in.

She glanced at the television, and her brows furrowed. "What are we watching? That doesn't look like something Sierra chose."

"That's because you weren't here, and I got outvoted." Sierra's eyes lit up. "But you're here now, so that means we can revote."

Rosemary's head tilted as she watched the beginning of the movie.

"Tell them you want to watch something else." Sierra clapped, expecting to get her way.

"Actually, this kind of looks interesting." Rosemary walked over and took the spot between Killian and Sierra, her eyes glued to the screen.

"What?" Sierra gasped. "I couldn't have heard you right."

Killian leaned forward and winked at Sierra as he said, "You lose. Now shut up and enjoy the show."

My cheeks hurt from smiling so widely, and I snuggled into Griffin's arms.

Everything was going to be all right. Cyrus would lead the silver wolves, and Griffin and I would change things in Shadow City. With the people here in this room, I knew we could get through anything that came our way. As long as we were together.

ABOUT THE AUTHOR

Jen L. Grey is a *USA Today* Bestselling Author who writes Paranormal Romance, Urban Fantasy, and Fantasy genres.

Jen lives in Tennessee with her husband, two daughters, and two miniature Australian Shepherd. Before she began writing, she was an avid reader and enjoyed being involved in the indie community. Her love for books eventually led her to writing. For more information, please visit her website and sign up for her newsletter.

Check out my future projects and book signing events at my website.

www.jenlgrey.com

ALSO BY JEN L. GREY

Shadow City: Silver Wolf Trilogy

Broken Mate

Rising Darkness

Silver Moon

Shadow City: Royal Vampire Trilogy

Cursed Mate

Shadow Bitten

Demon Blood

Shadow City: Demon Wolf Trilogy

Ruined Mate

Shattered Curse

Fated Soul

The Hidden King Trilogy

Dragon Mate

Dragon Heir

Dragon Queen

The Wolf Born Trilogy

Hidden Mate

Blood Secrets

Awakened Magic

Reaper of Wings

Reaper of Flames

Reaper of Water

Stones of Amaria (Shared World)

Kingdom of Storms

Kingdom of Shadows

Kingdom of Ruins

Kingdom of Fire

The Pearson Prophecy

Dawning Ascent

Enlightened Ascent

Reigning Ascent

Stand Alones

Death's Angel

Rising Alpha

CPSIA information can be obtained
at www.ICGtesting.com
Printed in the USA
LVHW100208021222
734458LV00016B/70

9 781955 616164